Robert Lewis is from the Black Mountains in the Brecon Beacons. He has been a silver service waiter, painter, barman, bookkeeper, banker, shop assistant, web editor, housing officer, and betting shop counterman, among other jobs. *Bank of the Black Sheep* is his third novel. Serpent's Tail has published his two earlier novels, *The Last Llanelli Train* and *Swansea Terminal*.

Praise for Robert Lewis

The Last Llanelli Train

'At times sordid, sometimes funny, occasionally bleak and sinister, this is a powerful if disenchanted journey, with echoes of Chandler, of course, but also of great mavericks such as James Crumley, Ellroy and Derek Raymond. Wonderfully misanthropic and sad, it's the sort of book that makes you look uncomfortably at the face in the mirror, for fear of recognising aspects of Robin in yourself' Maxim Jakubowski

'This debut from a talented young Welsh writer brings the detective genre bang up to date...an entertaining mix of classic noir with a twist of black comedy' *South Wales Evening Post*

'A jet-black comedy...emulating and updating the vintage hard-boiled style of Hammett and Chandler' *Western Daily Press*

'Written like a cross between Bukowski and Chandler' *Evening Herald*

'Riveting and exceptionally well written...dark, honest and guaranteed to keep you gripped' *Buzz*

'Lewis mines a buried seam in the national psyche with great subtlety and assurance...he is without doubt a writer of immense promise' *New Welsh Review*

'Has the requisite plot-twists, drama and sense of brooding danger and evil; as an anatomy of melancholy and addiction it could hardly be beaten' *The Crack*

'*The Last Llanelli Train* is Welsh Noir, a tour-de-force of squalor and desolation' *Planet*

'As a first novel it is quite an achievement; the writing is assured and confident, the humour gentle and dark, the plot classically private eye with the unexpected twists and double-dealings...A total gem; it kills dead the cliché alkie gumshoe for once and for all and breathes more life into the crime genre, which for me just continues to blossom' *Barcelona Review*

'It's Bukowski's *Pulp* gone West Country' *Uncut*

Swansea Terminal

'Charles Bukowski meets Raymond Chandler in this meandering yet keenly plotted tale of a man at the bottom with nowhere to go but down. Sad, darkly funny and quite, quite brilliant' Peter Gutteridge

'A crime caper with echoes of Ealing comedy, shades of James Ellroy and even a touch of Samuel Beckett...a compelling concoction, laced with dark humour and strangely life-affirming. Robin can't go on, but he does, and we go on rooting for him right to the very end' *Independent on Sunday*

'An edgy, twisted and blackly funny roller-coaster ride' *Metro*

'Robert Lewis' splendid creation Robin Llewellyn is a private eye of unsurpassed disintegration...a cracker of a novel...fizzy dialogue, superbly edgy writing and terrific humour' *The Times*

'Dark, bleak, sordid, sinister and very, very funny...Wonderfully poignant' *Guardian*

'Frankly, a betting slip written by Lewis will be worth reading' *Sunday Express*

'Beautiful prose meets sordid reality in this funny, dark and disturbing novel' *Sainsbury's*

'[A] wry, Chandleresque novel' *Daily Telegraph*

Bank of the Black Sheep

Robert Lewis

A complete catalogue record for this book can
be obtained from the British Library on request

First published in 2010 by Serpent's Tail,
an imprint of Profile Books Ltd
3A Exmouth House
Pine Street
London EC1R 0JH

website: www.serpentstail.com

ISBN 978 1 84668 745 7

Designed and typeset by folio at Neuadd Bwll, Llanwrtyd Wells

Printed in Great Britain by CPI Bookmarque,
Croydon, CR0 4TD

10 9 8 7 6 5 4 3 2 1

This book is printed on FSC certified paper

Mixed Sources
Product group from well-managed
forests and other controlled sources
www.fsc.org Cert no. TT-COC-002227
© 1996 Forest Stewardship Council
FSC

HONOUR ROLL

Many thanks to my editor and friend John Williams for his praise, faith, beers, hospitality and guidance. Further thanks to my agent and real-life literary hustler Antony Topping of Greene and Heaton. Both these men saw something in me when I was a very young writer indeed. I would also like to express my gratitude towards Pete Ayrton, who set up and then ran Serpent's Tail for the first twenty-odd years of its life. At Serpent's Tail I owe further thanks to Ruthie Petrie and Rebecca Gray, as well as former Serpent's Tail-er Lisa Gooding. I should also gratefully acknowledge the Writer's Bursary I received from the Welsh Academy whilst I was working on this book. And thanks too to Steve Roth, an ex-boss of mine, who helped me get some time away from the office in order to write it.

Hwyl far, Robin Llywelyn. Pob luc.

Some day we may return to some of the most sure and certain principles of religion and traditional virtue – that avarice is a vice, that the extraction of usury is a misdemeanor, and the love of money is detestable... But beware! The time for all this is not yet. For at least another hundred years we must pretend to ourselves that fair is foul and foul is fair; for foul is useful and fair is not. Avarice and usury and precaution must be our gods for a little longer still.

John Maynard Keynes, *Economic Possibilities for our Grandchildren*, **1930**

What's breaking into a bank compared with founding one?

Mack the Knife

ONE

SCHUBERT

I

You wake up in a room you don't recognise, wearing old cotton pyjamas that are too small for you, lying in a single bed like a boy would sleep in. The carpet is a fit of seventies swirls and on the wall hang some framed samplers telling you that every man who believes in him will not perish and that though you walk through the valley you shall fear no evil. The thick orange acrylic curtains are drawn shut but the dim day still creeps in, a dagger of light catching the dust in its beams.

You wake up and an old man walks in, small and hunched, with heavy black spectacles and a cheap plastic broom. He says nothing. You decide to get out of bed but instead you end up coughing blood, and you look to your bedside table for a tissue but all you see there is three or four bottles of pills and a bible. And you want to say something to the old man but your voice is thick with phlegm and fear.

And the old man walks up to you and pushes his massive glasses up the bridge of his nose and says:

'Aye. You're on the way out, son.'

And you want to scream but you have no mouth, you want to run but you cannot move. The old man stares at you quite openly and then walks out, trailing his broom behind him like a child with a toy, and once the door closes after him and your shock begins to subside, in that strange and empty room, you follow after him. But before you even get out of bed you are stopped short by a stabbing pain in the back of your left hand, which has a cannula sticking out of it. So you twist about towards the wall to see the drip they're feeding into you, but you're halted halfway again, this time by a cold jab around your right wrist.

And your right hand is cuffed to the metal railing that runs down the side of your hospital bed.

'He's awake,' calls the old man from down the hallway, and there are slow and heavy steps, and the jangle of a keychain, before a large screw in too-tight nylon trousers appears at the foot of your bed, black epaulettes on his stained white shirt. He feels his stubble with the back of his hand while he looks you over.

'What is this?' you whisper. 'What's happening?'

But the screw leaves too. He comes and goes. They both do.

You wake up alone in a room you do not recognise in a life you do not know, with the curtains drawn, and there are whole days and nights crouched in corners and in shadows just waiting to flutter past en masse, as light as moths. Weeks lay poised on top of the wardrobe, months crouch behind the tattered armchair. They sail by when you're not looking, the light and dark behind the curtains a slow but steady strobe. In the silent air you watch the dust drift and feel hysteria mount. Blink, and a morning goes, an afternoon disappears. The river of life is running fast underground away from you.

And you open your eyes and you have two new visitors: a copper and a small man with a scar on his face. The copper is cradling his cap under his arm all tidy and dutiful, but the other one is leaning against the wall with his hands in his pockets. That which befalleth the sons of men befalleth beasts it says, above him.

'What's happening to me?'

The thin man with the scar reaches into his jacket and takes out a dog-eared business card and hands it to you.

Robin Llywelyn, it says. Private Investigator.

'You're a private detective?' you ask. And your own voice sounds strange to you.

They exchange glances and the small man smiles gleefully and shakes his head.

'That's you,' he says.

You look down again at the card. It doesn't say anything more to you than it did the first time. You take a second run at the name, wondering if words can be haunted, listening for ghosts in every syllable.

Llywelyn, Robin. It does nothing.

'I'm constable Matt Roberts of the Dyfed-Powys Police,' says the uniform, 'and this is Detective Inspector David Knight, of Avon CID.'

DI David Knight is still smiling at you in his plain clothes, still showing you all his little yellow teeth.

'Just popping in to see how you were, old boy,' Knight says. 'Thought we'd pass the time with a little trip down memory lane, but I can see that'd be a bit of an uphill struggle for you these days.'

The smile on him. Massive and horrible, like the top half of his face might snap and flap upwards like a kitchen blind.

'Here,' he says, snatching your card back, 'let me write down my mobile on the back of this. Then, on the off chance you find anything creeping back, you can give me a bell, what?'

He's not posh, he doesn't look it and he doesn't sound like it, but he speaks it. An Englishman.

'We knew each other?' you ask.

'Oh yeah. We saw a lot of each other. It's that stuff, that's what it is,' he says, pointing at the drip. 'Turning your mind to mush. Junkies in St Pauls would go crazy for a bag of that stuff. Still, it's what you always wanted, isn't it? To be completely fucked up.'

He flicks your card on to the bed and the two of them shuffle wordlessly out of view, but you hear only one set of footsteps moving down the hall. A moment later, and DI David Knight sticks his head around the doorframe.

'Give my regards to your cancer,' he cannot resist, grinning.

Then they too are gone.

Even him you would have liked to stay and talk, or failing that, just to stand there while you tried to talk at him, at anybody, about anything, to help you from slipping into the strange dark abyss poised behind your eyelids, ready to swallow the tiny remainder that is all you've got left. Mornings and evenings eddy like seiches in a bounded lake.

Later in the day, or some other day, with the sun glowing through those heavy orange curtains like the world outside was burning down, another one of them arrives, a balding careworn man in a suit that could be twenty years old, a foolscap folder under his arm. He has brought a chair in with him, and he's sitting at your bedside. For a moment you think he might be your doctor, but he is your lawyer, he explains, careful to remind you he is legal aid, and you're not paying him for his time.

And you want to talk, if only to pass the time of day, but there is nothing you can say.

'Well,' he says, after the faintest of breezes has been shot. 'I have some good news.'

This you have to hear.

'The Crown has decided it's in the greater public interest not to prosecute. I mean, it caused a hell of a stink with Excise, because they're like Dobermans, they really don't like to let go when they've got their teeth in, but they're satisfied you helped them to recover the money as best you could, and more importantly, there's also your health to consider. If you pleaded not guilty it would be extremely unlikely you'd live long enough to hear the verdict.'

'That's wonderful,' you say. No one laughs.

'Bit of duty evasion, was it?' you hazard, seeing the Knock is involved.

'Yes,' he says. 'Of course, there is your mental health too. Your memory condition. And so on. A bit of duty evasion, yes.'

'I didn't make bail, then?' you ask, shaking your cuffed wrist against the railings of the bed.

'Well, no. I suppose they'll be taking them off as soon as the Prosecution Service has notified Group 4.'

'If you say so.'

And from out of a deep dry well you draw a little energy.

'I don't suppose you could fill me in a bit, could you?' you ask.

Not really, says the man's face, but he tries, just a little.

'Look, I tell you what I'll do,' he says. 'I'll get our clerk to send over a copy of your file. It might serve to ring a few bells.'

'It might at that.'

So he pats himself on the back for a job well done then makes his excuses and leaves, and three or four or some number of hours later, it's safe to assume, comes that jangling of keys, and in comes the man with the epaulettes, finishing off a scotch egg, and he takes his cuffs back and gives you some release papers and a badly-chewed pen.

'There, there, and there,' he points, rubbing dyed breadcrumbs off his chin.

'I'm too tired to read this,' you say. 'I'll sign it when I'm ready. I'm a free man.'

'You're not free till you sign the papers.'

Out of your box you may be, but you're not sufficiently orbital for this argument. Besides, you're too busy checking your business card to see how your name's spelt.

'Well done,' he says afterwards, unwrapping a Mars Bar at the foot of your metal bed. 'Free at last.'

You scratch your right wrist, cradling the cold damp band of flesh where the handcuff touched. When you look up some time a little later, or perhaps a lot, the warden at the foot of your bed has turned into a sincere, middle-aged Sikh in one of those jackets with patches at the elbow, all beard and turban, almost undoubtedly a doctor this time. He nods in the direction of your right arm.

'You're off the hook, then?' he says.

You raise your free, uncuffed hand in salute. It's hard work.

'Congratulations.'

He shifts his weight on his feet slightly and coughs with the air of a man who is trying to be delicate.

'Do you still want to stay on the drip?'

'What is it?' you ask.

'Morphine. A diluted but constant dosage. We've been pumping you with it for a week or so now.'

'It's that bad, is it?'

The man smiles awkwardly.

'In terms of your palliative care, you said you wanted to be absolutely sure you felt no pain. You wanted to be able to know you would be in complete comfort while preparing for your trial, you said.'

'Very sensible.'

'For you, yes. From a medical point of view it was not exactly best practice.'

'Most understanding, doctor.'

'Well, we did come to an understanding, didn't we?'

'I don't remember.'

'Good. I don't either.'

'No,' you say, 'I don't remember. I don't remember anything at all. My head's shot. When I came to, I didn't even know my own name.'

'Well,' says doc, after a heavy beat, 'you were of course aware that this treatment would be bound to adversely affect your mental and physical preparedness for court. Yet somehow this did not appear to bother you. In fact, I think its obvious negative effects on your soundness of mind had a certain legal appeal, from a defendant's perspective.'

The two of you lock eyes for a moment in that dusty and deathly room, and as the scale of your deception flashes into full view, you feel a little thrill of life.

'Patient choice,' you say, and you might even be smiling.

'You really don't remember?'

God knows what he got his end. Maybe there was a pay-off, or maybe some doctors just give you what you want, if you're dying anyway.

'I think I'll try to get along without it now, thanks, Doc,' you say.

'You probably won't feel normal again until it's left your system,' he explains. 'It's very strong stuff. If you had stayed on it for much longer the damage would have been far worse.'

'So,' you ask, with clammy hope lumped in your throat like another tumour. It just grows inside of you and no one can stop it. 'So I'm not dying, then?'

'No,' he says, 'I mean yes. You're a terminal case, I'm afraid. But you have maybe a couple of months.'

'Is this some kind of hospital then?'

'A hospice. A Methodist hospice. So the lost of the world can die comfortably.'

'You're a Methodist? I'm a Methodist, for that matter?'

'They've run out. The board looks at all sorts of cases these days. It's not very Christian to discriminate, is it?'

'And I am dying, definitely?'

'Cancer of the lung. It's very advanced.'

And you think oh, for fuck's sake.

So.

That's what this is all about, this morphine and memory loss, these consequences of unremembered acts by an unknown self.

The über-hangover. The morning after the life before.

'Open the curtains, will you?'

From where I was lying I could see the sun had passed its zenith over a few round green hills; Wales, definitely, and somewhere a way back from the border by the feel of things. Late afternoon on a pale day; obviously not summer, which meant it was autumn or spring, but there was no warmth out there or even the promise of it, and something told me the nights were pulling in. Summer and spring were over and done with now. I had no idea where I was, or even who I was, there was nobody there for me, and there were maybe a couple of months left. The most terrible morning-after of all my mornings. A normal person may have been able to take some comfort from the fact that the worst, surely, was now over with. But, you know, I had this funny feeling.

II

Morphine withdrawal proved to be a lot of fun.

I spent the night rolling around on my bed grinding my teeth. There were screams that could have been mine, or could have come from down the corridor. People here had screaming fits occasionally: physical pain they could dope out most of the time, but there always seemed to be a lot of other stuff to work through.

At one point I actually asked them to fasten me back to the bed again but the handcuffs had belonged to Group 4. Hospices don't stock handcuffs. It makes them look bad. They keep a little selection of leather restraints, though, which do exactly the same thing, and after I made myself understood they managed to put their hands on a set without too much trouble. After that I calmed down a little. There was nothing to be done but spasm and complain, and seeing as I couldn't tumble out, and that nobody was listening, I indulged in plenty of both.

I got the shits pretty bad, of course, which I understand is common. If you're a heavy drinker then shitting the bed may be something you've experimented with before, but being strapped into said bed at the same time can make it a much richer experience. I'd like to say I was deeply ashamed, but at the time I had other things on my mind. Later on I did feel a little sorry for the woman who had to clean up.

When the fits ended they unstrapped me and that night, or possibly the night after, I started to surface again. The corners of my eyes and mouth were dusted with a very fine salt, and my tongue looked like something you'd see hanging up in the window of a Chinese restaurant. When I blinked, I thought I could hear my scalp creak. The curtains were still drawn shut, but even so my insurgent consciousness was almost blinded by the light. It was like staring into the sun. With the backs of my eyes burning I looked around the supernova of my room and thought how awful and strange it was to wake up in your boyhood room a grown man. My mother, bless her, had put a jug of water at my bedside table, which I made short work of, and I was about to get round to wondering how I was going to explain this one, laid low again after another night on the tiles, when she came in, and turned out not to be my mother at all but some stern middle-aged blonde with an accent from the other side of the Oder, one of those imported carers, and I remembered where I was and what I was up to and how long it had been, and the familiar heaviness set in around me.

I could remember her then, though, my mother. I had not seen her for almost thirty years, nor hardly thought of her till then. They must come to you, these things, when you start to pull up.

The nurse or carer or assisted-living technician led me to the bathroom at the end of the corridor, and I think was even going to help wash me, when I told her for some reason that I could do it myself. Clearly, you are playing for stakes of consequence when you see fit to take a rain-check on a free rub-down. Then I went in all on my own like a grown-up and ran a bath and probably drank half of that too. There was a small hydraulic crane and a canvas gurney by the bathside, but I had no need of them yet, thank god.

She was still waiting outside when I came out.

'Come here,' she said, and sniffed ever so cautiously.

'You do smell a bit better,' she conceded. 'The weak ones just go in and they just splash about for twenty minutes. They do not actually wash.'

Then she took me back to my room and left me there. I looked at the bed where I had spent the last week, at its metal frame and rumpled sheets, the cradle of my precocious descent into a premature second infancy. When I had gotten into it the first time I had known who I was, and that was something that had just sort of fallen out of me while I was lying there. I looked at it for as long as I could, but it offered up no clues. Then I went and stood at the window and stared out with my hands behind my back, like Napoleon at Longwood House.

My room was at the front of the building and its high Edwardian window looked out over a long stretch of verdant, unkempt grass through which a pot-holed driveway curved down to a hedgerow-lined lane, which disappeared over a hump-backed bridge into some pocket-sized town not half a mile away. I could see a couple of chapel bell towers, a church spire and a market hall, and if I strained I could just about make out the words 'Agricultural Merchant' on an old brick warehouse. In the other direction those round, green hills I had mentioned earlier were still mooching about, and you could see the setting sun through their treetops. I stood at that window for almost half an hour, and the only things I saw move were birds and clouds. It was the countryside all right.

The doctor came back in a little later, while he was doing the rounds, looking a little nervous for a man of his profession.

'How's the memory, then?' he said. 'Coming back?'

I pointed out of the window.

'I couldn't even tell you what town that was,' I said. 'I only know my name because it was printed on my business card.'

'Well your recollection should come back. You know, if it had come back, you could tell me. I'm your doctor. Our professional relationship is entirely confidential. I shouldn't think it would cause you any sort of legal difficulties, if that's what you're thinking.'

'If it's coming back, it's taking it's time,' I said, and I wondered about the strain in my voice, if it was cancer or concern or if that was just the way I was now.

The doctor pulled lightly at the sides of his beard with both hands. He fiddled with his cuffs and then patted his pockets absently for nothing. When he spoke next his bedside manner was still there, but it had grown as brittle as pensioners' bones.

'I see. How about dizziness? Any dizziness? Sensations of faintness? Headaches, things like that? What about disorientation?'

'I can't remember how I got here or who I am. And I'm dying of lung cancer. Other than that, I'm tip-top.'

'I see,' he said again, in the same flat gentle tone, his fingertips playing nervously with the buttons on the front of his shirt. 'What about your levels of concentration? Or hallucinations? Any speech problems?'

The penny dropped.

'I'm not demented,' I said. 'I just can't remember anything.'

'Your mental state is affected,' he announced at last, with some decisiveness.

'Tell me about it.'

The doctor smoothed down the front of his shirt, which needed no smoothing, and put his arms straight by his sides.

'You cannot tell anyone,' he said, looking straight at me, resolved for the first time since he'd entered the room. 'I have a reputation to consider. Had I foreseen this development, I would not have helped you.'

'You can trust me, doc.'

'You can trust a person,' he said, 'but you cannot trust a disease. At least you can stay here, where I can monitor you.'

'I don't like it here,' I said, and it was the first real and true thing I had said to anyone since coming round.

'You mean you can remember not liking it here?'

'Let's just say I've got an inkling.'

'But what can you actually remember?'

'Nothing. I'm from the city. I drink a lot. And I don't like it here.'

'You have nowhere else to go,' he shrugged.

'So am I going to get better, or what? My head, I mean.'

'I'm a general practitioner, not a neurologist. But we must wait and hope for now. Another day or two off the drip, some rest and nutrition, and a little emotional adjustment: we shall see. Time is a great healer, as they say. Better than anyone in my business. Stay here and rest.'

There is a look that can haunt the human face sometimes the way a house fire will light a window, or like the way sunlight will look from underneath a fathom of water, when something familiar becomes suddenly alien and dangerous. It is the look of righteous authority, and my doctor had it then, when he spoke those last four casual-sounding words.

'You can't keep me here,' I said. 'You'd be in even more trouble if you did.'

And the doctor blanked out like he hadn't heard a word and left the room, picking invisible fluff off his sleeves as he went. It felt like a kind of victory, and then the room was empty again, except for me, and I was nothing. The dust was louder.

'Your mental health will get better or worse,' the doctor said from the top of the stairs, with a casual disregard for patient confidentiality. 'Either one will be fine. Even for you.'

Somewhere off in the maples, or the larches, or maybe the beeches, or in any case the fucking trees, some idiot bird chirruped gaily about his day. Morning follows night, I told myself, day follows darkness. It will come. Have faith.

I wanted it to come back and I had no idea what it was. We would rather know who we were, I suppose, whenever we didn't, and when we did we would rather be somebody else. The grass is always greener.

The low winter sun set soon after, leaving me and the black hills and that bed, taking up half the room, its mattress stuffed with the nightmares of countless dying deadbeats. It's not something you can wash out. I sat in a little armchair in the corner of the room while the light faded and tried not to look at it, but the lines and creases of its crooked sheets were fixed against me like a grimace, and its expression grew more terrible as the daylight disappeared. Me and the deathbed, with a meagre forty-watt bulb to keep the shadows at bay.

At six o'clock a lady came round with a trolley and gave me a bowl of brown soup, a cup of tea, and some digestive biscuits. Then I sat in the chair, and I must have dozed, or just kind of fazed out, for the rest of the evening. I was still pretty tired. Then I remember hearing the sounds of the staff putting the others to bed, we, the dying, and someone even offered to give me a hand, of all people, but I wanted to stay in my chair. I wasn't going back into that bed, not for one more night, if I could help it. I spent the night in my chair like a hitman, with my eyes more or less open, remembering what the doctor said, waiting for my past to pounce sometime before morning.

It didn't.

I spent the night half-awake, listening to the sounds of senility and despair, the howls and sobs and other such one-sided conversations with the void that lived on the far side of the bedroom door, and trying as much as I could to see that they stayed there. At least half the night could easily have been a bad dream, but when the screeching wheels of the breakfast trolley announced the arrival of another day, the dream did not end. I had a hot mug of tea pressed into my hands and a plate of toast put down on the small table next to me, a smile and a good morning, but I was still lost.

Nothing had filtered back. I told her, I told the lady with the trolley, that I was homesick – *hiraeth*, I wanted to say, that sickness for somewhere you couldn't get back to, an old word the gogs would use – and she told me to wait until the doctor's mid-morning rounds. I watched that glaze come down over her eyes – a glaze I saw a lot, in a bunch of different people – that appears when someone has decided they're not talking to a proper person any more, and communication is pointless, and it's not in your power to disabuse them.

Homesick. For what home, god knows.

I stayed put and kept my mouth shut and a little before midday a woman in gold-rimmed specs and corduroy trousers came in, a woman who could have been anywhere between thirty and forty-five, with arms full of documents and eyes full of fatigue, and asked me how I was.

'Doctor Narula told me about you,' she said. 'You're the prisoner.'

'You mean I was the prisoner,' I said. 'Although maybe it doesn't make much difference. Where is Dr Narula, then?'

Doctor Narula was off sick, as I guess doctors must be occasionally, which I suppose is one of life's little ironies, so I filled her in as best as I could and she sat there and listened and acted like she more or less believed me, although I don't suppose she had much choice about it.

'Well, that's interesting,' said the woman doctor eventually. 'Amnesia. Memory loss isn't really recognised as a side effect of morphine. Disorientation and hallucinations, yes, but not amnesia.'

I got a quick look-over then; follow the finger, touch your nose, a pencil torch in the eye. Motor skills and reflex response were okay, hardly ninja-quick, but at least they were there. Then a few simple questions: what year was it, how old was I, who was the prime minister? Apart from what did you have for breakfast, I didn't know any of them, and she wouldn't tell me either. I guess the test didn't end when she said it did.

When she asked me what I did for a living I told her I was a private detective and she nodded knowingly and smiled far too gently and said something about invented memories and something called Korsakoff's syndrome, and then I pulled my card out of my top pocket and waved it at her.

'Ring Avon CID if you want to,' I said, my temper flaring (it was nice to have that back). 'I have a memory problem, I'm not fucking insane.'

'I'm just trying to help. Korsakoff's syndrome isn't that unusual among chronic alcoholics.'

'Well, you're not helping,' I said. The bit about chronic alcoholism I let slide. Water off a duck's back, in the circumstances.

The lady doctor held her tongue and opened up a manila folder. A brief pause ensued which I decided not to fill. What it probably was, she explained to me, if all I said was true, was retrograde amnesia, which in fairness was a diagnosis I had reached myself, even deprived of years of medical training. The question was, she said, did it stem from cranial injury, or was it dissociative; had it been brought on by stress and trauma? A fugue state, she called it.

'Well I'm hardly the one to ask,' I said. 'I'm the one with the amnesia. But there was some trouble with the law, as I recall. Well, I don't recall, obviously. This bloke told me. My lawyer.'

'We'd have to put you down for a CAT scan,' she said, her head deep in her folder.

'There's therapy or something, I suppose.'

'Yes,' she said, face down, turning the pages, 'yes, but...'

And she looked straight at me and then through me and shrugged her small shoulders and shook her head.

'You don't really have the time. Sorry.'

I said nothing. Actually, I couldn't speak. It didn't seem much of a life, born middle-aged, alone and ill, into a strange house, with a past you didn't know about and a future that could be counted in weeks. Not much of a death either maybe, but then again that's how it usually happens, isn't it, dying? Unless you're one of the few that goes sharp and sudden, it takes a while, and bits fall off you as you go. You get smaller, inside and out. It was what my fellow corpses-to-be sang about in the night, that and other things. I felt a sudden tautness around my eyes and the corners of my mouth and looked away to the window and held my shortening breath until it passed. When it did all I could see was a lacklustre sky and those small, round hills. I hated those hills already.

'Otherwise you don't seem to be as bad as Dr Narula said you were, though,' said the woman doctor, brightening. 'I can't see why he thought that intravenous drip necessary. The pills are enough, right now.'

'I must have had a bad week,' I said, and the thought of our illicit arrangement gave me another little flutter of happiness.

'Look,' she said. 'You can still get up and around. Try and get out of your room today. It'll help you get your bearings. And I'll prescribe you some anti-depressants.'

'Do you think I need them?'

'You're bound to be depressed.'

'After talking to you,' I said, 'yes.'

'Mr Llywelyn,' she punctuated, 'there are some very

— 21 —

skilled people here who will give you all the skill and assistance they can. At least you are somewhere you can be looked after, by people who have some idea of who you are, even if you don't. Some amnesiacs, if that's what you are, are absolute mysteries. Like that piano player they found in Scotland.'

It had been on the BBC. I didn't know when, or where I was when I'd seen it, but it had been on the television.

'I remember something about that,' I said. 'It was on the news. He was a fraud, wasn't he?'

She had two plain brown eyes as tired as the leather buttons on an old cardigan and a full, round face that would probably have been attractive if she'd been sleeping properly. Now its net of etched lines was the most expressive thing about her, and even they said little, and the wrong thing. There had been a few gruelling weeks on the wards somewhere, and maybe some relationship or family trouble, and it had all gone on for too long. Two brown eyes as dry as stone. Both of them were still looking at me, or were parked in my direction, at any rate.

'Yes,' she said. 'Yes he was.'

She tucked a few pieces of foolscap back into my thin folder and left the room. In a busy city hospital, she would have made some kind of sense. She looked a little tragic here, like a breakdown without a crisis.

I was going to ask her about my clothes, but it was too late. Still, a little detective work, a little bit of the old tradecraft, and I'd tracked them down. Hanging up in the wardrobe.

When I plugged myself into the loopy juice and waved goodbye to the world I had been wearing a double-breasted woollen navy suit with a black leather belt, fairly shiny black leather brogues, a white shirt, and a Llanelli Scarlets tie. Seeing they were the only clothes I had, I put them on. It wasn't a bad get-up but I had lost weight and it was starting to look a tad Cab Calloway. In a transparent plastic bag by my bedside there was a set of the cheapest disposable razors and a can of Somerfield Value Shaving Foam, so I ran the corner sink and started to hack away. Clean-shaven I looked a little gaunt, but maybe not so much you could definitely tell I was ill.

My pyjamas, threadbare and oversized, I balled and binned, a small precautionary favour to the next guy roughly my size to come along, once I had gone. I was not the first man to have worn them, but I wanted to be the last. Whoever they had belonged to first, I had the very definite conviction that there was no chance of him coming round and asking for them back.

Once I was fully clad in the self-purchased garb of the independent adult I went through the pockets, where I found nothing, apart from half a pouch of Golden Virgina so stale it could have been discovered on an archaelogical dig, one pack of rolling papers that had HM Prisons printed under the flap, a plastic lighter from the Singleton Hotel and a stamped train ticket from Port Talbot to Llandovery. It was one-way. Port Talbot, Swansea and even the Singleton Hotel were all places that sounded familiar on the tongue, and I realised that I was getting bits of me back, even if they were just specks. Llandovery was a blank right then. Next I went though all the drawers and shelves in the room and found nothing, not even a bible.

I had no wallet, no watch, no phone, and no keys, none of the four talismans you always took with you into the real world. Worse, I had no money either. It was not, all in all, the personal inventory of a rich and successful man, and yet I had almost certainly had cash recently. Someone had bought the tickets; and possibly the doctor had needed some financial persuasion to get me on the intravenous morphine, from me or a benefactor, and benefactors seemed to be pretty thin on the ground.

Money, bribery, the law, prison: none of it felt particularly exciting or interesting to me. I wondered whether that was because I was used to it, or because I had more important things on my mind. Well, Narula would tell me if I pushed him, and I would the next time he came in. The past could take its time dripping back, but money I would absolutely have to get as soon as possible, one way or another, or I might as well climb back into bed and stick the drip back into my hand.

So I straightened my tie, took a final look at the impressive semi-shininess of my shoes, and left the room, which in itself was a lot more than some of the residents ever did. I glimpsed them through their doorways, like mummies without bandages, immobile on their beds. You saw the open door and you quickened your pace, but you couldn't help staring in.

In the hallway that woman with the East European accent and bottle-blonde hair was marking off her share of the duty rota on a wall-mounted whiteboard. When she saw me she said:

'Where are you off to then, all dressed up like that?'

I was going to ignore her, but I changed my mind before I got to the landing.

'If a man doesn't want to sit around in a dressing gown all day he shouldn't have to explain himself,' I said.

She gave a dismissive Slavic snort and I went down

one flight of stairs and through two sets of double doors and into a large room with a high ceiling that had the sort of cornice-work they make a big deal about on the telly programmes. There was a large but very old television set in one corner showing a presenter fawning over a sick rabbit in a country vet's, and the volume was set so low that even I couldn't hear it, and I was probably the youngest person in that room by twenty years. In another corner there were a couple of round tables with playing cards and dominoes on them, and along the back wall there was a long, low cabinet with a few food-stained paper doilies on it. On the far wall was a counter with a rolled-down grille over the hatch, where they must have dished out the sustenance, and lining the rest of the walls were long rows of pale green armchairs, lined in plastic for ease of cleaning. There were only four people sitting on them, and none of them looked much under eighty. Two of them were asleep and the third was a skeletal woman in a white cable-knit cardigan and an oxygen mask. Her eyes were open but I never saw them move once. I never saw any part of her move at all.

The fourth denizen of the day room I recognised. He was the old man in the dungarees and Jackie O spectacles who had swept my room. He was sitting in the middle of an empty row with his hands on his knees, staring at me unabashedly, as everyone seemed wont to do, if they had the energy to look.

'I thought you worked here,' I said.

'I help out,' he said. 'Look after the boilers, mostly. I'm a resident, mind. I'm the longest one. I've been in here seven years.'

'Hanging on in there, hey?'

'Liver or lung?' he said.

'I'm sorry?'

'It's one or the other with your sort.'

I was far from my physical peak, but I felt if I hit an eighty-year-old man square in the face as hard as I could then I'd probably do a fair bit of damage. I had the energy to hit him a good few times, too. It was a reassuring sort of a notion.

'We don't all get to claim our pensions,' was all I said.

'No,' he said, with evident satisfaction. 'I've seen you. Homeless mostly, and druggies, and the ones that are a bit slow. He's a bit slow.'

The man pointed with the absolute minimum of effort to the French windows next to the television. The back lawn had even longer grass than the front, strewn with the fallen leaves of autumn, and a large man was standing in the middle of it doing nothing, with a thick head of red hair blowing in the wind. He turned once to face some imaginary thing, and I caught a look at his profile, and realised he was even younger than me.

To my surprise, it didn't make me feel any better.

'So how about you?' I asked. 'What about fine upstanding voters like yourself? How'd you end up here?'

'Well…' the man began, eventually.

'Where's your family, then?' I pressed on. 'I know. Sat in a nice big house down the road, I expect, wondering if they should put a plasma screen in the spare room.'

The old man clamped his toothless gums shut, fixed his eyes at some faraway spot over my shoulder, and said nothing. I looked once around the room but everyone else still seemed asleep, except for the woman in the white cardigan and the oxygen mask, whose vision remained fixed on something only she could see.

The presenter on the television was stroking a Labrador and crying.

'Don't mind me,' the old man said eventually. 'With my remarks.'

'Fuck, don't worry, mun,' I said, leaning into his ear. 'I like you. At least you can actually talk.'

He gave me a helpless grin.

'You get a bit… You know, being a resident all this time. Anyway, it's good to see some new blood in here.'

Yeah, I thought, you probably mean that.

'You're the detective, aren't you?' he went on. 'Private detective, like the movies. You had some trouble with the law? Case go wrong, or something?'

'I'm afraid I can't tell you about that,' I said, which was quite true.

'Confidential, hey?' he said, and I gave a smile that probably looked more like a grimace to the trained eye, and left the room.

'See you around,' I said.

'Oh, I expect so,' said the seven-year resident. 'I certainly expect so.'

Nothing can explain how strange it is to be walking around with no idea who or even where you really are. Half the time you feel as if you're in a dream that belongs to someone else, and sooner or later he'll reappear and you'll be asked to leave, and then where will you be? If you can do it without constantly screaming and tearing your hair out you're doing very well, I think.

I found reception in a couple of minutes, at the bottom of a spiral staircase another corridor down, a long counter of fresh light pine that was probably the only new thing in the building. The reception was the first room I'd seen that was properly lit. Through the sash windows either side of the grand front entrance you could see the visitors' car park at the top of that winding driveway, its crumbling tarmac devoid of cars.

I pressed a buzzer on the counter and two plump women emerged one after the other from the back office behind reception, two women so young they could almost have been skiving school. They looked me up and down and made a show of clocking my suit and exchanging glances with each other before the first one said:

'Can I help you, sir?'

The tone sounded a little ironic but I gave her the benefit of the doubt.

'I was wondering if there was any mail for me,' I said. 'I was hoping for a parcel from my solicitor.'

Again, another exchange of glances.

'Sorry. Nothing here.'

And they were still looking knowingly at each other as I turned and left.

'I think he thinks this is his office,' one of them said.

It put a kink in my stride but I went without making a fuss. I didn't have the time, and I wasn't sure it would have got me anywhere. Instead I kept walking until my temper sagged, by which I time I was in a long, narrow conservatory running along the rear of the house. The simpleton with the red hair was still standing scarecrow-like in the middle of the garden, rigid as stone. There were patches of lawn out there that came up to his knee, and I watched the wind drive forking paths through the flexing grass, around legs rooted like trees. Although even the trees shivered.

The sky was the colour of cigarette smoke and already

the sun was too low, surrendered behind the leafless branches of that hillside copse. I edged past the bamboo tables and chairs to the far side and didn't notice her until I was almost out of the place.

Our eyes met and lingered maybe slightly longer than they should have done. Neither one of us was expecting to see somebody who was under fifty, whose eyes still held some life without being sat next to a drip or an oxygen canister. I would have thought she was visiting, or even working there, only she was wearing a set of red silk pyjamas and a thick quilted dressing gown. She had soft leather moccasins on and her hair was a curtain of rich chestnut that ran down to her shoulders, even if it was thin as straw. If you looked at her it was possible for a moment to pretend you were just in a very disappointing hotel.

God knows how she ended up here.

'Hello,' she said.

'Lovely view.'

She laughed, a nice, feminine, elegant laugh, but death was in it, the way the wind is in chimneys on stormy days.

'Are you a resident?' she asked, and I nodded. I was about to ask her the same thing.

'You're that private detective.'

I had the makings of a minor celebrity, it seemed. I suppose it was something to talk about that wasn't dying.

'Robin Llywelyn,' I said, and regretted it. I had no idea who Robin Llywelyn was.

'Hilary Price.'

And she stuck out a little ladylike hand. I felt like I'd short-changed her somehow, but I shook it anyway.

'I didn't think you were a resident at first. It's the suit you know. I don't think you're supposed to walk round all dressed up like that. They don't expect it. No one bothers. You're supposed to, you know...'

Sit around and die, I guess. She looked up at me and smiled awkwardly and I smiled awkwardly back. Soon we were both just staring silently out at the daily evening apocalpyse that was rural Wales in an approaching winter, which was, like a lot of the things I'd seen that day, the last thing you wanted to be looking at.

'Postcard material,' she said.

I pointed over at the catatonic hulk in the middle of the lawn.

'He seems to like it.'

'Still, I've sat out here a couple of times,' she went on. 'This time of year, sometimes, even when it's been a really terrible day, a day you'd think would have no beauty in it at all, something just comes together at the close, and you'll get an amazing sunset. A whole day of nasty, miserable, cold and rain and grey, and then for some reason when the sun starts to sink it sets something off and just for a few minutes the most incredible beauty comes out of nowhere. That's why I sit out here. Sometimes the sunset will amaze you. And of course sometimes the day just ends the way it began.'

'Yeah,' was all I said. I'd be bloody surprised if it happened any other way tonight. 'What's the date, do you know? When is it, exactly?'

She laughed again, a half-happy sound with a twinkle of doom in it.

'October. The fourth, I think. You do forget the time in here.'

God, it would be October, wouldn't it. Looking back, I had always hated that time of year. Nothing but cold and dark closing in, with nothing to look forward to but Christmas, which had never been anything to look forward to for me.

'You certainly do,' I said.

'Do you have any family?'

'I dunno. Probably. Maybe. Not a very close family, if I do.'

'No,' she said, and laughed again. 'They don't sound very close.'

'No,' I said, 'I mean I can't remember. I have amnesia.'

She startled and gave me the old up-and-down treatment.

'Really?' – all excited – and then a beat later: 'I'm sorry,' all sensitive and polite.

'Yup. Retrograde amnesia. The quacks say it'll wear off. But that answer must go for everybody in here. Anyone could have said it and it'd be true. About not having very close family.'

'Yes,' she said. 'Yes. I suppose.'

And a tear quickened in the corner of an eye, and the room was very, very quiet, and I left. I felt a little bad about it later.

In the day room nothing had changed. It had just got darker. The old man with the big glasses eyed me in a vindicated way as I walked listlessly around, as if he'd won some sort of argument. In the cupboards beneath the counter on the back wall I found an old record player, although I couldn't find any music. Behind me I could hear the woman with the oxygen tank breathing, a sound like rustling paper.

'What are you up to then, son?' said the old man. 'Got something to do, have you?'

Was this it, I wondered? Apart from the idiot in the garden and the lady in the conservatory, the only people who left their rooms were probably all in here. Most of them looked like they'd been carried or wheeled in. Certainly they would all soon be carried out. The day room. The end of days room. Four pale walls, some out-of-date furniture, crumbs from some birthday buffet or other forlorn attempt at gaiety, an old record player with no records, the smell of disinfectant and wood polish, plastic covers on everything, the sound of very laboured, very pained breathing. Nobody talking, nobody able to, perhaps nothing even to talk about. Was this it?

'Yeah,' I said, all matter-of-factly. 'I have.'

'Oh yeah,' said the old man, looking so smug that the area between his nose and his lower lip more or less disappeared completely. 'What's that then?'

'I'm going down the pub,' I said.

'You can't do that. You're not allowed. I'll have to tell—'

'Special privileges,' I said, and strode out as purposefully as I could muster, with a superior glance over my shoulder. Never mind him, I was walking out on my own two feet, which was one up to me, for the time being. While I was still able to stride purposefully anywhere. Of course, I hadn't reached the end of the hall before I realised I had no money. I double-checked my pockets, and went up to my room and double-checked my drawers, but reality prevailed. I didn't have a penny.

There were three or four rooms on my floor where the residents were reaching the end of their stay. You could see them from the corridor: the staff left their doors wide open so they could keep an eye on them. I hadn't been able to look in on them without flinching before, but now I watched them like a hawk. The first one I visited still had some kind of wits about her, but the second was almost gone. In fact, thinking about it, she may have gone already.

In the bottom of her bedside cabinet there was an old blue faux-leather handbag, and it had over forty pounds in it, which was mine now. She could have given it to a grandchild or somebody, I suppose, but I hadn't seen any visitors for anyone all day. It didn't seem like the sort of place that got them. At the far end of the corridor a carer was coming in through the first-floor fire exit from a fag break, and I gave it a minute and went out the same way.

I descended slowly, careful not to let my steps ring out on the dimpled steel, and when I hit the gravel I stayed as close to the building as possible, keeping away from the exterior lights, and already getting some small rebellious kick from it all. Hugging the stonework and walking on the balls of my feet I edged my way around to the front of the house, only to pass a pillar and find myself squarely exposed before one of the sash windows in reception. But the two girls had returned to the back room and their magazines, and it was probably already dark enough for the outside world to be more or less invisible from a lit room. All that was left was to take a deep breath, something that made my whole chest feel like a giant strained muscle now, and limp off towards that hump-backed bridge as fast as my knotted lungs would allow, my great escape almost complete. Fifteen minutes and I'd be there.

In the movie the lucky ones got to the Swiss border:

I got to the market square, a little open space not much bigger than a tennis court. There wasn't a soul about. I stood next to a miniature market hall, stood in the cool air between its stone columns, trod its flagstones, watched a nearby pub sign swing gently in the wind, and experienced a mild wave of panic. I had battled my way here with no more thought than a spawning salmon gives to the countercurrent, and now I'd arrived I had an instinctive suspicion I had swum up the wrong stream.

It was the sort of place, at first glance, that could have been any little town in inland Wales, the sort of gaff where a day of excitement meant a day return to Swansea or Shrewsbury (assuming you had a train station), and market day was still the liveliest it ever got, which is to say not much. Even so, would somebody recognise me from the hospice? Had they noticed I was gone? What would happen if they did? It would be terrible if they locked me in and it would probably be worse if they chucked me out. They would probably do one or the other, I reckoned, and a part of me believed they would do both if they could.

A fat man walked a mangy-looking Alsatian down the opposite end of the square and then disappeared from view. Two boys on bikes swooped round a corner and were gone. That was all the life I saw in five whole minutes. No sirens sounded. No searchlights combed the street. So my bold strike for freedom ended up in the White Hall Hotel, Llandovery, and anticlimaxed before the door had time to close behind me. I had forgotten what these country pubs were like. It probably wasn't busy at the best of times, and this must have been something like a Tuesday or Wednesday night. It was a chance to sit down, at least: the walk couldn't have been more than half a mile, but it had nearly done for me. I was the only person in there, apart from the barman, a lad with a scratchy goatee who couldn't have been a day over twenty-one, with his face in some kind of book.

'What brings you to our fair town?' he says, like he's the mayor.

'Cancer,' I said. 'I'll have one of those Watkin's bitters.'

He served it up without any more of the welcoming committee rubbish and then I went and sat down in a corner, under some low beams covered in desiccated hops, and watched it settle. A pale cloud rose and swirled within the glass, and as it disappeared there came that clear and perfect liquid amber where a man thinks he can swim forever. Even in the weak light of a dim, low-ceilinged pub, devoid of people, at the onset of winter, it cast a certain glow. Underneath that paper-thin head of foam lay a sweet and secret sea that seemed capable of swallowing all that was thrown into it; sorrows, joys, days, and years. I couldn't remember if I'd tasted a pint of Tomos Watkin's before, but I had feeling I probably had. I had a feeling I'd tasted most things, and I'd tasted them a great deal.

The full pint sat on the table in front of me. I was a chronic alcoholic, to use the doc's term, and I was sober. A week of intravenous morphine will do that to you, amongst other things. I didn't need my memory to know that chance had dropped me into the calm centre of a raging storm, and this was what it was like where the winds didn't blow. A moment of clarity is what I understand they call it at AA meetings. Real stone-cold sobriety, and it would come, wouldn't it, at a time when I had no real idea of who I was, or what I was, or the things that I had done.

— 35 —

I sat there and wondered if forgetting who you were made you a different person, if all that you had been and done didn't really have to matter in the end. Or if what mattered was in the mind or in the bones. I could have been anybody. And I didn't feel like anybody, or anything, apart from a drink. I turned the pint around slowly on the beermat while it called to me, rotating it anti-clockwise a dozen times without lifting it once, listening to its song, and for a spell it was the only thing I heard. I might have weakened, but somewhere nearby some tiny dog started barking over and over, somewhere in the room, but I couldn't see it. Couldn't see it anywhere, and I did look.

I wouldn't have said anything, only I needed to know if the hallucinations were coming on after all.

'Is there a dog in here?' I asked the barman, who raised his book at me in a gesture of explanation, and I saw it was not a book but a small plastic square.

'That a personal organiser or something?'

'It's a Nintendo DS,' he said, or something like it. 'I'm playing *Dogs*. I'm raising a little chocolate lab on it. Got a level five rottie too.'

'Yeah,' I said, eventually. 'All right then.'

That pretty much set the tone for the night, really. Me trying to teach myself philosophy with no textbooks and two months to live, and some post-adolescent with a fluffy chin and a little black box that made occasional barking noises. When they say there isn't much for the youth to do in those little market towns, they're spot on, you know. A little while later and I started thinking about going back to the hospice.

I had pretty much reconciled myself to heading back, and leaving an untouched pint on the table, when the door banged open and some huge farmer full of cider staggered in, wellingtons and woolly jumper and padded waistcoat, hair and pockets full of bits of wire and twine and hay. He was about two or three drinks away from being as drunk as an upright man gets.

'Evening Ger,' said the lad behind the bar, and Ger proceeded to conduct some large and incomprehensible conversation all on his own. Still, given the circumstances, he was the life and soul of the party. He was concerned about the prime minister in some regard, I believe, and I was happy enough to sit there and try and guess exactly how.

After he'd wet his whistle he leant back on the bar and had a good look around. He cast a familiar gaze over me and started in my direction, bringing a tumbler of Bell's with him. Sure enough, with some confidence, he sat down opposite me and gave me the nod.

'Didn't realise they let you out and about,' he said. He spoke like a farmer too, which is to say he wasn't very good at it; all that time on your own, see, speaking to nobody but animals, and then mostly shouting, probably in Welsh too. Miserable sods most of the time, they come to market and get all excited to be in town, booming nonsense and inanities all over the place with varying degrees of bonhomie.

I wondered if my condition was that obvious, that you could tell my address just from looking at me.

'I wasn't let out, as such,' I said. 'Just decided to take the air.'

'The air in here is lovely,' he said, and laughed, with tremendous force, the same way he probably shook hands, I thought. When he quietened down he looked at me expectantly and smiled.

'Do I know you?' I asked.

'Do you know me? Ha!' he said, and treated me to another gust of laughter. 'I heard about the memory. Fantastic. Expect you'll make a miracle recovery now you're off the hook.'

'The doctor did say it would come back, yes.'

Naturally, Ger saw the funny side of this and showed his appreciation in the usual way. It was like sitting on top of Pen y Fan in a storm.

'Terrific idea, that.'

'I wouldn't call it that.'

For a brief moment, we descended to about gale force three.

'Wouldn't call it what?' he said, wiping spittle off his chin.

'Terrific. Or an idea.'

'What do you mean, mun?'

'I have amnesia,' I said, very slowly, at some volume.

The laughter came on again, but started to tail off quite quickly until we were sitting in silence again.

'I have amnesia,' I said again, shrugging. 'Something to do with the drugs they were giving me, and stress maybe. I don't know who you are. I wouldn't know who I am, only I've got a business card.'

I took it out and showed it to him, and he glanced down at it, hardly taking his eyes off of me, the jollity draining from his face as if he was holding a poker hand. He was grave now, serious as a man waiting for his test results. In an instant he had reverted to the state of high grimness that was probably his usual manner.

'Amnesia?'

He stole another quick glance at the card, turning it over in his hands.

'Not so handy, for a private detective,' he said.

'Yeah,' I said. 'Private detective, or private investigator, I forget what it says.'

Another hard stare.

'At least you're up and about. We should talk,' he says. 'In private.'

'What do you want a private detective for?'

He leant in towards me.

'Maybe I don't,' he said, draining his tumbler. Then he got another double at the bar and stayed there, although he kept looking back at me in a strange way. I wondered if it was just because he was legless or if he really was turning something over in that addled, Wurzel Gummidge brain.

'Private detective?' said the barman with the electronic barking box. 'What d'you want one of them for then?'

'It's a matter of security,' Ger said to him, after what might have been a little contemplation. 'Security is very important, you see. Security is paramount. The running of a farm requires certain equipment and machinery that can be very expensive. It's the machinery.'

Gerald paused for breath. Then he looked about him in a bewildered fashion as if he'd forgotten where he was, and I thought that'd be the end of it, but his eyes fell on me in my corner and it seemed to egg him on.

'The machinery. There are thieves, you see. Steal your machinery. Scousers probably. Come over from England. Steal your fucking sheep! Ten thousand lamb gone in the middle of the night just like that. But it, it's the…'

Ger paused, careful to select just the right word.

'It's the machinery, you see. Where are the police? Fucking miles away, mun. Asleep. This is the countryside. There's no police here, there's not enough of them. I need to know about cameras and so on. Special fences. Landmines!'

And he cackled without feeling. In fact it looked to me like the whole speech was pretty much for the barman's benefit. Ger showed him my card, although he didn't let him touch it, and then he came back over and sat down, although next to me this time, not opposite, and started talking into my ear.

'Don't worry about all that,' he said. 'I'll get you all up to speed tomorrow night, never fear. Tomorrow night at my place. Seven o'clock. High Farm. Can you make it?'

'What's in it for me?' I asked. Perhaps this was a sensible thing to ask, perhaps it was something else, something in the bone, like the drink.

The corners of Ger's mouth began to rise upwards and tremble ever so slightly. Two minutes ago his old self would have been in hysterics.

'What's in it for you?' he repeated. 'Oh, I don't know. We'll see.'

'I'll need something up front,' I said. 'Just a kind of bond, really, it's quite common.'

Yeah. Some things are in the bone all right.

'Of course,' he said, reaching into the frayed tweed jacket he wore under his torn bodywarmer. 'Naturally.'

Like a magician producing a rope of brightly coloured handkerchiefs, Ger started pulling out crisp new twenties one at a time. After he'd put a hundred quid on the table he tapped the side of his nose and told me:

'There's more where that came from. Tomorrow night at High Farm. Seven o'clock at the latest, can't wait any longer than that. You've got people to look after. Ask Gary for directions. Now if you excuse me, I have to go home and have my tea. Been a long day. Been up since five.'

He sank his last double and after nodding goodbye to the barman, waved my business card at me from the door and disappeared.

We listened to the sound of his lumbering footsteps on the wet cobbles outside, to the slam of a car door and the burr of ignition, to the hapless grinding of gears and a small engine receding as it disappeared between the hedgerows. If he crashed into anything, it wasn't within earshot of the Red Lion.

'Your dog is lonely,' said an electronic voice.

Pretty much on reflex I got up and got myself another pint.

'You Gary?' I asked.

'Yeah.'

'And that was?'

'Gerald Williams. He's been on the pop, mind. He's solemn as a priest when he's sober.'

'Aren't we all,' I said.

The barman already had his eyes back on his electronic gizmo but he lifted them long enough for another quick appraisal.

'Ger's all right,' he said.

'Is he serious?' I asked.

'Are you?'

'Christ,' I said. 'They get enough in subsidies.'

I asked Gary if he was on shift tomorrow night and he said yes, and then I took my drink back to my table, where my first pint still lay entirely untouched. I put the second one next to it to keep it company. I'd only bought it out of habit. I wasn't going to touch either of them tonight; not for a while, most likely. It'd be nice, but that particular avenue of investigation wouldn't help the memory, and a man in my situation has to hang on to what he can.

'Beer all right?' asked Gary, looking at my two little friends.

'Is there much to do round here?' I asked. 'Apart from go down the pub?'

He shook his head.

'There's a little theatre. Got some sort of musicians from Estonia in at the mo.'

'No thanks.'

I watched another Tomos Watkin's settle in the glass. It surprises me that there isn't some superstition about the swirling clouds of hops and foam in freshly drawn beer, that some mystic has never insisted there are omens and auguries in its swirls and vortices. I sat there and tried to read them, but I think it's harder without drinking the stuff. In short order I probably would, but not yet. Farmer Gerald, with his security evaluation, if that was what he wanted, if, for that matter, he actually wanted anything at all, would probably appreciate some temperance. Doubtless he required and expected something that looked at least a bit like professionalism. Not that I really cared. Mostly I think I just wanted my card back. It was the only thing I had with my name on it.

III

The nurse that came into my room the next morning was very happy.

'You made the bed,' she said.

'People get into those things and they don't get out, you know,' I said, when I'd come to, sat in my armchair. I had to grip the armrests pretty tight when I remembered where I was.

'Nobody ever makes the bed,' she said, 'hardly ever.'

Not for the first time, I wondered where she was from. Poland, maybe, or the Baltic states, I don't know. Somewhere bad enough to make working here a cheery prospect. I decided not to tell her I'd slept in the chair.

'Sure,' I said. 'Well, I like to help you. You're nice.'

She gave me a sardonic smile that I found oddly flattering in its mistrust and puffed up the back of her bottle-blonde hair and checked her medication chart with an overly solemn expression and sailed out.

'Breakfast is being served in the day room,' she told me. 'It's important that you eat. It doesn't matter whether you're hungry or not.'

'Fine,' I said, and I was not hungry, had no appetite at all, but went downstairs anyway, seeing as she'd smiled at me. It wasn't a bad start to the day.

Downstairs I found myself in a small crowd of people who were going to have nothing but bad starts to their days until the rest of their days ran out. And muesli too, would you believe. I would have thought at this stage a few fried eggs and black pudding wouldn't do anybody any harm, but it was a breakfast that would have passed muster in a health spa, which this place certainly wasn't.

There were less than a dozen residents present, and half of those would probably go upstairs again once they'd spooned down their gruel. It wasn't a heart-warming sight. I filled a cup of tea from the urn and decided to take it out to the conservatory, if only because I didn't know where to look. I couldn't cope with the sight of a dozen dying people having to eat muesli first thing in the morning.

Outside there was a fine frost on the ground, and a faint ribbon of pink running along the bottom of the sky, promising bad weather later. She was in there too, that woman, working her way through two slices of dry toast, still in her dressing gown. We nodded good morning to each other and sat there watching the pale white sun lift itself into the cold grey sky. It was warm in the hospice, at least, a thick blanket of heat steaming out of the old building's Victorian plumbing. I didn't relish the thought of going outside later, but I preferred it infinitely to the idea of staying in.

'Have you got much planned today?' said Hilary Price dryly, from the other end of that long conservatory, once we had finished our breakfasts. You could tell it strained her to project that far. I got up and went over, although I wasn't sure whether I should sit down or not.

'Thought I'd go for a run,' I said, 'and then do some weightlifting.'

'I'm going to pop into the sauna and then get a massage and then order some champagne. Probably with lobster.'

'I believe I had a cup of the house champagne just now. Very fine.'

Then we two comedians sat there silently and watched the fog coming through the trees until it seemed to be pressing up against the glass.

'How's the memory?' she asked.

I tried a Gallic shrug.

'Still shot,' I said. 'It comes back in little flashes, a couple of little irrelevant details a day. Thought I might try and dig up whatever paperwork there is on me, see if it'll help jog the cogs.'

'Are you sure you want to remember?'

I couldn't tell if she was joking or not.

'There's not much else to do, is there?' I said, at last.

'Tell me who you are, when you find out,' she replied, and I told her I would, and then I got myself out of my chair and headed for the gorgons in reception. As I edged my way past her she reached out for my arm.

'But I might not be here,' she said. 'My son is coming today. He's been trying to arrange home care for me, if I stay with him. He owns a marketing agency down in Cardiff.'

I put a hand on her shoulder.

'I'm glad,' I said, and I was. She didn't deserve this, I was sure of it, without knowing the first thing about her. To die in a single bed tended by strangers, in a house not your own, full of awful silences and laments, surrounded by residents who have lived far longer than you will, and whose added years have bought them only the curious blessing that they are now only partially aware they are alive at all. Better, surely, that the sound outside your bedroom door is the soft tread of a husband or daughter on the landing, and not the boots of night-time security or foreign nurses. Better to hear the voices of loved ones talking softly to each other from the kitchen or the lounge than the inchoate complaints of your survivors howling from their own little rooms that they, on the other hand, are waiting too long to die. Better a hand to hold occasionally than to have to sit there wringing your own. All this, I think, was understood.

'I'm glad,' I said again, and gripped a delicate shoulder, and felt the rare glow of a little happiness, a little hope. It felt like the most daring thing in the world. 'Good luck.'

The girls in reception weren't any more useful than they'd been the day before. In fact, much like yesterday, they weren't even in reception. I paced up and down past the doorway until I caught their eyes and then the pair of them trotted reluctantly out like teenagers, the same two as before, two fat brunettes in twinsets.

'The reception is for visitors,' the least fat one explained to me. 'What is it you want?'

'I'm expecting some mail,' I said.

'It'll be delivered to your room, if you have any.'

'Nothing came this morning? Nothing from my solicitor?'

'The mail is delivered to residents' rooms.'

'So there's nothing to go up for me?'

'The mail is delivered to residents' rooms,' she repeated.

'You can't tell me?'

'I'm not your secretary,' she said, with a copy of *Heat* in one hand and a cherry yoghurt in the other. 'If there's anything for you it'll be up by lunchtime.'

'Mid-afternoon,' piped up the other one, and they returned to their back room and closed the door.

Not for the first time, I wondered what sort of person ends up alone like this. I wondered if I deserved it or if it was just bad luck, or if maybe there was somebody out there waiting to find out where I was after all, somebody who would come through for me.

A grown man shouldn't have to hope he's a good person, like some schoolboy waiting for his end-of-term report, but I did sorely want to be a good person. It meant it was slightly more likely there was someone out there who cared about me, although I was not optimistic. On either count.

If the file from my solicitor had not arrived, then there were still my medical records. The doctors' office was signposted from the reception area, and turned out to be a locked blue door at the end of a narrow corridor, which nobody answered when I knocked. Two small steel and leather chairs were backed up against the wall right by it, so I sat down in one a little nervously and waited. It was kind of like running a stake-out on myself.

It was the woman doctor who appeared first. She had a Tupperware container of steaming microwaved pasta in one hand; cutlery and a cup of coffee in the other, and a broadsheet newspaper under her arm. Because the seats took up half the corridor there was no real way she could have ignored me, although you could tell she did think about it.

'Hello,' she said, side-stepping past me, as fast as she could.

'Dr Narula still off?' I asked.

'Afraid so.'

Then she was on the other side of the door, and soon after I heard a key turn in the lock.

'I'll wait until you've finished your lunch,' I said, through the keyhole.

Sometime after two o'clock she reappeared with carbonara sauce on her jumper and asked me what it was I wanted.

'Really you have to file an official request invoking the Freedom of Information Act,' she said.

'I know about that,' I said, and to my surprise I did, or half-knew, anyway. 'And you have six weeks to comply. If you don't, I can write to the Ombudsman, and I'd be very surprised if I heard back from him inside a fortnight. A week or two after that, the ball might start rolling. Bloody hell, I'll be dead by then. If my records are in there I don't have to take them out of the room, you know.'

The doctors' office was a lot smaller than you'd think: two tiny desks pressed up against each other in the middle of the room, a filing cabinet, and a small potted plant on a low corner table that was browning nicely. There was a small window that looked out on to the breezeblock wall of a nearby shed and not much else. The receptionists got a better deal, really.

'We don't consult in here,' she explained. I almost began to feel sorry for her. 'You can sit at Dr Narula's desk while I dig out your file.'

While she had her back to me I had a quick rummage through his drawers, just on instinct, I suppose, but there was nothing revelatory in there. Actually there wasn't anything in there at all. Completely empty. If a tidy desk is a sign of a tidy mind, Narula's was in a state of divine innocence. Which it wasn't.

'Here we are,' she said at last. 'Seeing as you insist. Llywelyn, Robin.'

'That's me,' I said, feeling pretty ambiguous about it. 'Looks pretty slim.'

'Did we lose your records?' she asked herself, thumbing through it. 'No. Guess you just haven't been one for visiting the doctor. Well, here it is.' She tossed it on to the desk. 'Hope it helps.'

I sat down and felt the weight of it; as you'd expect, it was light as air. Three or four sheets of paper tops. And yet there might be an entire life in there waiting for me.

'How come I ended up in here, Doc, of all places?'

'It's up to the board,' she shrugged. 'They run the admissions panel.'

'And who's on the board?'

'Oh, I couldn't tell you off-hand. There's about eight or nine of them, mostly from the county set, the farming and hunting types, and a few members of the big local families. Or what were the big local families.'

I took a punt.

'Is one of them a man called Gerald Williams?'

'Yes, I believe so. Not that he's very involved. Are you going to read that or not?'

So old Gerald was more than just a drunken idiot after all. I was not in the least surprised: all drunken idiots are more than they seem. It is the parts of them you cannot see, their stories and secrets, that help make them like that in the first place. Not for the first time I wondered how much, if anything, we'd had to do with each other. But first things first, I spread my hands open over the beige cover; braced myself for whatever lay inside.

'You're not nervous about what I'll find in here, are you?' I said, perhaps just because I was nervous myself. 'I've heard about you doctors and your acronyms, writing all sorts of little messages in your notes because you think no one'll ever see it, or they won't be smart enough to work out what it means if they do. PIA for pain in the arse and all that.'

It didn't lighten her mood any, or mine, come to that. She just looked at me coolly and waited for me to get on with it.

'Did you see me before I lost my memory?' I asked her. 'Did you know me at all?'

She shrugged.

'What sort of person would you say I was?'

'Ill,' she said.

I took one final moment to steel myself and then opened it up. I needn't have bothered. I would have learnt more about myself reading a bus timetable.

I was only forty-six, which was about ten years younger than I'd have guessed. I'd been born in late winter, in Prince Philip Hospital, Llanelli. Prior to the hospice in Llandovery I had been living in a hostel for the homeless in Swansea. Something was probably wrong with my liver, and I had lung cancer. I had no next of kin, or rather the space for next of kin was blank. And that was all there was.

'What do you put if there's no next of kin?' I asked. 'Do you write "none", or do you leave it blank, or what?'

'Well, we should put "none", I suppose. Usually we do, I think. Some of the time doctors probably don't.'

'Why is mine blank?'

'You'll have to ask Dr Narula when he's well enough to come back in.'

'And what does GIT stand for?'

She gave me that cool glance again, neutral and professional but also decidedly unimpressed.

'I don't think it stands for anything,' she said.

I left the file on the desk, shut the door behind me, and walked down the long and narrow corridor until I came out into reception. There was nobody there this time either, just that grey mist hanging thickly outside the window. It looked cold out. Upstairs in my room there was no solicitor's parcel waiting for me, but the second floor was high enough to see over the fog. I sat on the edge of the bed and watched a bunch of starlings take off from their branches and circle the treetops.

I knew a bit more about myself, I suppose, but it was knowledge without memory, and the strangeness of it didn't really make things feel any better. Anyway, we are more than names and dates, than blood types and allergies. I watched the birds grow in number, following some strange and unpredictable pattern unknown maybe even to the tiny starling subconscious. They moved as one, like smoke. Soon they would be joined by small clouds of other starlings from roosts nearby, until the sky blackened with their numbers, or else they would leave themselves to join up with others elsewhere, and as night fell they would descend as one in their thousands on some safe, secluded spot, and sleep.

Surely we don't go through all our years without reaching somebody, somewhere.

It's impossible.

Downstairs, Hilary Price was still sitting in the same seat in the conservatory. I don't know why I went there but I did.

'Well?' she said. 'Did you look at your medical records after?'

'The jury is out,' I said. 'Didn't discover much. I was born in Llanelli.'

'Oh, I wouldn't worry about that,' she said.

'Do you want to go out tonight?' I found myself asking.

'Where?' she said. I could tell I'd thrown her a bit. If you're trying to die peacefully in a hospice you probably shrink your horizons a good whack, or you end up ripping your heart out. Myself and the red-headed retard were the only residents that ever left the building, far as I knew.

'I hear there's a little theatre in town doing a concert. I could get tickets if you like.'

Hilary had a good long look at the wall behind my shoulder, but when she finished I was still there.

'That would be very nice,' she said finally.

'Right,' I said, 'I'll see to it,' and strode off like a man taking care of business, instead of one who barely knew his own name. I nicked a pen from reception, which wasn't difficult, found a payphone, and got the numbers for the theatre and a local taxi firm from directory enquiries, booked a cab and reserved two seats, all the time not quite believing I was actually doing it. According to the woman in the theatre (Gary was right) tonight's performance was a classical concert from touring East European musicians. Could be worse, I suppose. Hilary would probably appreciate it, I was pretty certain. She seemed like the sort.

'Six o'clock all right?' I said, on my way back through to nowhere in particular. 'I've got us a car.'

'Fine,' was all she said, so I left it there, and went up to my room to do nothing for what little of the afternoon was left. It was how most people staying there spent their time, in their rooms, or in the pale lime seats of the day room, or in Hilary's case, sat in a rattan chair in an empty conservatory. Feeding off their memories, perhaps. Obviously, that was a bit tricky for me.

When I came back down Hilary was still in the same seat, although the dressing gown and slippers had gone and she was wearing a dark, elegant overcoat that came down to her ankles, a long patterned dress, and a black jumper with some ethnic-looking necklaces hanging down it. They were probably the clothes she had on when they checked her in.

'I thought it might be a bit cold out,' she said, waving some gloves and a scarf at me. 'What is it we're going to see again?'

'Some quartet from Estonia playing Schubert,' I said, doing my best.

'Okay.'

She gave me a brittle smile, and I realised this was the first time I had seen her standing up. She seemed fine, if a little nervous, but people can seem anything. Something like guilt or fear tugged at my sleeve, and I was going to ask her if she was really all right to do this, but instead for some reason I found myself saying:

'Don't suppose you fancy a quick drink first?'

The White Hall Hotel wasn't any cheerier than it had been the night before. Gary was still there, serving a dark-haired brick shithouse in a Barbour jacket and army boots, bald on top but compensating with a thick moustache, a good third of which was probably nostril hair. There were already four or five empties on the bar next to him. He didn't speak once the whole time we were there; didn't even turn his head. I had the feeling it was probably a good thing.

Hilary said she wasn't allowed alcohol but I asked what difference that made now and she couldn't answer, so I got her a large schooner of sherry and a pint of Tomos Watkin's for me and we sat at our own table and looked at them, too afraid to raise a glass, her because her doctor had told her not to, me because I had a feeling I wouldn't be able to stop once I did. I could already hear the wanting humming in the blood behind my ears.

'Do you like classical music?' I asked Hilary, when the awkwardness became unmanageable.

'Oh, yes. Of course.'

'I thought you might,' I said, and then she excused herself to go to the ladies, probably because it was more interesting than being sat next to me, and I sat and stared at our drinks and thought about dropping the sherry in the bitter and downing them both. Maybe I would have done it too, but then I noticed somebody standing behind me.

'I thought you were supposed to be seeing Gerald,' said Gary.

'If Gerald wants to play funny buggers he can wait,' I said. 'I've got other things to do right now.'

And I nodded in the direction of the ladies, like I was on some kind of hot date. Don't ask me what I really thought I was doing. Just trying to keep the number of dying people around Hilary Price and me to a minimum, I suppose, for one night only.

'That doesn't seem very professional,' said Gary, as if he cared.

Had I slightly longer to live, I might have cleared up a few pointers with young Gary, but curiosity got the better of me.

'He knew me, didn't he?'

Gary shrugged.

'Knows everyone,' he said, and went back to his little Nintendo, and then Hilary came out of the ladies and said she didn't feel up to a drink after all, and I wasn't really in a position to argue with her seeing as I hadn't even picked my glass up, so we left.

'Tell Ger I'll go round tomorrow night,' I said, and Gary stood behind the bar and stared down at the little screen in his hands and said nothing. I nodded good evening to the back of the Barbour jacket and we stepped outside.

I spied one of those brown information signs pointing towards the theatre, and took Hilary's arm, for some reason, and we went over the flagstones towards the other side of the square. Two or three young teenagers were standing round outside the Spar, and back by the river I could see somebody coming in from the fields with a Welsh sheepdog on the end of a lead. As we passed the market hall Hilary was about to say something but this rumbling noise began to draw near, and as we turned the corner a lorry with a second unit towed behind it barrelled down the little street, maybe not much more than a foot away from us on our sliver of pavement. For a deafening instant there was an overpowering smell of diesel and animal shit, and then it was gone already, leaving the dirt to settle in the gutters while the bleating of hostage livestock disappeared off towards the border.

Nobody batted an eyelid, of course.

'The locals call it the meat train,' said Hilary. 'There's a couple of them every hour.'

'Day and night?' I asked.

She nodded.

'When I came in about six weeks ago there was a warm spell and I slept with my window open for a couple of nights. You could hear them passing through. I didn't mind it, actually. Not from that distance.'

I thought of some guy doing the night shift in a factory abattoir on an industrial estate somewhere, standing by a conveyor belt of endless mutton, chain-mail gloves and a knife sharper than anything else in his entire life, or rubber mittens and an electric gun, snuffing out lamb after lamb, or gutting the carcasses, stepping out into the dawn with offal in your hair every morning for year after year. There were people that did it their whole lives. Serial killers, probably.

'It does taste lovely with a bit of mint,' I said.

'Llandovery's always been about the drovers one way or another,' she said, and I got a little slice of local history then, that I might have known once. About how these wild souls would come down from the lonely hills and open spaces of mid-Wales with a flock of thousands, and march them all the way to the London markets. About how they gathered here before setting off east, rough characters walking an untrustworthy road, vagabonds smart enough to form their own bank so no one could steal from them. It was a bit of a stretch comparing them to some agency truck driver in a Leyland DAF, but I let it slide. I liked the sound of them.

That took us up to the façade of a very forlorn-looking

theatre, and we went in and it was everything I expected. Some damp, cramped little place that still managed to seem as empty as somewhere two or three times its size, maybe because of the air of failure in the foyer, the broken hopes that hung over the empty seats. The whole place was a labour of love for some displaced thespians, and that love was not being returned. Mind you, even the famous ones never seem to get quite as much as they would like.

Then these four guys from Estonia came on, four pale and thin musicians whose last gig had probably been two hours' busking outside British Home Stores in Newport, with an open violin case on the ground in front of them. I'm far from the expert on classical music, but they weren't too bad at all, two guys on violins and two guys on cello who looked like they hadn't eaten since the airport.

It was beautiful music, but there was something else to it too. It took a while to get into it but I tuned in eventually. Sadness has a melody that you can recognise anywhere if you've ever spent much time in its company, and that makes most of us, I guess.

Hilary didn't seem to mind it either.

'This is the quintet in C major,' she whispered. 'He was dying when he wrote this. He died two months after.'

'What did he die of?'

'Syphilis. He had this friend who was a bit of a boy, you know, and he led him astray. He was only thirty-one.'

One of the cellists went into a coughing fit so bad it looked like consumption, and the few of us there had to wait for him to recover, the racking of his chest reverberating beneath the wide, high ceiling. When it was over they started from the beginning again.

Thirty-one and two months to live. Still, it happens, I

thought, people get worse deals, and then I realised what had happened: he got dealt the bum hand and he still wrote this.

I sat there and strained my ears but bitterness wasn't in it.

'It's really not bad at all,' I said, and Hilary nodded and her eyes began to well up so I looked to the stage and it all washed over us again.

Some time later, much later, although it didn't feel like it, Hilary and I were the only people left in the seats, and the Estonians, who hadn't said a word all evening, were shuffling around putting their gear away. She still looked pretty depressed.

'The taxi will be waiting,' I said, because it was the only thing I could think of saying.

We went out through the little foyer, stepped through the double doors into the cold night, and saw our driver idling down the street in his Volvo estate.

'Took your time,' he said, and we climbed into the back seat of this car that reeked of cheap deodorant and even cheaper cigars, took off towards the deadhouse, and it was almost as if Schubert had never been born at all. That's the problem with music. It always leaves you with silence, in the end.

The lights were still on in the day room, and reception was empty, just like it was during most of the day, but I took us in through the ground-floor fire escape at the side. I think maybe I was trying to put some adventure into it, seeing how Hilary had been sobbing quietly in the taxi all the way back. But she didn't really stop.

'I'm sorry,' I said, as we stood at the foot of that once-grand sweeping stairway. 'Probably not the most uplifting gig to go to. I'd have suggested something else if I'd known.'

God knows what. An evening spent staring at alcohol, perhaps.

'Oh no,' she said, 'it's not that. The concert was lovely. It's just, I saw my son today. He said it wasn't practical. For me to live with him.'

'What about your own home?'

'I signed it over,' she said. 'It's a tax thing.'

I don't know if talking about it made things any better, but she stopped crying. She couldn't very well talk and cry at the same time, I suppose.

'I'm sorry,' I said, again.

Hilary tugged some frayed old tissue out of her sleeve and dried her eyes and nose.

'Listen to me going on,' she said, with little bits of tissue paper left dotted on her face. 'You don't even know if you've got any family.'

'Well, we'll see,' I said.

Hilary stroked my cheek once with the back of her hand.

'I'm sure you've got someone somewhere,' she said, and tried to smile. 'People that are really alone, they don't worry about it so much. Goodnight.'

I stayed there in the hall and watched her ascend, even though our rooms were on the same floor, just to give her some dignity. She almost made it, but as she turned the final corner I saw her shoulders tighten as she suppressed a sob.

I counted to fifty, and then I decided I would give it five more minutes, and maybe I would have stood there until morning but for the footsteps of some carer or warden approaching down the parquet. Then I went up those same stairs myself, and down the lonely corridor, past the closed doors and the open ones, with their little wheezing parcels of humanity inside, and into my own room.

I drew the curtains, turned on the bedside lamp, and took up my vigil in the armchair. From the bottom of the garden I heard the hoot of an owl. A little while later I thought I could hear Hilary crying, through the walls, but I was imagining it. Or it was a man crying, maybe, an old man. Somebody who wasn't on Prozac yet. Opposite me the deathbed lay there immaculate, awaiting my ascension. It could wait a little longer. I sat there in my chair and thought about family and sadness and alcohol and Schubert and morphine, listening to an owl telling me the night was supposed to belong to him now, and waiting for the distant rumble of the meat train.

IV

'Again, you made bed,' said the bottle-blonde Florence Nightingale from the doorway.

'I did it especially for you,' I replied, and the woman who was normally dour enough to make a bowl of boiled sprouts look like a summer cornfield tilted her head, gave another one of those sardonic smiles that suggested I had half a chance, and walked out.

'Breakfast,' she commanded, over her shoulder, and I followed obediently after, back down to the slow, solemn queue for toast and muesli and tea, with its pained but proud ambulators, the upright few.

You could go and sit at one of the tables and they'd come and serve you if you wanted, but I guess you didn't want to let things slip if you could help it. Once they'd slipped, they'd slipped for good. So you popped your pills and held it all in and waited, and waited, and waited. There was a woman in front of me who spent most of the morning trying to get a boiled egg off the hot plate. Nothing you could do about it but let her work it out for herself: you're on the way out, love, as the old guy in the dungarees would put it. Last thing you wanted was somebody rushing you. And you didn't need a five-star memory to work out there were people here even more fucked up than you, you just needed eyes for that, so I shut up and took my turn like everyone else. I wasn't hungry anyway, wouldn't be hungry ever again, by all accounts. Doubt any of us would.

I took my cuppa out to the conservatory so I could try pretending I was just in a bad hotel. I couldn't manage the hotel bit, but maybe a drug rehabilitation centre or something similar wasn't too much of an imaginative stretch. I wondered if I'd ever done any drugs. I suppose I could try them all now and not have to worry.

'How you finding it then?' this voice piped up, and I looked around and there he was, the seven-year resident, a little crumpled old body sat in a big green armchair that made him look like a very wrinkled eight-year-old, clutching a cup and saucer of the old Chateau Aldershot.

'Well it's off-season, isn't it,' I said. 'Probably better in the summer.'

'Yes, it is nice,' he gurgled. 'Expect you'll be gone by then, though.'

'You're on form today,' I said. I wondered if it was his medication or just something sour inside of him. Maybe it was the sourness which kept him going. Either way I wasn't in the mood to pick him up on it.

'Have you really been here seven years?'

'Seven and a half. Longer than any of them, including the management.'

'What did you do on the outside?'

The old man squinted at me though his bottle-ends, and the boiled eggs behind them became a pair of pickled mussels.

'That's a prison term. You been in prison?'

I thought about the Rizlas that had been in my jacket

pocket, with 'property of HM Prisons' stamped under the flap.

'Maybe,' I said.

He kept up the squinting for a good half-minute, more than long enough for me to understand that despite his rheumy vision he could see me perfectly well. This was just a little display of moral superiority. It felt like something people had given me plenty of times before.

'Printer, I was,' he said, once he'd established his moral altitude. '*South Wales Evening Post*, *Llanelli Star*, *Carmarthen Journal*, you name it, all that. I was a printer for nigh on fifty years, man and boy.'

I bet he was wearing the same dungarees when he started too, from the state of them.

'Suppose all those computers would have you out of a job now,' I offered.

'Computers? Tell me what a computer can do for you. Can it tell you when to go the toilet? Can it tell you when to lie down? Can it tell you when to have a shit? Can it?'

'Probably, these days. Maybe if you plugged in some special sensors.'

'Sensors? What's a sensor going to do for you? Is it going to tell you—'

He stopped himself, much to my disappointment, and drew the back of his hand over his whiskery chin.

'They still need a printing press to connect the computer to,' he concluded. 'They'll always need printers.'

'Just maybe a few less,' I said. He didn't rise to it.

The two of us sat there without speaking, taking it in turns to raise our tea to our lips, like two in-laws at a christening party.

Four more mouthfuls of tepid tea later and I had finished

the cup, which left me just as deficient of purpose as everyone else in there. A couple of dozen corpses-to-be, loitering in armchairs and plastic seats and steel-framed beds, with nothing to dwell on but the memories of the past, the pain of the present, and the fear of the diminishing future. The memories were probably the best part of it, and if you didn't have memories, where did that leave you?

The old man got that familiar vindictive grimace again. It was the only time his face didn't look like a death mask.

'I know about you,' he said.

'Oh yeah? Know what?'

'Coming and going any time you please without so much as a by-your-leave. This place isn't a hotel, you know.'

'So that's why I can't get my shoes shined.'

'I could tell them. Could tell them about your fancy lady too.'

'Hilary?'

I didn't disillusion him about the fancy lady bit, which wasn't chivalrous, but it gave me a boost.

'Oh yes.' The old man took a beat just to savour it. 'They'd throw you out on your arse.'

'Bollocks,' I said. It had occurred to me. 'No one's told me I can't go out, and if they had, they should have told me again, because I have memory loss.'

'Memory loss? Dead loss more like. That's what you are. Bloody jailbird alkie, come in here with your own warden, chained to the bed. Everybody knows about you.'

Everybody apart from me.

'What was I in for, then?' I asked, 'if you know that much?'

'They don't say that, do they. Data Protection Act.

Suppose they'd have to say if you were a child molester or a psycho or something.'

It was some consolation that they hadn't, I suppose.

'But everybody knows,' he went on. 'We all saw. I could tell them.'

'You didn't though, did you?' I said. 'You're just jealous, that's your problem. You've been cooped up in here almost eight years.'

'Aye, and I've made myself bloody useful too, unlike some. Do the boilers, and the sweeping, and help out with the private ambulance people. I'm a grafter. Look at you! Can't be much over fifty and you wouldn't lift a finger. Dead loss.'

'I'm forty-six, and I could lift a finger or five right now, if I was that way inclined,' I said.

But threatening a geriatric was no way to start the day, and we both knew it. He gave me a victory cackle as I fled, and he was welcome to it. If you can last seven years in a place like this and end up nothing more than a complete cunt you're probably doing all right. I had to sort myself out.

'What do you want change for?' said one of the two gorgons at reception, looking at a two-page feature on Ben Affleck's holiday luggage.

'I need to phone my solicitor,' I said.

'Ooh, he needs to phone his solicitor,' said a voice from out back in a fake posh falsetto. I don't think I was supposed to hear it.

'There's a payphone in the cubby at the end of the hall,' said the woman, without looking up.

'I know. That's why I need some change.'

The woman turned the page. The other side showed a

collection of bags you could carry little dogs in, and where you could buy them.

'We don't do change,' she said.

I stood there and watched her studying all those little bags for Chihuahuas and puppies and the like. I don't think she was any more interested in it than I was.

'We don't do change,' chorused her second, coming out of the back room with a giant book of word puzzles. It occurred to me people can spend decades waiting to die and not even know they're doing it. Neither of them could have been much over thirty. One was married and the other was engaged, if the jewellery was anything to go by. It wasn't doing them much good from the looks of things.

I got some help from the canteen in the end, from a worn-looking woman behind the food counter who was not so much trying to feed the five thousand as persuading them to eat, and without much more than a frayed smile at her disposal, although the smile was sincere. It was the fact that it was frayed that gave it away. She looked like she could do with a bit of feeding up herself.

'What have you got, love?' she said. 'A tenner? I'll see what I can do.'

She talked to the security guard, the nurses, a couple of care workers, some cleaners, even the pair in reception, I think, but she came back with a fiver and five pound coins and put them in my hand and said, 'There you go, love,' and went off to let the lost souls know there was still solace in a boiled egg if they would only raise a spoon to their pursed lips. It's always the ones that don't even seem to know they're doing it who keep you from passing sentence on the whole fucking lot of us, who keep the jury out a little longer in your trial against humanity.

'Thanks,' was as much as you could ever say. Then I went and stood by the phone and held the coins in my hand and weighed them and thought about it: just a couple of quid fed into that and who knows what self-knowledge would unfold. Money can mean everything in the world, when you haven't got any.

According to the directory enquiries service, my solicitor had an office in Carmarthen, but he wasn't in it, of course, or rather he wouldn't speak to me. I didn't get any further than the secretary, and I didn't get very far with her, but the tone of her voice was awkward enough for me to realise he was certainly available. I wondered what was wrong with my own, wondered if it contained the slur of the lifelong alcoholic, or the insincere slime of the salesman, or the unwelcome desperation of the terminally ill, or maybe all three.

'I think he might be around today, I'm not sure, but he's very busy with a lot of meetings, so perhaps I could ask him to ring you?'

Sure, busy as hell. I'd seen the guy's jacket and it had frayed cuffs and threadbare elbows. He was probably sitting at the desk opposite her trying to add a few personal touches to some old biddy's will. I kicked up a fuss about the case notes I hadn't received and didn't get any joy there either. So I hung up and left the handset on top of the box so I could keep the credit, and promised myself I would ring her every twenty minutes for the rest of the day. There wasn't much she could do about it. After a while I got the feeling that I was enjoying myself.

By early afternoon I got lucky and the guy picked up the phone himself. The case notes, he promised, were going out in the next post. I had the feeling he ran the sort of practice where a lot of things were always going out in the next post.

'Is there much in them?' I managed to say before he could hang up.

'What do you mean?'

'Family, friends, next of kin, that sort of thing? I'm sort of stuck on my own here.'

'I'm afraid you're a lone wolf,' he said. 'Or at least you are to me. There's your previous solicitor, if you want to try him. I believe you chose to dispense with his services.'

He gave me the number, which I scrawled on to the base board between the phone and the wall with an empty biro, and then he spent the next five minutes alternately apologising and telling me how busy he was.

'You want to get caller ID,' I said, and hung up.

It was a Swansea number. I recognised the code straight away, and I waited for more but nothing else filtered through except the way the bay looked in the sun. I rang in and said who I was and got kicked upstairs to the senior partner straight away. My hands began to shake.

'Where are you?' he said.

And I opened my mouth but my throat was locked, like a door to a bad room. It was a perfectly innocent, understandable question. I tried another run-up at it but it was like trying to jump out of a plane.

'Where are you?'

It was the tone, maybe. Or I'd like to think it was the tone. In fact a little natural truth had started to unravel, and it was difficult to swallow.

There was a reason why I was alone. I had thought about it a lot. Thought there was something wrong with me, that I was stranded and adrift because of the person that I was. Worried about every phone call and file because it would tell me I was doomed and deserved it. But it's not always about you.

Cause and consequence and character, sure, let it occupy you when the empty nights start to pull up short. Your conscience is supposed to be a problem, but it's only your problem. Karma is an accident that only children believe in. Maybe I deserved all this and maybe I didn't, but I wasn't here because life made sense. I was here because I was hiding.

'You'll have to excuse me,' I stalled. 'I'm a little messed up.'

The answer that doesn't require any faith is the one that matters. It was time to grow up.

'I've rung the hospitals,' said the man, 'you're not in any of them. And you were lively enough to pick up a little work before they took you in, weren't you?'

I gave a good chesty cough into the phone for effect.

'There aren't many secrets round here, Llywelyn. We got word from Port Talbot you were up to something.'

I wiped the blood off the receiver, and thought, all this time worrying if there was anybody out there who gave two fucks about me, and there was. Just the wrong sort of person, and for the wrong sort of reason.

'Did you hear that?' I said. 'I am in a bad fucking way. I'm being looked after. And my fucking head is shot.'

'I heard about them dropping your trial. Who'd have thought cancer could be so lucky?'

'Yeah. Fate smiles.'

'Fate grins like a bastard. Where are you?'

It was a strong, stern manly voice. It was the first one I'd heard speak to me like I wasn't a sympathy case or a nut job, but there was nothing pleasant about it.

'Why the fuck did you call?' it said, eventually. 'What is it you want?'

'My head's a little messed up.'

'Yeah, we know that. That's pretty well established. But listen: just because you decided to take the rap it doesn't get you off the hook. Facing the music isn't the same thing as paying the fiddler, not with this. You owe us a lot of money, Llywellyn. And operating out of town doesn't give you a concession.'

'You're pretty candid for a player who isn't on a private line.'

'I think you and me and the Blethyns ought to have a little word, Llywelyn. Bit of company for you.'

'I have to go,' I said.

'I'll find you,' I heard him say, as I put the handset back in the receiver, ever so gently, like it might go off in my hand. It rested there in its cradle, under its big brown plastic hood, halfway up the wall, so people could say goodnight to their grandchildren.

A little while later it would ring, maybe in an hour, or five hours, or sometime the next day. Some passing person would pick it up. A friendly voice would ask for an invented name, and when the misunderstanding had been passed off, would ask innocently where he'd called by mistake, if he hadn't already been told. He would get his answer. Then I probably had a couple of hours at most.

I stared at the phone, at that faceless human interface, that little metal box that had told me that I had nobody, was worth nothing, that you could waste an entire life the way you could stub out a cigarette, and realised that even with the memory back, there would be little comfort and no excuses. I didn't want my memory back. I wanted a new life, and these last few decrepit, institutional months were all that was left to me.

I ripped the receiver off the cord, punched the buttons out with both fists, cracked the LCD display, and tore the connection cord from its socket. I cracked the surrounding acoustic hood with right and left hooks until it lay in fragments on the linoleum. I jabbed at the solid metal that remained until my knuckles gave out, and then with hands running with blood, picked up a nearby chair, wrenched the plastic seat away from the metal legs, and swung the blackened steel down on to the casing until my vision swam and my legs went and my chest concertina'd into a tight, breathless envelope of jagged pain. A rich clot of blood-flecked mucous reverberated on my rasping, awkward breath, and the room shrank and darkened, and I fell to my knees, and then my side, and lay prone amongst the debris and hoped I would never have to get up. But I only passed out for a brief spell.

I stayed down there with eyes shut tight, waiting for my futile, pointless pain to recede to its usual baseline. It hadn't been enough to do me in. When the dizziness went I stared upwards until I was able to focus clearly on the little holes in the foam ceiling tiles, and then I took a deep breath, or what passed for one, and got to my feet.

The seven-year resident was standing silently behind me, with his dungarees and his broom, and a look of stern indignation that would have seemed something like hatred if you couldn't spot the self-righteousness.

'You should be locked up,' he said.

And I laughed long and hard, from the unspoken place from whence all real laughter only ever comes, where you can see for an unflinching moment that we are all lost and doomed and rootless, though some of us are happier than others. I laughed and it hurt me and I laughed some more, and then I went smiling into the dank, disinfected gloom of the ground-floor toilets, to rip up some towelling to wrap around my knuckles.

Time to grow up. Easier said than done.

For no sensible reason I could discern, the next thing I did was search the conservatory with my bloody hands wedged out of sight in my pockets. It was empty. She wasn't anywhere on the ground floor.

'Have you seen Hilary Price?' I asked the medicine-trolley lady.

'She's not feeling very well,' she said. 'She was in a lot of pain in the night. She asked to be sedated.'

I nodded. Maybe something showed on my face, I don't know, but she took my arm and said:

'I don't know if she's going to be up and around for a good while, you know.'

There was no such thing as a good while in the deadhouse. I smiled back to let her know I understood, and left her to wheel her little chemical mercies around to the ones that were never going to be up and around again.

Hilary's door was closed shut, which was unusual. The carers liked to keep it ajar so they could keep an eye on you. Guiltily, because it wasn't as if I was in any state to cheer her up, I knocked against it as softly as I could. Then I put my ear up to it and listened and heard nothing. Goodbye, Hilary Price.

I went back to the chair in my room and stared into space and rolled my fear around in my mouth like you would with a fine wine. Then I wrung my hands so the knuckles throbbed some more, and I must have worn myself out downstairs because then, unbelievable as it sounds, I think I fell asleep, and the next thing I know it's late afternoon and the sun is rolling slowly down towards those bloody hills again.

I could smell the meal trolley coming down the hall, tinned vegetables boiled to death, oily gravy and meat that never smelled of anything. There is such a thing as a free meal in this life, but you wouldn't want to eat it.

I drew a hand over my stomach and there was nothing there: my belt was down its last notch and it still hung loose by a couple of inches. I should eat something, it occurred to me, but not in my room, like an invalid. So I trotted downstairs to the day room, and Christ that was worse. A big empty room dotted with silent diners fighting to keep their faces from falling into their food. I should have known.

Round by the fire escape I limbered up against the wall like a marathon runner, rolled my neck and shoulders, took a few long breaths, judged the wind direction and available light, and set slowly off.

'Renting another beer?' said Gary, as I took my stool. 'What drink would you like to look at tonight?'

He still had his little Nintendo, but there was a mobile phone and an iPod on the bar in front of him as well, and something else I couldn't identify.

'A pint of Watkin's will do. And a packet of pork scratchings.'

'Why not have a half?'

'Aesthetics,' I explained.

Mr Biffo's Pork Scratchings. I would be getting my daily intake of fat, if nothing else. I sat there diligently chewing with a dry mouth, watching the beer settle, eyeing the dust motes drift through the air, reflected in the glass. We were the only people there.

I eyed Gary's little exhibition of the latest solid-state consumables, and thought of the seven-year resident back in the hospice, the former printer stuck in a forlorn age of inky fingers and grease.

'Like your technology, don't you?' I said.

Gary looked me over before he replied.

'Yeah,' he said defensively. All barmen are defensive creatures at heart. 'I've got a degree in graphic design, you know. University of Glamorgan. Going to be an animator.'

I couldn't tell you a great deal about the job market for animators in this country, but I'm guessing there isn't one in Llandovery, and especially in the White Hall Hotel. He didn't look like he was going to be an animator anytime soon, but I didn't say anything. He still had his life ahead of him, I suppose, as much as it pained me to think about it.

'I know an old printer back at the home that would hate you,' I said. 'Mind you, I think he hates everyone.'

Beyond establishing his reputation as something other than a barman, Gary was not interested in conversation. I watched the head thin out on my pint and did my best with the pork scratchings.

'Did you tell Gerald Williams I'd be over tonight?' I asked.

'Haven't seen him,' he said, without looking up. He had the pale face of somebody who spent a lot of time indoors, and you could see the coloured pixels in the little screen dance across his brow.

'Where's his farm?'

'High Farm. Up over towards Llanwrda, off the A482. Must be five or six miles. The taxi driver'll know it. If you go, take his mail, will you? He's got a couple of bills here, by the looks of things.'

'His mail?'

'Yeah, it's half a mile up a mud track, so the postie leaves it here for him.'

'He comes in often enough, I suppose.'

'That he does.'

I picked a number at random from the business cards around the pub phone and in less than ten minutes I was sitting on a beaded seat-cover and inhaling a noxious fug of something that called itself Alpine Freshness Delight, or so the little plastic dispenser said, off to see Ger Williams, who the cabbie reliably informed me was a character who would live to a million. We passed a private boy's college and a church and crossed over a steel bridge, and then we were out on an A-road with the main beams on, one car travelling in the early night off towards Carmarthen. If you kept going you would get out to Pembrokeshire and Cardigan Bay and the Irish Sea.

After ten minutes of desultory Welsh countryside, empty fields and holiday cottages and hobby stables for the horsey types, we turned right into some dense woodland and pulled uphill for about another mile on a narrow lane before turning onto an uneven track. You could see an orange outside light shining dully through the branches up ahead.

The place looked like a kip. There was a rusty five-bar gate resting off its hinges against a mossy stone wall, and beyond that there was a wet, muddy courtyard with an old squat farmhouse backing onto the hill and a big corrugated iron barn off to the left. There wasn't a single light shining in the house but a door must have been open on the far side of the barn, where a harsh fluorescence was spilling out and away from us, casting long shadows up into the paddock. In its clinical, alien glow you could see a pile of hay bales two or three seasons too old, practically compost now.

To our right was a low stone garage with a metal roof, jammed to the rafters with farming machinery that looked like it hadn't been used since the Suez crisis. God knows what any of it was for. Next to the garage was an old Lada and a Rover 2000, with a couple of ancient tractors behind them, and there was an old Peugeot 306 by the house, which could have been the car Gerald had been driving when he stopped by the White Hall.

'Twelve quid,' said the cabbie.

'I'll just see where he is,' I said, and headed round to the front of the barn, into the glare of a couple of industial spotlights, hanging by chains from the the middle of the ceiling. If I was making a delivery then old Williams could pay for the car fare.

Unlike the rest of the place, the barn was pretty tidy, oddly so. There was a pyramid of big cardboard boxes stacked up neatly against the nearest wall, with a half-drunk mug of coffee resting halfway up. In the middle of the cement floor was a full-size Portakabin, a building within a building. The veneered door was ajar and the lights were on inside. It all looked fairly new. Between the door of the Portakabin and the open door of the barn there were two guys lying on their back, both wearing heavy black leather jackets and some very chunky gold: not the farming type, I have to say. They were dressed so alike they could have been twins. Perhaps they were. It was hard to tell, because one of them had been shot in the face.

The first thing I did was turn my back on it, whipped round tight as a dancer and stared at the wall instead, but there was a fleshy smudge there about head height, so I just closed my eyes until I remembered how to breathe again.

They looked like they'd got it up close all right, one in the head and the other in the chest. I got round to wondering why I wasn't being sick. Maybe that's what living in the deadhouse does to you, or maybe I had seen it all before. Maybe I just needed to have something more substantial inside me than a packet of pork scratchings. I was scared, though. I could feel a high-voltage current of fear humming through the hair on my scalp.

'Well, is he in?' cried the cabbie from the courtyard.

'Hang on there a minute,' I said somehow, over the beats of an exploding heart.

A private detective would check the temperature on the bodies, feel the warmth of the coffee, examine the area, scout for clues, light up a cigarette and wait for the police. Instead I walked up to the one with the gaping chest wound and put three fingertips to his forehead like a doctor, like there was some chance of him coming back. It was as cold as graveyard stone, but his eyes still seemed alive, although they looked hard and completely unscared. He hadn't died afraid, if he had ever been physically afraid of anything in his life. Not like me. I was scared out of my skin, so far out I was practically vapour.

'He's not here,' I yelled, like a man who wasn't set to argue about anything, and went out to the car. 'We'll go back.'

I don't remember much about the return leg. He dropped me at the pub without any of his nosy small talk satisfied and we descended, without purpose, into a blazing row about the fare, or three pounds fifty of it to be exact, with a pair of corpses before my eyes the whole time. In the end Gary chipped in just to shut me up.

Then I went and sat down drinkless in the far corner of the empty pub and pined badly for my room in the hospice, like going back there would make everything go away, like being there made nothing outside matter. It was true enough for some of them I suppose. Not me. But right then I would have surrendered to it all in an instant if I had the choice, the boiled eggs and the bedpan and bathside gurney and all. I would have got back into bed and stayed there if senility would have taken me.

Gary rang the bell for last orders and I had to ask him for a lift up the lane, in exchange for a tenner the next time I was in. He didn't trust me, but it was almost certainly more than he earned in two hours for ten minutes' work, so he said yes.

'You're staying in the hospice?' he said, when we crunched up the gravel driveway in his modded Renault Clio.

'Yeah. I'm a bit out of shape, you know.'

Gary looked me up and down, as I stood under the little portico.

'Yeah, well if I don't see you down the White Hall in the next couple of days I'll come up for it,' he said, and pulled down hard on the wheel so he could get his hatchback out in a single arc, and accelerated off towards town, aftermarket dump valves hissing as he went.

The ground-floor lights were on but no one came out

right away. Somebody had probably seen the headlights or heard the engine and doubtless would want to come down for a look, so I spent five trembling minutes in the shadows but no one appeared. Then I went up the fire escape where the carers went out to smoke, and tried the handle, and it opened. And before I could feel lucky I bumped straight into two of the staff around the next corner.

'Where've you been?' they said, in unison, hands on their hips and fierce expressions on their faces.

I gave a little pathetic cough, and tried my best to look sad and confused, and succeeded perfectly well.

'I'm going home,' I said, like a child. 'I want to go home.'

One of them took her hands off her hips.

'You're supposed to be in your room,' she said. 'It's past your bedtime.'

And she put an arm round my shoulder, as if she was comforting me, and steered me back to my room, which was just as I'd left it, except there was a large brown parcel on my bed.

'Do you want any help?' she said.

'I'll be fine, thank you,' I said, perking up enough to sound sufficiently independent.

'Are you sure?'

'Yes, I'm sure, thank you, I'll be fine now. I'm sorry.'

For a moment I thought she was going to watch me undress, and in fact she did stay to watch me take off my shoes, hang up my jacket and unbutton my shirt.

'You shouldn't be wandering about like that at this time of night,' she said, on her way out. 'It's very bad for you.'

Yes, I agreed after she closed the door behind her, quite so. Then, once I was alone and the two of them had moved off to wherever they spent the nightshift, I sat down on the armchair in my trousers and my vest and with my parcel on my lap. I laid my hands on its brown paper and asked myself what I'd really been so scared about back there in the barn. Not dying, surely?

I held the parcel up again and felt the weight of it, which was about the same as a six pack of beer, with something solid rolling around inside of it. There was no stamp on it, just my name and address in rough capitals with the words 'Private and Confidential' underscored five times. Whatever it was, it was about as subtle as a brick. It sure wasn't a legal file. I sat there not opening it.

The owl was silent. I didn't hear the meat train. Even the residents were quiet, for once. Downstairs, in some little room, the carers were watching late-night television or listening to the radio or reading magazines. In the barn, under the spotlights, two dead men were spilled out over cold concrete. In the morning the lady would come with the toast and tea.

There was nothing else for it. I tore open the paper, four or five layers of it, then found myself wrenching a thick lip of sellotape from the end of a jumbo-sized jiffy bag, and inside that there was a letter and a shoe-box, gaffer-taped shut, with the same Private and Confidential warning scrawled over it. I peeled off the gaffer-tape and inside that was what looked to be about two grand in twenties and a sawn-off shotgun.

'Well then Robin,' the letter began, 'you did say the drugs might mess with the old marbles a bit but I could of done with you the other night mind.'

Two

Shotgun

I

That letter took up no more than one side of A4, and I spent the whole night reading it, over and over again. Nothing really sunk in the first ten or twenty times. It was one sheet of paper, covered in handwriting that would shame a child, but it felt like something worse than a death warrant. Although it raised more questions than it answered, the one thing it unequivocally killed off was the chance I'd been some kind of innocent. I read it so many times it could have been a catechism for the fucked. Sometime in the early morning, in the aubade, before the birdsong, when the sun had not yet risen but the night was somehow a lighter shade of black, I ran it over one last time.

Well then Robin,

You did say the drugs might mess with the old marbles a bit but I could of done with you the other night mind. Hope you can still read. You've been doing some laundry for me. This is your cut from the first lot. Don't spend it all in one place. You tell me they have been picking it up in Port Talbot for twenty in the pound but I don't suppose it could of lasted. They are awful nosey down there after all. I won't say goodbye because you never know. So from one black sheep to another, good luck wherever your going.

I'd burn this if I were you,

cheers.

He hadn't signed it, and there was nothing about the gun. There was black tape around the short wooden handstock and another strip of tape halfway down the stubby barrels. I went to sniff them but recoiled so badly I did my neck in: it looked like there was blood around the muzzles, but I rubbed it with my thumb and it was only flecks of rust. In the end they smelled just like any shotgun would, I guess, of gunpowder and metal. I flicked the catch on the top of the stock and broke it open and there were two blue cartridges inside. God knows who or what for.

At the bottom of the letter was a mobile number with Port Talbot written under it, and a reminder not to use a landline, which was good advice. I tore it off and tucked it into the top pocket of my blazer, and then fought with the sash window until I got a foot's grace out of it, and burned the rest on the window ledge with my lighter from the Singleton Hotel.

It didn't occur to me to count the money.

Out in the hall I could hear the gentle encouragements of the carers leading the mobile down to breakfast, and the wheels of the breakfast trolley on parquet coming round for those who weren't going to be led anywhere. I managed to get everything in the wardrobe before the door opened.

'Hot toast and a cup of tea love? Or are you coming down?'

I said I would take it in my room.

'Feeling a bit under today, are you? Well, not to worry. The nurse is coming round with the prescriptions soon.'

At about the same time the peroxide blonde Slavic carer, or nurse, or whatever she was, reappeared in the doorway and showed off all her communist dentistry with another big smile.

'Again he made the bed! He makes the bed every morning,' she explained to the breakfast lady.

'He doesn't!'

'He does. Look, perfect. Better than some of the staff do it.'

'I do it because I love you,' I said again, and tried a wink.

'You don't have to do that, you know, love,' said the breakfast lady. 'You shouldn't tire yourself out like that. You're here to be looked after.'

'He's feeling a bit tired today,' she explained to the Slav. A thought occurred to me.

'When do you change the sheets?' I asked.

'Why? Have you had an accident?' asked the blonde, in a conspiratorial tone.

'No,' I said, although she was already in the room and checking. 'I just wondered.'

'Another three days. Do you want them changed?'

'No,' I said. 'It's fine.'

After they'd gone I shoved the armchair up against the closed bedroom door, took out the package and put everything under the bed, save as much money as I could comfortably fit in my pockets. It was a divan bed with two drawers underneath, and I took one of them all the way out and put everything in the cavity underneath. The police will surely be here soon, I thought. The sensible thing to do would probably be to ring them up and put yourself on the level. That would be the sensible thing to do. But it didn't seem likely.

God knows how I was going to get through this, I remember thinking, and then in came another one of them, another one of this endless stream of busy well-meaning women, broadcasting casual sounds of comfort and checking you hadn't pissed yourself. This one was definitely a nurse, or I hoped she was, because she was pushing a cart that had more drugs on it than you'd get if you shook down an entire music festival.

'Bit down, are we dearie?'

Well, I think I might be involved in two murders, I wanted to say. I could have, too. I could have said anything. I could have told her to fuck off sideways. It wouldn't have made the slightest impression.

'Here we go,' she said, taking two blue and white capsules out of the top drawer on her trolley and passing them to me in a paper cup. 'Dr Catherine says these ought to cheer you up a bit. Do you have any of your tea left?'

Yes, I was going to say, but she checked the cup herself.

'There you go. We've got it all here, you know. No need to worry. Anything else? Anything else you think you could do with? Any little problems? Don't be shy.'

In fairness, she was asking for it. She had half the pharmaceutical industry right there for the taking.

'To be honest,' I said, and I almost had to bite my tongue while I was saying it, 'I could do with a little pick-me-up, you know, a boost. A bit of energy.'

Which was perfectly true.

'Couldn't we all! Rest and tea and regular meals, that's what you want. You relax now.'

I put on my sad face.

'I'm just so tired and depressed. I'm eating my food.'

And I pointed to the breadcrumbs on my plate like a child showing off his latest finger painting.

'You take that Prozac there then, that'll help you out, okey dokey?'

'But I can barely bring myself to move, and my mind wanders all the time. I don't want to be like this,' I pleaded. 'There must be something for me.'

Inside, part of me was already laughing like a schoolboy on glue.

'Well, there's that Ritalin,' she said, lifting up her glasses from the chain around her neck. 'There's two of them on it in here. Terrible slow they were before. One of them's not much better now, though, I have to say.'

It didn't matter what it was called. Pep pills, go tablets, there was bound to be something. She picked up a yellowish bottle from the first shelf on her cart and read the label absently.

'I think that, you know, that Eminem is on it. The rapper. Or is it Madonna? Oh, I don't know, they're all on something or other.'

'Would it be possible to have some of that, then?'

'You speak to Dr Catherine about it, or Dr Narula, when he's back, all right? I only hand out the prescriptions.'

'Yes, thank you,' I nodded, as she wheeled herself out of the room. On the way out she turned round and smiled at me again.

'"Will the real Slim Shady please stand up, please stand

up, please stand up,"' she said, moving like her hip was giving her a bit of gyp. ""'Cause I'm Slim Shady, the real Slim Shady and all the others are just imitating." That's how it goes.'

'Right you are,' I said, and after she'd gone I gave her a two-minute start and then went to shuffle around in the hallway behind her, which is the sort of loitering that would look suspicious anywhere else, but was par for the course in there. Then, when she was jabbing something into the veins of an invalid three doors down, I swiped the bottle. There were eighty pills in it, the label said. Enough to put me on the fucking moon, I should think. Then I nipped down to the day room for an alibi and some more food: I wasn't hungry, but I had a feeling I would need it today. Today I had to go back to High Farm.

The kind canteen lady who'd got me my change seemed happy with the morning's turn-out.

'Start the day on an egg – isn't that right?' she said, 'That's what they say.'

The day room was still the same sorry sight it usually was, but it was undoubtedly better than prison. After I'd stuck my tray into the rack with all the other dirty dishes I went back upstairs so I could come out down the fire escape. I would have made another call to my solicitor, but I'd smashed the phone to pieces and I didn't feel like bringing it up with the girls in reception.

Hilary's door was still closed, I noticed.

Out on the metal plate of the fire escape I stood in about an inch of fag butts until I could be sure the driveway was clear. Two fields away I could see a farmer trying to bat a herd of cows through an open steel gate with a crooked branch. I wasn't close enough to hear exactly what he was shouting, but you could tell even from that distance that he was more than adaquately expressing himself, although his physical movements showed no sense of urgency. The cows weren't exactly imbued with a sense of mission either. I stood there and wondered if maybe there was some way the cows were slowly but subtly herding the farmer, and then I necked a handful of Ritalin and tried to speedwalk into town.

Running anywhere was beyond me, but I managed a decent pace, I have to say. By the time I reached the market square my eyes were stinging from the sweat, and even my jacket had damp patches under the armpits. The valves of my heart tapped out a furious SOS, desperate to get away from the arson I had committed in my lungs. I felt just fine, though. I could have kept going till I ran out of land. Instead I managed to grind to a skidding halt on the other side of the square, half-convinced I was seeing things, because there, on a triangle of land on the eastern edge of a small town behind the back of beyond, somebody had decided they would own a car dealership. I blinked a few times but it was still there, the showroom and the forecourt and the cars. Second-hand, of course, if not third or fourth or fifth, but a car dealership nevertheless. Well, I thought, why not? I had pockets full of cash, and taxi drivers remember things.

Behind the big glass front there were two cars in the showroom, the real flagships of the fleet: a four-year-old Renault Megane with some ill-suited alloys and a Volvo saloon, one of the first ones to get the new shape. They wanted seven for the Volvo and four and a half for the Megane but outside in the yard it got cheaper, and quickly. I jogged past the first three rows of vehicles and went straight to the back, where the prices were in three figures and they hadn't even bothered to wipe the bird shit off the bonnet.

There were a couple of Ford Fiestas and some little Fiats, a Mini Clubman and a Vauxhall Cavalier and a couple of other motors that were never going to be admired if you kept them for another hundred years. I kicked a few tyres and dug a handful of rust out from under a wheel arch, and after a couple of minutes the man came out to catch me before I did any real damage.

'After a bargain?' he said, false smile, false cheeriness, false teeth. The teeth were the newest-looking thing on the property. Everything else about him was worn down, but in a smooth, not unpleasing way. He had a big soft fleshy head, almost bald save for a band of white around the back, and was my height but six or seven stone heavier, mostly around the gut. He wore a pair of grey-brown worsted trousers, a faded checked shirt, and a chunky green cardigan with big leather buttons. There was an old Seiko on his wrist and a signet ring on one of his fingers, the vestiges of younger, more flamboyant times. Which were a while ago now, I expect. He was well on the other side of sixty.

I had stood still for almost two minutes now, but inside I was still surging breathlessly forward, a pharmaceutically induced headrush pressing hard against my skull.

'Fucking great,' I blinked.

'Right, well, look away,' he said, unruffled. 'Look away. What sort of car do you go for?'

I smiled despite myself: a man his age, tripping out to put the spin on the sort of guy who felt up the wheel arches on a two hundred quid Mini Clubman. He was probably quite the salesman once, at least for a town this size.

But anyway, the cars. I had no idea. The only thing in my head was the druggy buzz of the Ritalin.

'They're all fucking great,' I said.

'Well, what about this Cavalier? Very tidy. Good size, decent engine. Man's car.'

I wanted to tell him that was fucking great too, so I clenched my teeth together instead, only I found they were already clenched shut and grinding too.

'Nice,' I managed to let out.

It looked like shit.

The sticker price said six hundred quid, but it was the sort of thing you could pick up in the small press for a hundred if anybody had thought they could sell it. It was a 1987 Vauxhall Cavalier in faded white with a generous flecking of rust, Opel mudflaps, a crumbling black rubber spoiler, and a long, sloping hood. The upholstery was a mottled brown with patches of yellow foam showing through. I danced around it a couple of times while I tried to calm down.

After a token inspection I put my hands in my pockets but they were too full of money, so I folded my arms instead, and thought about saying something that would make sense. My left leg had a bit of a tremble on it, I noticed.

'Does she go all right then?'

'Oh, she'll start all right,' he said. 'How are you going to get her off the forecourt otherwise? She's got four months' MOT left, look. Only two on the tax, mind.'

'Two months is enough for me,' I said.

'Let's step into the office, shall we?' he said, rubbing his hands. 'I'm Dai, by the way.'

The office was partitioned off the corner of the

showroom by a wall of painted chipboard with a sliding window in it. It had a couple of metal filing cabinets in beige laminate, a cheap standing fan covered in dust, a corner table with an electric kettle and a couple of mugs, and an old desk under the partition window. It smelled of Panatellas, oil and Brut. There was a captain's chair by the desk and a striped, seventies recliner in the corner facing it. Dai moved some very old-looking invoices around on the desk, from one pile into another, for no reason I could see. Then he pointed at the armchair and asked me if I wanted a cup of tea, and we both settled in for a good long haggle over a car you could have swapped for an electric teasmaid and a digital watch.

I got him down to five fifty, which took the best part of an hour. He had nothing else to do, I guess, and I was still working through the tablets. We talked about caravans, Margaret Thatcher, roast pork, women, the taxman, Rod Stewart and the A44 as if all of them had some sort of bearing on matters, then he started to sag a little and my leg finally became still again so we called it a day. Looking back I think I may just have been trying to put off the return to High Farm.

'Insurance?' he asked, just the once, in as cursory a manner as he could.

'I'm covered,' was all I said.

We shook on it and he produced some documents which I signed off under the name of a guy who I think played fly-half for Ebbw Vale one time, now living happily on a non-existent street in Cardigan, and then he handed me the keys.

He had to come back out to unlock the chain around the forecourt so I could drive away, and naturally he insisted on waving me off, which I could have done without. I didn't even know for sure if I could drive, although like most people I thought I probably could, and not badly either.

It took me a couple of minutes to get it together. I tried the indicators, the hazards, the rear demister, the wipers, the heaters, the radio, and anything else I could think of while I waited till I was calm or almost calm enough to drive. Dai stood beaming proudly by the gate, ushering me out with a regal wave the whole time. His professional façade did not falter once, not even when I pinged the front wing against one of the short metal posts at the exit.

'No harm done,' I shouted through the driver's window.

'You won't notice it,' he said.

Then I was out on the Queen's highway for what I was fairly certain by now couldn't be the first time. At the end of the road I sailed out of a T-junction with the sedate obliviousness of a royal yacht, and almost wrote off a couple of cars in my first sixty seconds.

The first one, a red hatchback, came to a shocked standstill and honked angrily at me a couple of times before shooting angrily past. The woman behind the wheel was the East European nurse from the home, but she didn't recognise me, although she was staring hard, she just shot me the finger and mouthed a few obvious swearwords at me as she went. It felt vaguely uplifting.

Once I made the road west out of town I knew I'd cracked the worst of it. Two miles out I caught up with one of the empty meat wagons, rolling out to the farms of west Wales for another bleating load, but overtaking seemed a mite ambitious. I might as well have tried to fly a plane. So I sat there trundling along behind it, despite a chemical impatience, and waited for the turning.

It was on me too soon, that old forest track, still full of shades in the middle of the day, but I caught it in time. The five-bar gate was still rusting quietly away against the low stone wall. There wasn't any yellow police tape stretched across the gate posts. I pulled into the muddy courtyard and saw that the tyre tracks from last night's taxi were still there, and now mine would be too. Ger's motor was still parked by the side of the old garage.

I did the house first, chiefly because I didn't think there would be any corpses in it. It was your typical old Welsh farmhouse, leaning and low with thick walls and lots of damp, flagstones on the ground floor and wooden floorboards upstairs. There was running water and electric but they both felt a little out of place. Everything else was spot on. It was filled with crap right up to its big crooked beams: old furniture, dirty dishes, leftover food, unwashed clothes, and bulging cardboard boxes.

The house told me nothing, in the end. There was a Welsh dresser with the usual crockery on it, along with two-dozen spark plugs and a shovel. Judging from the dust it hadn't been touched for years. In the front room there were three television sets, one from each decade since the seventies by the looks of things, and a rabid old tomcat that nearly killed me when it sprang out from under a threadbare settee. I booted it out and went upstairs.

There were three bedrooms, one impenetrable with junk, another a child's room with the bed covered in bicycles, and the third was the master, containing a four-poster bed and rumpled sheets. They were filthy, but they'd been slept in: Gerald's room, and his parents' before that, I expect. God knows how many generations had passed through it, had lived here in this dim, unwelcome house. Maybe they had even been here when it passed for a decent home, which was a couple of centuries back by the looks of things.

I rummaged through a couple of drawers, all of them stuffed full, but there was nothing in there of any use. The most recent document I could find was a council tax statement from the previous March (Ger's little estate was in a band that set him back over two grand a year) but most of it was a lot older than that. There was a warranty on a three-piece suite from a Carmarthen furnishers that was paid for in pounds, shillings and pence and a visitor's brochure for the 1972 Welsh Challenge Cup, Llanelli playing Neath away. And there was an MOT certificate for a Morris Minor Traveller from a garage in Sennybridge, and shopping lists and receipts faded beyond reading and a load of other pointless paper.

There was a stack of photos in one drawer, with the most recent at the top, and the bottom of the pile must have started back in the nineteenth century, a couple of studio shots against a painted backdrop full of battlements and ivy, a Victorian couple who looked like they'd never had it off in forty years, surrounded by a bigger gaggle of kids than the Von Trapp family. I rifled through them, flipping quickly through the decades, but there was nothing tucked away in there for me. There was one of the farmhouse, with a bunch of tweedy gentlemen out front under some bunting and flags, which must have been taken around the Great War. High Farm could have done with a lick of paint even then.

Fast-forward almost a century and on top of all that there was a yellow Prontaprint envelope with a load of wedding shots in it, some young couple with a little girl getting hitched in a garden marquee by the sea. Gerald made a few appearances, looking a bit worse for wear in most of them.

I grabbed one, a shot of the young newlyweds and their kid with Gerald beaming proudly in the middle, arms around each of their shoulders. There was a long, jagged headland stretching out into the sea behind them, and I knew I had seen it somewhere before, not too far from here. The Gower, possibly, I knew the Gower, and I cast my mind back but I only got a dull throbbing pain behind my eyes, like the ache you got from staring into the sun.

I put the processing envelope back but slipped the photo into my jacket pocket. It would be handy for identifying Gerald if I had to, or if I took it into my head to track him down. It was a fairly recent shot after all, but there were a lot of other recent shots I could have chosen. Instead I picked the one with the young man in it, and the young woman and the little kid.

I wondered about that, afterwards. When I wondered if there are some connections we do not need to remember to feel.

I checked out most of the front room and had my head under the Welsh dresser in the kitchen before I conceded defeat. Hanging on the walls in there were some of the old hand-sewn biblical samplers they had up in my room at Howell Harris, that same virulent strain of local Methodism rearing its head, full of commandment and authority and stark spiritual advice, none of which I was inclined to think at all helpful in the circumstances. Maybe there was a nice tidy file somewhere with all the pertinent stuff alphabetically ordered, and god knows there had to be some records someplace, but you could have looked for a week and not found anything, so I gave up. I couldn't put the next bit off any longer.

It took twenty-seven steps from the front door to get

to the barn. I counted them. The two dead men were still there, with the last surviving bluebottles of the summer buzzing around them, and a smell that was something like rotten eggs, which I guess if you felt inclined you could call the smell of death. I stood above the one nearest the door, the one with the eyes of stone and a gaping chest cavity, and looked at him for long enough to make sure I wasn't going to throw up. He was lying down with his arms neatly at his side, almost as if someone had laid him out for a wake. I went through his pockets and came up with a wallet, loose change, two mobiles (a cheap Nokia and something smart with a touchscreen), a disposable lighter, a set of keys and a packet of Sovereign cigarettes, and then I went over to the other one, the one with no eyes at all, and searched him too. The other one didn't smoke but other than that the contents of his pockets were exactly the same, right down to the brands of the phones.

I took it all across the courtyard and put it down on the bonnet of my Cavalier. The batteries on all four of the mobiles were flat, so they'd been out here a while. I had a feeling that ordinarily if you'd called the Port Talbot number from the black sheep letter one of them would have started ringing.

Doubtless someone used to corpses could have told you how many days they'd been there at first glance, but I couldn't and I didn't mind not being able to. The departed had something close to sixty quid in cash between them, some house keys, three unused condoms, and a dozen plastic cards, not all in the same names.

Twenty pence in the pound. No, Gerald, I thought, it didn't last, did it?

The next thing, the main thing, was to get rid of the

bodies, or at least move them somewhere out of sight. I couldn't hope to fool serious investigation, but just getting them to the other end of the paddock would be enough to prevent casual discovery for the time being, providing I cleaned the place up a bit. I didn't want to end up back in jail for something I didn't remember getting involved in. Actually, I didn't want to end up back in jail at all. God knows, though, they weren't small men, even with bits of them blasted away. If I rolled them onto some tarpaulin I could drag them out, that was probably easiest, and I wouldn't have to look at them while I was moving them either. I took another one of my go pills for luck, stuck one of their Sovereign cigarettes in my mouth (although I did not light it) and went back into the barn.

Now that I could stand in it without hyperventilating it became pretty clear this was not your typical farmyard barn. Tarpaulin, or any kind of tarpaulin substitute, was in noticeably short supply, but so were the rolls of fence wire and containers of sheep dip and buckets of worming mixture and all the usual sort of things you might expect to see. Up by where the wall met the roof space there was a dense mesh of wires, hanging like clothes lines, which served no obvious purpose. What with the Portakabin, it could almost have been an industrial unit.

There was a chunk of machinery that ran the whole length of one wall with a big green plastic cover on it, which I thought would do the job perfectly if I could cut it in two. I yanked it off and Christ knows what was underneath it, some great metal trapezoid that looked like a miniature World War One tank, as tall as a man and half as long again. Knobs and levers stuck out on its sides like little pontoon-mounted guns.

I felt the width of the cover and it was obviously going to be impossible to rip up with my bare hands, so I left it in a heap on the floor and went off to find some suitably sharp instrument. Inside the Portakabin, within the barn, were a couple of workbenches with some presses and plastic bottles on them, their surfaces a mess of bright paints. In one corner was an office guillotine which looked handy.

Next to the guillotine was a two-inch-thick ream of oversize paper. On the paper, printed neatly side by side, were the frontispieces of the Bank of England's twenty-pound note, four across, eight deep: thirty-two Queen Elizabeth the Seconds staring beatifically up at me in browny-purple ink. I took the top sheet and turned it over. A flotilla of Adam Smiths looked blankly in profile towards the door of the Portakabin.

'Fucking hell,' I said.

Still clutching the sheet in my hand I walked back over to the World War One tank by the wall. This time, rather than facing it from the side, I walked round and looked at it head-on. You could see a series of paint-stained rollers reaching into the depths of the machinery, each one with a series of oblong-shaped imprints on it, containing in reverse the details of some element of a twenty-quid note.

'Jesus Christ,' I said.

I had wondered. Gerald Williams was probably a bit long in the tooth to be doing banks, although older men had pulled it off. But this was the philosopher's stone. This was the fountain of youth, El Dorado, the cotton candy mountain. I looked again at the thirty-two fake twenties in my hand, felt the odd granularity of the paper, traced a fingertip along the white spaces between the notes, touched the canvas of dreams. Every hope the human mind could conceive of for tomorrow and ever onwards could take form from these rough-hewn, uncut notes, in their audacious and costless abundance.

In the barn at High Farm Gerald Williams made counterfeit money. A lot of it.

I turned and looked at the two dead men in the middle of the floor. I felt better about them now. For a piece of this, or maybe all of it, perhaps it was worth staring down a shotgun. I didn't think of them as victims so much any more. They were mountaineers who had got caught on the final ascent, who had died within sight of the big peak. Two operators from Port Talbot taking the biggest chance of their lives.

Were it not for the pills I would have had to lie down.

'Worth a punt, mate,' I said to the guy with the chest wound. I put the plastic cover back on the printing machine, where it belonged, and went back into the farmhouse for the bedsheets off the four-poster and the curtains from the window.

Rigor mortis had already set in, but they had died with their arms by their sides and their legs straight, felled like timber. It made things a little easier. I did the one without the face first, rolling him onto one of the dusty red curtains from the Williams' master bedroom, some ancient bit of tapestry that had kept the sun off snoring farmers and their wives for generations. It was too short, and his legs poked out, but I would rather them than the other end.

I had in mind a spot on the far side of the field nearest the barn, an unused paddock covered in high grass. Underneath the dry stone wall that backed onto the steep hillside behind, impenetrable with bramble. There. Getting him to the gate was the easiest part, although both his shoes came off, and one of his socks and as I staggered puffing and heaving and coughing, looking down at his bare foot, I thought of Jesus washing the feet of the disciples, which was a lesson I had forgotten a long time before the morphine got to me.

I had a full sweat on by the time I made the wall, but I managed it in one run without a break although it left my trousers sodden with the damp from the long grass. There were wet patches spreading up my thighs and squishing sounds in my shoes. My ribs and my arms hurt the most, though I think all of me was in pain, as I walked back to the barn, lit up against the darkening sky, its big doors leaking light into the late autumn air, treading a path back through the flattened grass in leather brogues. I nearly fell over twice.

I was sweating so bad I could barely see, but I didn't feel hot, was barely conscious of temperature at all. The one who had been shot in the chest, I was worried about him, about parts of him falling out of himself when he moved. I laid out the stained bedsheets from the master bedroom, half a dozen of them, all the colour of cold tea, on which countless sturdy Williamses had farted and fucked, and turned him over onto them. There was more than enough to cover him completely. Before I had got out of the barn I could see that the underside was turning a dark, wet red. And I didn't look down again, not until I was at the wall.

I don't know how I did it. From the bar to the wall and back again twice without stopping, two bodies, across the concrete and the mud and the long grass. After I dropped the second next to his brother I had to put a hand on the mossy stones of the low wall to steady myself while the world heaved itself into a tiny pirouetting speck of white light, and I stood there as still as either of them until the darkness rolled back. I kept my hand on the cold stones and my eyes fixed on some vague but defined spot at the top of the trees until reality evened out and was still. I did not look down. I kept my sight level, while my blood hummed in my ears, and I did not move an inch in case I broke into bits.

Some time later I found some waterproof sheeting from the old garage to cover them with, and when I stumbled back to the wall I dropped it at my feet, kicking it out over the bodies while I stared out into the trees, not looking at them, not thinking. When it was done I started to weigh it down with some stones from the top of the wall, and I put down two or maybe three of them and then I was walking without reason to the brook that ran down the lower part of the field, where I found myself on my knees, with my hands in the cold, clear flowing water. Then I wept briefly, for reasons I did not understand, and was sick.

There was blood and vomit in the stream and I watched it curl and dissipate downstream. Somewhere in the narrow valley a wood pigeon was calling. There was the sound of rushing water and wind through tall grass and the rasping hunger of my own damaged breath and over and above all the high-pitched whine of my own blood in my eardrums. The pills, perhaps, had not helped.

I left my amateurish burial mound unfinished and headed back to the barn, where I flicked off the bright glaring lights and closed the heavy doors. Then I was alone in the coming night, in an old and empty farm where you could print as much money as you liked and men had killed and died dreaming of it.

I wondered where Gerald was. I wondered if he had killed them or even if I had, and how many more people I was going to have to meet before this was even halfway over, and if they were all going to be alive. Then I closed the farmhouse door, sank into the front seat of the Cavalier with my wet, muddy clothes and let the heaters build up to full. I turned on the main beam and the radio, heard a man on BBC Radio Wales talk earnestly about New Orleans jazz, and turned it off again. The engine started and I turned her around, slicing through the mud, wondering how I expected to get away with any of this, whatever it was. Then I put a few miles behind me and the woods and the fields rolled by in the night until I was in that little market square again.

Christ knows what I looked like when I walked back into the White Hall. There were a few locals who gave me the eye-over, briefly, then went back to the low murmur of their banter. Gary did not say anything, not even anything sarcastic, and I owed him a tenner from the lift.

I asked for a pint of Watkin's and a double of Famous Grouse and he put them on the bar without a word. And I downed the Grouse and washed it down with half the beer in a single go. And I ordered another round and thought already of the round after that and the one after that.

It was what I was, after all. An alcoholic and a criminal. It was a homecoming of sorts.

The only other person in there drinking on his own was that tall balding brick shit-house who was here when I'd been in with Hilary, a guy about my age, by the name of Doc as it turned out, hard as nails, with the regulation moustache and Barbour jacket of the off-duty army NCO. From the infantry training centre down the road in Sennybridge, he said. A little while later we talked to each other, in the way that preoccupied drinking men will do: infrequently and making no sense, exchanging oblique glimpes into each other's troubles – vistas on which we did not dwell – one highly trained professional killer, and one possible amateur.

II

I woke up fully dressed in the deathbed with no memory of how I'd got there or anything much about the White Hall at all after the third or fouth round. Prior to the pub I could remember the events of yesterday perfectly well, although perhaps not in too much detail, something which was fine by me.

After that old terrible realisation of waking up and realising where I was, after that had passed, I have to say I did feel a lot closer to an older self, after my night on the tiles. True, the cancer and the corpses were not welcome developments, but those aside, to the extent that such things can be put aside, I was easier in my skin. Because I was still pissed.

From the sound of things I had woken up with the rest of the house. From the other side of the door came the distant creaking of wheelchairs and the gentle tramping of walking frames; weak noises of effort and discomfort; a steady incantation of generic, professional consolation. It forced me out of the deathbed and into the armchair, and then sitting there, opposite the wrinkled sheets, I felt an urge to get up and straighten them, make the bed look as though I had never been in it. After a couple of minutes I actually got up and did it. The East European lady popped her head around the door a little later, and I smiled and pointed like a child.

'Made the bed,' I said.

But she just looked at me sadly, and with a hint of disgust, and walked silently away. The woman with the breakfast trolley didn't come round either, and the plump brunette with the pince-nez gave me my pills without a word. Downstairs, in the breakfast room, the friendly canteen lady only grinned awkwardly, and the seven-year resident just tutted his head and turned away. I was standing in the middle of the floor with a boiled egg and a cup of tea, stubbled and hungover, my pockets still full of fake notes, when the woman doctor appeared with constable Matt Roberts of the Dyfed-Mercia police at her side.

'I think we're going to have to have a word in the office, Mr Llywelyn,' she said sullenly.

So that was it, I thought. Don't ask me how I'd thought I would get away with it. At least I had one night on the piss, I told myself, it was more of a break than a lot of other people probably got.

We walked without speaking down the tight corridor, squeezed past the metal chairs, and filed into the tiny doctor's office, with the close-up view of the breezeblock garage. Dr Narula's desk still showed no sign of his existence.

'We're very disappointed,' said Dr Catherine, sounding like she meant it. The policeman said nothing.

In the silence I went and sat down on Dr Narula's chair and stared at my lap. It was all I could do to stop from crying. Truly, there are things in life which you just cannot cope with. You have no choice but to give up and break down, even if there's no possiblity of ever regrouping yourself into a single normal person ever again. The best I could do was to wait until I was on my own before it happened. I sat there and bit my lip and wondered if I could hold off that long.

'What on earth made you think of money at a time like this?' said the doctor.

I will be chained to a bed and left all alone until I die, I thought.

'We look after you here. You don't need money. You should be concentrating on your own wellbeing.'

Whether I had a friend in the world or not, no one would be able to come and rescue me from this. And the person that I really was, that I might have been, the person I'd been looking for, he was gone now, eclipsed forever by the sensational story of the murders at High Farm. Something I may very well have had nothing or almost nothing to do with, and which could not, in any case, god forbid, have been the real summation of my forty-six years. I began to well up.

'Mrs Probert has reported that twenty pounds has gone missing from her purse,' said Constable Roberts. 'Her daughter has confirmed it.'

This didn't sink in straight away. I was too busy trying to hold my face in a rigid vacant mask. If death came to me at that moment I would have run up to hug it.

'And the payphone has been completely destroyed.'

Something was not right.

'This is the behaviour of an adolescent,' said the doctor. 'I understand you may be going through a lot, but this is not helping anyone. It's not helping you and it's certainly not helping the people who are here to care not just for you but for dozens of others, many of whom are worse off than yourself.'

No, this didn't seem to be going along quite the right lines at all.

'More serious,' said the copper, 'is the theft of one bottle of Ritalin. That's a highly controlled substance. It could do a lot of damage in the wrong hands.'

I couldn't say anything. I wanted to laugh out loud but even in my state of mind that didn't seem like a helpful thing to do. Suddenly the reason behind my struggling poker face reversed completely.

'The phone,' I chipped in. It was all I could say without cracking up.

'We can't have this kind of behaviour here,' said the doctor. 'We simply can't.'

They let me stew a bit then, to think about what I'd done, both of them looking at me like a pair of headmasters.

'I'm...' was all I said, after a minute or two.

'If you return the property to its rightful owners,' said the policeman, 'and make amends for the phone, I have been told neither Mrs Probert or Howell Harris will press charges.'

'Hywel?'

'Howell Harris House. The hospice.'

'We can only help you if you accept our help,' said the doctor. 'And if you accept you are in a place of care where a job of work is done. Good work. Important work. But most of all you need to accept your situation.'

That's easy for you to say, I thought.

'Terminal cancer is never a simple matter to deal with,' she went on. 'But we do know that every case is different. Every case brings its own troubles.'

'Amen,' I said.

She laid off the sympathetic bit then and the two of them looked at me like school teachers for an awkward minute.

'Do you admit to this?' said the constable. 'Do you admit to taking the money from the old lady's purse, and vandalising the phone, and stealing the medicine?'

Why not?

'Yes,' I said.

The doctor gave Matt Roberts a proud and knowing look.

'So will you return the property?' said the constable.

'Oh yes.'

'Now?'

'We could have searched your room,' said the doctor. 'But I told Constable Roberts that wouldn't be necessary.'

'Oh, no,' I said, but not because I was agreeing with her. Oh, no as in oh, god, no fucking way.

'Please wait a moment,' I said, and before they could respond I walked out of the room.

'It's much better this way,' I heard the doctor say as I closed the door. 'You have to give them the chance to do it themselves. Thanks so much for coming down.'

Outside I had the hallway to myself, so I took a twenty from the crumpled stash of money in my pockets, and retrieved the pill bottle from inside my jacket, keeping a dozen or so for later. They surely weren't going to count out all eighty tablets. If they did I'd just say my head was going and I couldn't remember. Then, on the off chance I was hallucinating, I spent a moment gently slapping myself around the head and the face, but nothing changed, even when I started pinching my neck. When I went back into the office they were still there, the young lady doctor doing the good and important work and the wholesome young constable with his helmet under his arm, come to give the doddled old rogue an edifying fright. I put the note and the bottle on the desk and apologised to my feet, just in case I couldn't pull it off facially.

'Well,' said the constable. 'Does that seem to be in order, Dr Penrose?'

Dr Catherine Penrose looked briefly at the pill bottle and nodded solemnly.

'It appears so. Now, what about the phone?'

I came over all helpless and gurgled something about getting the money later. Neither of them would have thought it legitimate if I coughed up enough readies to pay for a new phone now.

'Well, we'll have to see about that, won't we?' said the doc, looking knowingly at her new-found police friend. 'I'm sure you'll want to make amends in due course.'

'Is that it?' asked Roberts.

'Yes, thank you, officer.'

'All right then. But if there's any more trouble, Mr Llywelyn, any more touble at all, I will be back. By all rights you've committed some serious offences but you have found yourself in very understanding company. You've been extremely lucky.'

'I have,' I managed to say.

'We will have our eye on you,' he said, as he closed the door.

I stood around waiting to be excused, knowing it was not quite over. When I looked up Dr Penrose was leaning against her desk, looking at me levelly over folded arms.

'There's something else,' she said. 'I didn't want to go into it when the policeman was here. But we've heard that on occasion you are not in your room when you ought to be.'

Out on the drive, I heard Matt Roberts' panda car start up and crunch down the driveway as he sped off to lecture some schoolchildren on the importance of road safety, or check on some over-filled bins, or possibly just spend the rest of his shift watching the racing at this girlfriend's flat. It wouldn't exactly be the fast-track to promotion, working for Dyfed-Powys. I doubt he was promotional material anyway, sergeant in ten years or so maybe, if that. At least when this finally hit the fan, I thought, there would be something for him to talk about that would have been on the telly.

'Sometimes I just fall asleep where I'm sitting,' I bullshitted happily. 'Other times I can't sleep. I go and sit in the conservatory or the day room or somewhere.'

Not that it mattered too much what I said now. I was a free man, for the time being. Odds on it was almost certain no one was going to arrest me for at least ten minutes.

'That's no good,' said Penrose, rubbing the end of her button nose in a slightly distracted manner. 'That could get us into all sorts of trouble. Look, we'll check you in at nights from now on, all right? It'll be a lot less worry all round.'

I can't say I cared for the idea particularly.

'According to Dr Narula, you should barely be able to walk.'

I pointed at his spotless desk.

'Where is Dr Narula?' I asked. 'Still sick?'

'Actually, he's resigned. He's starting his own practice in Sydney, apparently. I can give you something to help you sleep.'

'Came into money, did he?'

'Would you like something to help you sleep?'

'If you think it's a good idea.'

Then, with her eyes closed, she dismissed me. When I left her she was holding the bridge of her nose in a pained way that did not seem entirely necessary.

Back in the day room my cup of tea and lone boiled egg awaited me on an empty table, both of them stone cold. The canteen counter was rolled shut and the tea urn was empty. The four skeletal figures had taken their habitual places on the lime-green seats, the woman with the oxygen tank and the chunky-knit cardigan amongst them, the rheumy eyes above her mask still focused on something that couldn't have been in the room. On the television an orange man was commiserating with two people in red tracksuits because their carriage clock had only fetched twelve pounds.

I had no idea what to do. Coming clean was still the only sensible option I could think of. Perhaps it wouldn't be so bad. I could still give it a day or two, make the most of Howell Harris House before I went back into custody, assuming no one from the wrong side of the law got to me first, whoever they were. Whatever making the most of Howell Harris entailed I had even less idea. Maybe I could just ask for the pills and the dope and drift off again, for good.

Upstairs it was even quieter. A few of the residents had televisions in their rooms, and from the sound of things were all watching the same programme. The television, if there was one, was not on in Hilary's room. It didn't occur to me to knock or go in. I didn't have the nerves left even for that. I went into my own room and closed the door behind me, wondering if it would be easier once I'd been on the Prozac a bit and got on the sleeping pills, and I may even have been gliding into some miserable acceptance when the door opened again.

'More mail for you,' said one of the women from reception, tossing a thick white envelope onto my bed and leaving the door wide open behind her. I closed it again and picked up the envelope, which was stamped Everard Solicitors Carmarthen; my case file, most likely, and I sat myself down in the armchair and opened it up without any curiosity or excitement. It felt too late for any of that.

The case file was in a beige folder tied up with red ribbon: lawyers will have their little indulgences. It was a good thick file, but it was mostly boilerplate, I was sure of it, the sort of endless clauses and pointless terminology that is the lifeblood of the provincial solicitor. I scanned it absently, wondering what it would be like when the key turned on the other side of the bedroom door tonight, if it would be a comfort or a torture. Terms of engagement, contract details, legal-aid conditions and provisos, addresses for the ombudsman and the Law Society: it was a cheap and quick way to fill a file.

And then, unexpectedly, came the meat. The Crown versus Robin Llywelyn, in grave black Courier on stiff watermarked paper that was incandescent with authority, and without reading the next page an interest awakened in me that put all my immediate concerns at the back of the pile. You owe yourself this, at least, I thought, throwing the rest of the chaff on the floor. I felt my fevered brow and dived in. And it was good stuff. Background was scanty, but the run-up was this: Robin Llywelyn, forty-six, of no fixed abode. Last known address was a street in South Bristol, near where I had an office as a private detetective; had done for years. The flat and the office were gone now. By the time the law picked me up I was Swansea-based, living in short-term accommodation, addresses undisclosed.

Then came the main act, or two of them: a VAT fraud carousel and a bonded warehouse rip-off. The VAT fraud involved shipping mobile phones in and out of Ireland and claiming the intra-community VAT each time they crossed the border, under a couple of fake companies that folded whenever they came near a quarterly excise return. The bonded warehouse involved shipping stuff in without the duty, and then flogging it on direct to whoever would take it. Between them the two schemes could easily have netted over a million quid, according to prosecution. And I had run them. I had overseen the whole shebang.

I had run them and someone somewhere along the chain had grassed and when the law came knocking I corroborated the lot. That was the finale. I'd made takings of twelve hundred thou or thereabouts off the booze and a fifth of that again from the VAT fraud by the time it fell apart, although the precise figure had been the subject of some debate between myself and the Criminal Assets Bureau, and it was all my own show. Warehouse, drivers, delivery people, distribution; I'd managed all that. I was the boss man. And when it looked like the gavel was going to come down, I'd taken it like the captain of the ship. Confessed complete culpability to everything so the crew could scramble for the lifeboats. The would-be prosecution had lined up no witnesses.

As a tactic it appeared to have worked. There were no charges being brought against any accomplices. Some of them may have been mystery men, guys known by a single name who took cash in hand and could leave in a second, but there would be others who had more at stake, especially in a place like Swansea. Swansea isn't all that big. I closed my eyes and pictured without effort, and for the first time since they took the cuffs off, the long curving strip of sand and the grey sea, the steep rising hills leading up to the twin council icecaps of Townhill and Mayhill. It was coming back. It was returning to me, a chunk at a time.

I had been sold out, but I had not sold out. I had run two tidy scams for a fairly lucrative period, and when my time came I had faced the firing squad all alone and without flinching. Then, filling in the rest from what little I knew, came the amenable Dr Narula and his magic drip, and a last chance at a little freedom and some spending money to go with it, if High Farm was anything to judge by.

Outside my sash window the Carmarthenshire countryside bumped and rolled in its little oblivious way, all hedgerows and hillocks and babbling brooks, herds of wormy cattle sitting blankly on the damp grass, droves of worthless sheep nuzzling mud, fast water flowing over smooth stones and big banks of pale grey sky. And me sat there with tears brimming on my cheeks, about to throw it all away. Sat there as if I was eighty, ready to be locked in and doped up by a couple of NVQs in adult care, the only choice in my life whether to have my boiled egg upstairs or downstairs.

Plainly, it was time to buck up my ideas.

That sort of shit didn't happen to men like me. It wasn't our lot. A man like me would know what to do in the clinch, even if he didn't remember beforehand. And he might have allies as well as enemies. I shuffled the papers back into some kind of order and stuffed them back into their envelope, took out the shoebox from under the divan and wrapped the shotgun in my hand-me-down dressing gown. Then I put a hand on the doorknob and breathed in, listening to my struggling chest rattling in that empty room, wondering if I was really going to do it.

I did. There was nothing else for it. There would be no more leniency from the Prosecution Service if I tried the same trick twice.

Out the door, down the corridor, out the fire escape and into the lane. No one saw me. No one stopped me. The Cavalier wasn't in the driveway, but it didn't matter. I popped a few Ritalin and tried for the railway station on foot. There would be a few hours' grace before the alarm sounded. I'd get on the train, put in some distance, and regroup.

That was as far ahead as I'd got, and then I came across the car, the front half deep in hedgerow, two long skidmarks stretching ten or twelve feet behind the rear wheels, a Police Aware sticker already on the windscreen. I guess I hadn't been in any state to drive myself home. Still, I'd almost made it.

To my surprise, she fired up eventually, after a long high whine from the starter motor, and the wheels got enough traction to take them back onto tarmac. I pointed it in the right direction, took one last look in the mirror at Howell Harris, laughed at it, turned the radio on (to Carly Simon's 'You're So Vain', as it happens), and laughed again. Or at least, it almost sounded like laughter.

Before I got into town I already had a plan to buy myself some time.

'Is Gary in?' I asked the woman who eventually

answered the door at the White Hall Hotel. Bleary-eyed at midday, she squinted into the pale autumn light and tugged at the quilted collar of her dressing gown.

'Gary? He's the barman. We're not open.'

'I need to find him. He does know me.'

I got directions to a bungalow half a mile over the wide, free-flowing Afon Bran on the High Street bridge, a little way out on the Brecon Road. There was a sloping lawn out front, neat but not striped, with a few flowerbeds at the bottom and a couple of plastic Grecian planters dotted around the place. There was a two-car garage attached with bright blue doors, although all the cars seemed to be out front in the drive: a little Mercedes A-Class and a Renault estate, both of them about four years old. Gary's hot hatch lay off to one side, black and wet and sparkling, and I would have tried the doorbell but there was still a patch of watery suds trailing down the driveway.

I went around the side of the house and caught him winding up a yellow hose.

'What do you want?' he said.

'I've got the money I owe you for that taxi,' I said. I handed him a twenty and told him to keep the change, and we were friends then. He moaned about the landlady at the White Hall and I moaned about Howell Harris House, and I won that one. It was no contest.

'Listen,' I said, 'if they don't know you in there, I need you to go in and tell them you're my nephew or something and that some relatives have picked me up.'

'Fucking what?'

'Honestly, it'll cause all kinds of fuss if I just bugger off. And I'm not staying there. Tell them I've gone to stay with your Aunt Gladys and I'll give you two hundred quid. I'll give you two hundred a week, starting now. I don't want to see my days out in a place like that.'

The lad didn't say anything to that. I tugged ten of the fake twenties out of my jacket and offered them to him.

'All right,' he said, stuffing them into his back pocket.

'Any time this afternoon will do,' I said. 'Just feed them some crap. You won't have to sign anything. You'll do it?'

'I might.'

'We can make it a grand a month if you like,' I said, with absolutely no intention of ever seeing Gary or Llandovery or Howell Harris House ever again. 'I don't have any relatives left.'

'As long as you're not staying here,' he said, at last.

There was nothing else I could do unless I was going to frogmarch him into reception himself, and I was taking a big enough gamble as it was, so I turned around and walked back down the drive, sank back into the foam seats of my eighties saloon, held the key until the ignition caught and pulled away.

I stayed on the Brecon road. To the north was nothing but mountains and reservoirs, to the west there was only the hospice and the town, and behind that only towns smaller still, until the cul-de-sac of Cardigan and the wet wall of the Irish sea. To the southeast lay Cardiff and the valleys and the distant English border with all the attendant urban allure beyond, London and Soho and even Heathrow airport. But to start with there was only a creeping A-road behind an empty horse box, trundling slowly through small clusters of stone houses hemmed in by steep hill and woodland, places that were barely hamlets, without names or sunlight.

A few miles out of Trecastle I stopped at a garage shop

that lay in memoriam to the ghost of the tourist trade, with the Ddraig Goch, the flag of St David and even the banner of Llywelyn ap Gruffydd hanging forlornly from its awning, unbought souvenirs gathering dust in the window, toy fire engines and miner's lamps and statues in slate, groggs and love spoons and miniature dragons smiling at nothing. Behind a box of bath salts was a triple figurine of the Pontypool front row from the old Viet Gwent days.

I filled the tank and a bell above the door tinkled as I went in. A round woman with a grey bun and a ragged navy jersey sat behind the till with a stern vacuity that a couple of decades ago the people round here might have called god-fearing. I half-closed my eyes and tried to imagine in her in a stovepipe hat and shawl and didn't have too much difficulty.

Inside, the shelves were bulging with stuffed toys and sun cream, which you might need all of three days out of the year round here, camping stools, inflatable dinghies, cheap fishing rods you couldn't catch a cold with, travel blankets, tins of mints, tinned food, canned drinks, anything that wasn't perishable and that you could leave standing until the tourists decided to come back again. I bought a leather-effect holdall that said Cymru on it for my gear and some clean clothes: three pairs of pants that also said Cymru on them, a jumper with a small Welsh dragon on it and three pairs of socks that were mercifully blank. The lady gave me a nod that was so small it might not have been there at all and took my dodgy notes without looking at them. I could probably have paid her in ten-shilling notes.

A couple of miles outside Sennybridge, just as the rain

began, I got stuck on the verge with one of the meat trains while an army convoy rolled past, a dozen jeeps and just as many canvas-topped trucks with teenage platoons in the back, knees bobbing and bergens bouncing and quiet for once, subdued by the prospect of spending a few days squelching through the wet Welsh undergrowth and shitting in bushes. I thought of Doc back at the White Hart, with twenty years on all of them and a few wars on him, grim as a bad x-ray. Christ knows what good camping in Carmarthenshire will do the boys when they arrive in Basra or Helmand, but a couple of hours in a room with Doc would probably go a long way.

I passed through Sennybridge – two pubs, a tractor dealership and a few redbrick houses – just as the wiper on the passenger side gave out. The clouds had started to roll in five miles back, and the rain was falling in big drops. At Brecon I took a right on to the A470, probably with Cardiff in mind, and began the climb into the Beacons. There was hardly any traffic at all by now, just an empty snaking vein of worn tarmac weaving between the steep scraggy tendons of the hills. Look behind you after ten minutes and there would have been half of mid-Wales laid out like a model in a vistors centre, but that afternoon there wasn't anything in the rear view but cloud bank and the shrouded solid portents of the peaks.

The rest, all that was visible, was just dripping conifers and the unworked fields of useless farms. Even the road signs were rusty. Somehow, despite it being quieter than the road to perdition, somebody had managed to have a shunt seven miles up. I stopped behind an anonymous white transit while I waited for a policeman on a motorcycle to wave me on, and found myself staring at a stretch of farm fence by the roadside, its soft wooden posts green with algae, each one pointing in a different direction, the chainlink sagging like a clothesline, a fence that kept nothing in and nothing out, and hadn't had to for decades. A little while later and I would end up in a town of roughly equal purpose.

The Cavalier rolled out of the Beacons and the valleys opened up beneath me, wisps of rain rolling across them like smoke over a battlefield. I passed a disused viaduct on the left, stretched across the Cefn Coed, with a great country house on the opposite bank, all turrets and battlements and old money long gone. Then, out of the rain and the cold, the next thing I could see were those old, ubiquitous golden arches, atop that familiar red rectangle, aloft on their metal pole, that said the countryside was finally over. And an out-of-town Carphone Warehouse and a JJB Sports and three or four other units that were just as generic and omnipresent and thoroughly reliable as indicators that you were finally back in the land of the living. You can moan about them all you like, but I caught a glimpse of myself in the rear-view, as I passed the turning for Swansea Road, and I saw that I was smiling. By the time the next junction had appeared, I had decided to pull off and head into Merthyr.

III

It was getting on for seven o'clock when I left her parked in the Tesco multi-storey and crossed over the end of the Taff Vale railway line, headed into town at the onset of that magical hour when the pubs start their evening shift, with pockets full of money or something very like it, a town where no one had heard of Howell Harris House, or probably Robin Llywleyn either. For a little while it felt like I could have been walking through the gates of Eldorado.

I skipped down a narrow path on to the High Street and into a rain so fine it was like walking in mist. There wasn't a soul about. A way off in the distance you could hear the sounds of a small group of men starting a fight, or pretending to. The High Street had five discount shoe shops, a place where you could dress a schoolkid for under a tenner, a bakery that did six sausage rolls for a pound, and a chapel that might as well have been a stone-age obelisk for all the currency it had in modern day Merthyr. The rest of the place was boarded up, apart from the amusement arcade and the tanning salon and the pubs, which were where the good townspeople drew their solace these days, in moderate and inexpensive doses of glamour and gossip and alcohol and violence. And if the streets were silent the pubs were heaving, a bright and busy island of humanity behind each foggy window. I managed to walk past the first one somehow, but fell effortlessly into the second, a red corner-boozer called the Wyndham Arms.

'Hello love,' said a woman who was smoking outside, bar staff or a friend of one most likely, and I tilted my head and winked at her on my way in, to stand on the rough boards underneath the low rafters. There were flags on the ceiling and old boxing posters on the walls, a few local bouts from decades ago, heavyweights still waiting for their punches to connect after all these years. I stood amongst a small crowd of men not much shy of seventy, whose laughter and arguments and ailments formed a steady throaty chorus that never dropped once, that came from years upon years of sitting exactly where they were now, and doing exactly the same thing.

I ordered a can of lager, Breaker or Kestrel or whatever everyone else was drinking, and a tanned woman in jeans and blonde pig-tails broke one of the twenties for me, and only too late did I glimpse the UV note-checker on the counter, but she didn't use it. I leant to catch a glimpse of myself in the mirror behind the spirit rack: a tired sallow man in a worn suit, too quiet and desperate to look like trouble, too shat on to be shifty. Keep the twenties coming in a place like this, though, and they would check soon enough. It was not a town for flashing the cash.

I drained my glass and it was hard work, much harder than it should have been, and ordered another, listening to the boozy mantra of the ancients as they chanted away, the bastard children of absconded industry approaching their dotage, their frames and faces still full of futile, grey-haired energy. I guess it was all very well if you had twenty years to spare.

I wondered where their children were. It would have been a strange kind of virility, theirs, if they had not spawned. Out of town now, I suppose, if they'd had any luck. The ones that stayed, a lot of them ended up killing time on faster stuff that booze, time and more besides. Round the back of town rose the Gurnos estate, where even the panda cars went in pairs.

Around the pool table in the back a gaggle of teenagers were doing their best to stay out of trouble. Next to me at the bar there was a small poster inviting local hard-nuts to enter an upcoming all-styles fighting tournament. There wasn't a man of fighting age anywhere in the pub, although give it another drink or two and they'd all be happy enough to offer you outside if you asked. It was the sort of pub that needed seat belts on the bar stools. Ordinarily I would have been happy to join in. Or happy enough, maybe. Instead I swirled the dregs of my flat pint, downed it, and went out to find somewhere to spend the night.

I crossed the road and found myself in the town bus station, some optimistic post-war construction from the fifties, a great concrete semi-circle that turned the cold, still air into a gale. It was devoid of buses, and passengers, and any life at all, save for a lone black people carrier parked forlornly in the centre, the taxi driver idly biting his thumb. An idiot in an anorak, loitering by the public toilets, said hello without facing me, his eyes fixed on the empty road.

The office blocks around the bus station were all creations of the fifties too, and just as empty, to-let signs up on every one. The biggest of them still had some tenants, all public sector, of course, a driving-test centre and a few employment initiatives, and next to that was a five-storey building with blue neon letters down the side that said it was the Cyfarthfa Hotel.

A little plaque by the entrance showed that once upon a time someone from the RAC had given the place three stars, probably back when Britain burned with Harold Wilson's technological white heat, when service stations were glamorous and the hovercraft was going to take over the world. It must have taken some nerve to build a five-story hotel in Merthyr even then.

I walked into a reception area that was trying far too hard to impress with nowhere near enough money and got a room for the night for forty quid. I handed over more of the twenties and waited to see if I was going to be arrested. Instead the man just tapped the guest book and pointed a pen at me, then lifted himself halfway out of his chair to give me a key from the rack behind him.

'Room forty-two,' he said. 'Top floor. Drinks are being served in the saloon bar and the resaturant is still open.'

He smiled again, ever so briefly, and then settled back with well-practised ease into staring hard into space, thinking about some bothersome thing, or most likely not thinking about anything at all.

In the saloon bar a table of men drank and ate quietly in the corner, some road gang or a team of shopfitters maybe. A lone Brylcreemed pensioner sat on his own, nursing a can of Carling, ignoring the glass they'd given him with it; he was being equally chatty. I got a bottle of Magners and a glass, without the compulsory ice the TV ads are always trying to shove down your throat, and took it up to my room.

I pulled apart the thin blue curtains and looked out on Merthyr town in the settling night from the fifth floor, traced the orange lights of the A470 as it struck out down the dark valley towards Cardiff, over the horizon. The Millennium Stadium and St Mary Street, the Bay, what was left of the docks, the fast-food places on Catherine Street: all these places I knew and could remember, without knowing why or what they meant to me. Fragments from a spinning world.

Somehow the photo from High Farm found its way out of my pocket and into my hands, and I stared at the smiling people without knowing why, wondering if there was something in it I was missing, some trick or clue. Wondering if there was something in it I wasn't getting, apart from decent company. I may as well have been staring at a bunch of Kays catalogue models. The only thing it told me I was missing was my life, or what had passed for one.

The surroundings didn't help: it was the sort of hotel that could have been especially designed for the low-level fugitive. Rooms like this one, and nights like this one, in towns like this one, were all you'd get, ekeing things out with a bellyful of booze each night and holding on to see if you went in your sleep or got arrested first. But I was too sick and old to last long now, two or three hard nights of it and I would be in hospital with a records check on me, and that would be it.

It was, I realised, what a part of me had wanted all along. A little dalliance with freedom for dignity's sake, a few more cheeky nights on the pop just for fun, and then they could drug me unto the grave. It was all I had the money for, and maybe it was all I had the guts for too. The next few months frightened me more now than they had in the home.

The people in the photo, the happy couple, the little kid, a doting Gerald, were all still smiling. They would always be smiling; the sun would always be shining down on Worm's Head, and they knew and loved each other. I remembered something that Hilary Price had said to me back in the home: people that are really alone, they don't worry about it so much. We would see.

There is a fine distinction between breaking out and running away. Miss it and you can waste a lifetime. I put my drink down on the windowsill half finished and kept staring out over the town. The kebab shops and fish shops were starting to get the first of the evening trade now, a few punters calling it an early night or taking on some ballast for a big one. What you needed was to make the most of what you had, or try to. What you needed was a plan.

From the top floor of the Cyfarthfa I could see the windows of the pubs shining like little yellow gems, the empty streets, the shut-up shops, the supermarket squatting there like some crashed mothership, disused Victoriana, terraced streets, stunted tower blocks, the valley and the sky, both of them almost the same coal-black shade by now. Down past the Texaco, a bingo hall.

Bingo, I thought.

Caer Bingo was a big new building on the other side of the centre, perhaps the only big new building in town. It didn't take more than ten minutes to walk there, and it was just as well I did walk there, because the car park was rammed. It was built of light sandstone and glass brick, with white steel and blue signage, all very art deco. The foyer was tiny, although they had managed to get a baby grand piano in there with a candelabra on it, and next to that was a small counter with a big fat ginger lad behind it.

'This a chain, is it?' I asked.

'Yeah,' he said. 'There's thirteen of them. This is the flagship branch though.'

'Thirteen? Lucky for some.'

He gave me a smile that looked more like toothache and passed me a membership form, and two minutes later I had my very own identity card, with my name on it and everything, the only one I owned. I wondered if I could use it anywhere outside Caer Bingo.

Inside the double doors lay a vast open floor, most of it taken up by a tables pit that must have held five hundred people easy, and it was full. It sort of broke your stride, suddenly stumbling upon so many perfectly silent people, each grey head held in rapt attention to the more-or-less monotone voice of the caller as he ran down his numbers. He didn't bother with any of the old bingo lingo, two fat ladies, legs eleven, all that stuff: just a list of numbers. It sounded like a less evocative version of the shipping forecast. And after it, if you listened carefully, you could hear the sound of five hundred black dabber pens descending on their tickets.

Along the back wall there was a recess full of fruit machines, and even an electronic bingo game, for those who just couldn't get a big enough bingo hit out of the real deal, and in the corner beyond that was a bar, which I instinctively found myself drifting towards. When I got there and saw all those shiny brass pumps lined up it was a hell of a job, but I managed to pull myself up short and asked to see the manager instead.

'What's it about?' said the barman, who had one of those pre-tied elastic bow-ties hanging loosely about his neck.

'I'm a detective,' I said, and the man just nodded and walked off. I had forgotten about that too: there are a few magic words in this life. I parked myself on a stool and waited, and tried not to make any noise. At all. Even the fruit machines had been set to run on silent.

It wasn't as old a crowd as you might have thought. There were a lot of housewives there who couldn't have been over thirty, a few blokes, even the occasional young lad. I found the attraction of it all a little hard to work out. It was cheap, I suppose, and it got you out of the house, it got your mind focused on something for a little while, but how boring did your day job have to be for you to be pulled in by this? Then again, the last serious burst of employment this town saw was building the Sinclair C5. I guess it didn't have to be better than working. I guess it just had to be better than doing nothing at all.

'And now we're playing for the linked game, big money,' said the caller, running straight into the next game. It was relentless. That was probably why they'd got rid of the old bingo lingo, it was too slow for decent profits. I didn't think it was much of a loss to the world.

Then, while I was waiting, the big double doors flew open again and a dour, heavy-set woman in a damson woollen jumper marched purposefully in and straight past me, to a table not four places away, and punched another woman straight in the face. The other woman slid half out of her chair, although that was probably the shock more than the impact, and put her hands to her face.

'You're sitting in my chair,' hissed the woman, and the

one on the floor regrouped herself sufficiently to offer a slap of protest, which got her another jewelled fist in the smacker, at which point the barman reappeared with two of the floor staff, and the pair of them were swiftly escorted out without protest, while the game continued uninterrupted around them.

'Sorry about that,' said the barman when he returned. 'They think it's a lucky seat, see, and they fight over it. The boss'll see you now. Just through that door.'

You wouldn't think it to look at it, but there is prestige at stake in the sport of bingo.

The boss's office was behind a door in the far corner, to the right of a gigantic electronic screen which showed the called numbers and the value of the current prize. Ordinarily, walking around in front of as many people as that, you would have felt a hundred eyes on you, but I think I could have been stark naked and no one would have noticed. I opened the office door without knocking and went on in.

It was a large room with a big dark wooden desk in the centre and another white desk up against the wall. On the rear wall was a map of the valleys with thirteen red pins in it, in case anybody forgot how many branches they owned, or where they were. On top of that there were a couple of bookcases with sliding doors and a long counter full of lever-arch files. On it was a water jug and a couple of glasses and a portable television showing *You've Been Framed* with the sound off. With the door closed you couldn't hear the bingo caller or anything else.

Behind the wooden desk was a wide-faced man only a few years younger than me, whose dark hair had turned to silver at the sides, with the blank but curious face you'd expect to see if you were a visiting detective. At the other desk was a younger glum-looking guy of about thirty with blonde spikes and a Warner Bros Tweety-Pie tie.

'You're the detective?' said the manager, with enough disbelief in his voice to make the question more than rhetorical.

'You're the manager?'

The man nodded once.

'Managing director.'

I liked that. I liked that a lot.

Then he sat there and waited, without looking like he had any high hopes for the conversation.

'I'm a private detective,' I said. 'I don't suppose I could have a word? In private?'

'Don't suppose you'd care to tell me what this is about?' he asked.

I shook my head, just the once, and the man looked over his shoulder at his young deputy without any kind of expression on his face at all, and the lad with the cartoon tie smiled with something like sympathy and walked out.

'Thank you,' I said, when we were alone. 'You'll be reimbursed for any assistance you're able to give us. My name's Dan Jenkins. My client was recently defrauded in a business deal.'

'Derek Hughes. What's that got to do with me?'

'Well, Mr Hughes, your business handles a lot of cash,' I said. Somewhere in the region of five grand in prizes a night, according to the big electric screen, and five grand a branch meant the whole chain was doling out over fifty thou every night, easy. 'I wonder if you'd be so kind as to have a look at this for me.'

I took my wallet out of my pocket and unfolded one of the twenties from it. Hughes took it without looking at it, and just held it for a while as he sized me up. Without taking his eyes off me he scrunched it up into a ball and then let it gently unfurl in his open upturned hand. Only after it uncrumpled did he look down at it.

'The paper's all right,' he said. 'Maybe a bit soft. And maybe the engraving effect is a bit flat like, if I had to say.'

Then he got up and and held it over a lamp on the counter.

'Watermark looks real enough. Commercial printers can ink that on these days no bother. It's a nightmare. Watermarks are no good to man or beast. The thread's not the best, but it's not bad. Hold it up to the light and you'd have your doubts that was a continous strip, but it's only foil, after all. It rubs. It can end up looking iffy on the geunine article. And maybe the printing could be finer but you'd need to compare it to know. The hologram doesn't shift, that's the only thing.'

'Well,' I said, 'my client isn't used to handling large volumes of cash.'

'Christ mun, I only know it's fake because you practically told me. Let's see how it tests.'

From a desk drawer the man took out an orange marker pen and a small black UV box.

'One of these costs about two quid,' he said, holding up the pen, with which he drew a fat orange line over the note. 'You seen one of these before?'

'Oh yeah. Not too sure how they work though.'

'They use iodine to pick up the starch in the paper. If the paper's wood-based like normal paper you get discolouration, that yellow strip turns dark brown. If the paper's fibre-based, if it's proper rag paper, and unless I'm very much mistaken that's what this is, it just fades away.'

The man sank back in his seat and looked at me quite openly and without any hurry. I did my best to look calm and counted to thirty. When I got to thirty I promised myself to say nothing until he did. I was pretty sure he was as good as mine, but it's so easy to blow these things. Anything at all can do. Shifting in your seat the wrong way is enough.

'Takes a few minutes,' he said, after an eternity. 'Sometimes quarter of an hour. Which makes these pens fucking useless, really. You're not going to wait that long at the supermarket, are you?'

The note was in his hand again, and he was turning it over and over and trying not to look at it too much. Then he held it up between us and the faint yellow line was still there.

'The paper's the right kind,' he said. 'Wonder if she glows.'

He flicked a switch on the side of the little black box and slid in the twenty.

'No fluoresence,' he pronounced.

'No?'

'No. I think maybe a little on the watermark.'

'What does that mean?'

'Security paper is a hundred per cent UV proof. Some of the fakes glow.'

'And the ones that don't?'

'Well, they soak them in suntan lotion, is what I'm told. A couple of hours in Factor 50. Of course, it's possible to get hold of security paper legitimately, it you know where to go and you don't tell them what you want it for.'

'It must be a problem,' I said.

Hughes stroked his chin, leant back on his swivel chair and crossed his legs.

'Well,' he said. 'I'll be honest with you. I did the training course and I bought the gizmos, but we don't use them really. The problem with dodgy notes is if you keep an eye out for them you have to do something with them when you spot them. I mean who actually checks every single time they get a note whether it's authentic or not? And if they do check, it's not at the point of receipt is it, more likely some time later, when it's too late. The bank won't reimburse you. What are you supposed to do? It's better not to look at all. It's not ideal, is it, but there you go.'

'No,' I agreed. 'Most people pass it on. The problem is when you get swamped in it.'

'Your client's deal just a little bit too good to be true, was it?'

'Probably.'

'How come he knows, anyway? If I hadn't have known, if you hadn't said nothing, and I'd have looked, I might not have had any doubts myself. Real notes go funny in all sorts of ways. People stick them in the washing machine when they does their jeans. Why'd you think they were fake?'

I know they're fake because they were printed in a barn in Llandovery. I was up there the other day. There were two dead men on the floor.

'I have some pretty reliable information,' was all I said. 'I haven't performed any independent tests on them. Neither, as far as I've been told, has my client.'

'Well, anyone professional tests it, they're legally

obliged to hand the whole lot into the police. Bit of a fucker, but I tell you this, if someone wanted to pay me a pile in folding, I'm going to have a proper look at it.'

'Sensible policy,' I said, and I got up and made to leave. 'Thanks a lot for your time.'

The twenty-quid note still lay in the UV machine.

'I'll leave that with you. If you happen to see any like it, I'd be interested to know. My client is rather keen to track down the source. Naturally, his priority is to recoup his losses. It's not something the police could help with.'

The man's face had turned blank by the time I'd got to my feet, and for a moment I thought I'd lost him.

'I'll drop off a couple more with you if it helps,' I added, when I was at the door. 'Stick them on the walls of the branch offices or something. And I can promise you that your time and discretion in this matter will be rewarded if we get a result.'

The man just shrugged. It was just more work to him at this point. The Neighbourhood Watch shtick didn't appeal to him any more than it did any other working person. But a seed had been planted.

The lucky table was still empty when I passed it. It was the only empty table in the house.

'All right?' said the barman as I made my way to the double doors. A detective, an audience with the boss, it can get people's interest up in far more exciting workplaces than bingo halls.

'Yes, thanks. Throw them both out, did you?'

'We can't have the game disturbed. We had a lady in here one time and she keeled over and died. Her daughter caused a hell of a storm afterwards, she expected us all to drop everything and make a fuss about it. But you can't stop bingo because you think something might be wrong, can you? Wouldn't have saved her, anyway.'

'Probably not,' I agreed, from my position of equally absolute ignorance, and crossed the wide expanse of carpet to the exit, watching five hundred heads bowed in silent concentration over something so transcendentally boring it could almost have been meditation. When I left the big screen said the house prize for the current game was a hundred and twenty quid. Enough to cover you for a month in Tesco, maybe, or to get something for the patio, if you didn't game away the winnings. But then that's practically impossible. You couldn't really be reckless in a bingo hall, although I was trying my best.

Over the road I bought a jiffy bag from the Texaco garage and, in the shadow of the car wash in the corner of the forecourt, stuffed it with a thousand pounds exactly. Too many notes for mere samples, but not a big enough bribe to cause any panic. Just a little moral splinter that would get under his nail and stay there, until the way of the world took over. A thousand pounds in cash, in a brown envelope. It had an oddly familiar weight in my hand, that little grenade I was about to toss into somone's life. For there hath no temptation taken you but such as is common to man. And so on.

I knew these things.

I sealed and addressed it to Mr Hughes, marked 'Strictly Private and Confidential', and handed it to the fat ginger lad in reception. I waited there until I saw him off. Just to be sure I even watched him cross the floor and enter the office, absently tinkling a couple of high notes on the baby grand while I watched, two high notes over and over again. They slowly reverberated around the room, like a police siren in a world where the worst crime was using the fish knife to butter your bread. And then I buggered off. You have to give people a bit of time, after all. People overreact. Sometimes people don't see things the way they are.

I had a couple of gentle nightcaps in the hotel bar, probably the only quiet bar in town, me and the Brylcreemed widower with his liquid pension, in our crumpled suits, not talking, not even looking at each other.

Sometimes people don't see things at all. In the Portakabin at High Farm, next to the guillotine, there was a slab of printed notes, eight to a page, as thick as your fist. All I had to do was go back and cut them up. Must have been over a hundred grand easy, and if Hughes had never been naughty before, he'd snap it up for twenty per cent of face. Might even be worth doubling that.

I carried a double whisky upstairs to my room and eased myself into bed, although I still coughed long into the night. I was starting to have trouble sleeping lying down. Soon I would have trouble sleeping full stop.

The orange glow of the streetlights reflected off the ceiling and I found myself smiling, despite the pain, between the cramps in my chest. After all, you could probably spend a lifetime's worth of fake twenties in a town like this, and no one would ever care.

IV

The following morning I came down to breakfast in my Cymru jumper with my dragon socks showing above my unshined shoes, unshaven, a little greasy, a little giddy. One night in Merthyr and already it looked like I had lived there my entire life.

The restaurant and the bar room were completely empty. So was the coffee percolator. There was a variety selection of miniature cereal boxes gathering dust in a wicker basket, offering all the variety of a month of Mondays. I passed.

Outside the morning air was cold and damp, and a grey sky hung over the wet valley like a shroud. The only thing moving up on the black-and-emerald slopes was the grass waving in the wind, wherever there was some, anyway; it wasn't even real soil up there, just old slag, Wales turned inside out.

A few truant schoolkids ran by shouting, and on the high street the old women with the tartan shopping trolleys were starting to appear, up at the crack of dawn to spend an hour and a half nipping into town to buy some mince. A woman with a blue tabard and spiky blonde hair smoked so listlessly outside the amusement arcade she could almost have been there all night.

I looked at the arcade window, full of stuffed bears and dried flowers and cycling clowns, a tinted screen rising up behind them so you couldn't see the punters. I don't know why they make such a big deal about the anonymity of arcade patrons. Plopping yourself on a stool for a couple of hours and feeding some loose change into a machine that will usually give you about seven tenths of it back doesn't seem like much of a vice. Perhaps it's more to do with embarassment than guilt.

I went in, looked in the booth for a UV counter and found none, and had broken a couple of my remaining twenties when the woman came in from her fag break.

'Does anyone buy those things?' I asked, pointing to the window.

'Some do,' she said, gurgling a little phlegm in the back of her throat.

'What? They walk home holding a cycling clown?'

'Some do.'

I went and sat down in front of a machine called Do You Feel Lucky, idly popping in a few quid until I got on to the features board, flickered around on there until I started getting the odd quid back. When you got into the swing of it, it was no more expensive than parking a car.

Derek Hughes probably needed a week, or ideally a fortnight. Enough time for it all to sink in. He couldn't find me to return the counterfeits, and if he went to the bother of handing them in to the police then there might be all kinds of questions. At the same time, he was unlikely to just throw them away either. So in the end, he would have to do something about them, distribute them through his own business, which was easy enough, or get a friend to do it, and either way he would be taking the plunge and making a cut. Once he'd done that, then you'd approach him to see if he'd like any more.

A fortnight, I thought, watching the three drums roll, while a nearby London-themed fruit machine exhorted me to 'come and have a butchers' in tinny cockney.

A fortnight. It was out of the question. A week was too much.

I got three lemons on a diagonal and won eighty pence. Scooping whatever the machine had given back to me out of the plastic pay gutter I went and stood in the doorway, and thought, without any desire whatsoever, of smoking a cigarette. Hughes would bite, I was sure of it, but it's not wise to rush a man when you're counting on him to do the wrong thing. He's likely to kick you back just to keep his own idea of himself intact. The only question was how long I could wait.

Well, one thing, I wasn't going back in the arcade. I'd have as much fun if I went into the launderette and pumped money into the washing machines. On a whim, seeing I had pockets full of change, I stopped at a phone box and asked a directory enquiries service to put me through to a Bristol private investigation agency.

'Hello,' said the voice at Clifton Detectives.

'How much do you charge for a background check?' I asked.

'What sort of thing did you want to know?' said the voice.

'The guy I need to know about is a former private detective, worked out of an office in Totterdown, hang on—'

I searched in my pockets for my tattered business card, but Gerald Williams had taken it.

'Well, somewhere around there. Guy's name is Robin Llywelyn. Left Bristol a couple of years ago. Someone in your office probably knows him, I expect. Shouldn't be too hard. Just ask around, check with the police, the usual sources, all that. See if you can get me a two-page report on what sort of work he did, how he was regarded professionally and personally, why he came to town, why he left, that sort of thing.'

'That's not what we'd call a standard background check,' said the voice. 'A standard background check would be criminal records, work history, credit rating, that sort of detail. Objective, verifiable stuff. That's how we like to work, see, sir. We write a two-page report of opinions and hearsay, you might very well decide you don't like it and then we'd fall out, the two of us, wouldn't we?'

'I know how it is,' I said. 'Believe me. I know.'

'What did you say your name was?'

'David Jones,' I said.

'And your relation to the party in question?'

'Prospective personal creditor.'

'That's it?'

'That's as far as it goes. And I'm a curious guy.'

'Well, it's not the usual sort of work we handle.' The voice droned on, about variables and difficulties and allocating resources, until it became a single humming tone I realised I recognised all too well: it was the sound of the grift, working my way. It came with the trade.

'Just give me three hundred quid's worth of work,' I cut in, 'and your bank details. I'll call you when I've lodged the money.'

'You'll need to sign the paperwork,' was the best the voice could do.

'Can't. I'm out of town.'

'We don't like running around for someone without a signature.'

'You'll have to skip it.'

And I hung up before he could argue. They'd take it or they wouldn't, they were busy or they weren't. Everying else was just haggling with its hat on. That's the nature of the private investigation industry in this country, and probably any other, for that matter. I knew it, without remembering a thing about it, the way a croupier could lay on a perfect faro shuffle while staring at a pair of breasts.

It must have been a vocation of sorts, my job.

If I'd the money, I'd have stuck him on it there and then, but I wasn't even holding three hundred in fakes so it would have to wait a while. The smart thing to do would be to nip up to High Farm and recover the sheets before anyone could find them, but I wasn't up to High Farm just then. I knew I would have to do it soon, but High Farm gave me the shakes. It had two murdered men in it, just lying there, in the top field. Which is very bad for feng shui.

In the café at the bus station I ate a cheese sandwich that came wrapped in cling-film and drank a cup of tea from a polystyrene cup, watching the passengers come and go. There weren't many of them. Oldsters and housewives and the odd embarassed-looking man, gossiping quietly with each other under the vast plastic awning. A few little kids ran around in small circles shouting at each other. Most of the bus bays were unused, I noticed. All you had now were a couple of local shuttle services to the outskirts of town and an occasional run into Brecon or Cardiff or Abergavenny. I watched the X15 from Aber to Cardiff pull in, and counted three people get on. No one got off.

The next bus came in with its wipers on, and I looked up to see the cloudy sky had turned a notch darker again. I took a few steps backwards, into the safety of the shelter, and listened to the sound of the rain hitting the plastic roof.

Give it a good two hours to Llandovery, to be on the safe side, swipe the sheets and the guillotine and whatever else was handy, and two hours back. I'd be in the Wyndham again by nightfall. The best thing to do was to get up there straight away.

I still wasn't up to it.

I moped around town with my hands in my pockets, trying to gather some nerve and instead feeling it drip steadily away. Perhaps I'd wait until I had the green light from Hughes, to give me that bit of motivation.

It was dole day in Merthyr. The benefits queue stretched halfway down the high street, old people mostly, standing there with cross faces and cagoules and barely moving at all. I'd never seen anything like it. I thought again of High Farm, and tried to remember the money that was there too. It was a strange town to be waiting in, when you were waiting for the mother lode.

Round the next corner an empty travel agents advertised package holidays and coach tours, the two saleswomen inside chatting idly to each other with blank faces. It was too late in the year to get any sun out of the Med, but there were deals to Florida and Egypt and Mexico; cruises round the Caribbean; fortnights in Goa and the Gambia. They all seemed like nice ideas, in the same way that a caring god seemed like a nice idea, or pacifism. I looked at the poster of the Canary Islands, where the sun shone till late in the evening and it was still warm after midnight, even in winter, where the living was cheap and the lager flowed, and then I thought about me going to the moon and playing golf there. They both seemed about equally likely.

Next door was a little second-hand mobile phone place, and I almost walked straight past it until I remembered.

'Hell of a dole queue out there,' I said to the lad behind the counter. 'Is it always this bad?'

'That's not a dole queue,' he said, lifting his head out of a tit magazine. 'That's for the bank. There's been a run.'

'What?'

'Yeah, it's run out of money. People want to get their accounts out before it goes belly up.'

'That's not supposed to happen,' I offered, seeing as I was a man of age and experience who had been around a bit. The man put down his soft-core and pondered.

'Don't you watch the fucking news?' he said. 'The whole system's shot. They'll all be running out of money next, you watch. It's all going tits up.'

'Things don't change that much,' I said. 'They never do.'

With the pound coins from Do You Feel Lucky I got myself chargers for the two pairs of mobiles I'd picked off the bodies at High Farm and left him to console himself over the supposed collapse of the capitalist system with pictures of topless women and sports cars. Back in my hotel room I wiped the drizzle off my brow and plugged them all in.

When they had all tunelessly bleeped into life I took

the phone number from Gerald's letter out of my jacket pocket and tried it on the room's landline. One of the two grey Nokias fired into a tinny rendition of 'Who Let The Dogs Out?'. So those two were the Port Talbot connection, and all of it, hopefully. It kept the number of people involved to a minimum. We would see.

The two cheap Nokias were obviously the work phones, pay as you go, most likely, and they hadn't been used much. The call logs went back about five weeks, and almost all the calls on them were from one phone to the other, with the number simply stored as 'business' in each. There were only three other numbers in the address books and the logs, and one of them was my mobile, apparently, or at least it was listed under my name. God knows what had happened to that. I didn't have it when I checked into the hospice. From the looks of things we chatted about once a week, even when I would have been handcuffed to a bed in Howell Harris, which was a bit of a puzzler, so presumably I'd handed the reins over to Gerald before I went in.

It had some legs, as a theory. The second number was to an 01550 line, which was the area code for Llandovery, and that was only five days ago. And the other number was an out-call to a Swansea landline, made only once, last Saturday.

So: I pass the phone over to Gerald, something goes wrong, or Port Talbot gets some sort of a lead, they close in, make a stand-off, and get shot. By Gerald, most likely, who almost certainly would have had a shotgun or two kicking around the farm. Then Gerald takes off, but not before sending me my so-called cut, an illegal weapon, and a pointlessly euphemistic letter, any of which, if intercepted, could have landed me straight back in the dock. Then again Gerald had just shot two men and was about to disappear himself, so he would have been pretty spooked, and he may well have been an idiot in any case. Desperate idiots are the rank and file of the criminal world. And it did occur to me, in a realisation which wasn't exactly uplifting, that it wasn't as if I had anything to lose either.

Anyhow, I liked the theory. I liked the fact that it put the killings squarely on Gerald and then got him out of the picture, which meant there wasn't much I could do about them. Then I went and stood by the window and ran it around a bit in my head. The wheels fell off at the first corner, and it only got that far out of cowardice.

I thought some about the sawn-off. It was the sort of thing you could hide pretty well under a three-quarter-length leather jacket, a mean vicious little thing that would be just the job for putting the shits up someone if you were paying a visit. All you'd have to do would be to hold it in your hand. I reckoned odds on it was theirs. Gerald wouldn't have carried it, or been the type to shoot two unarmed men in cold blood. I liked that idea too, although you could have demolished it in the same breath as the first.

I tore the frontispiece off the room's Gideon and wrote down all the numbers and dates. There were no texts and no voice messages and if there ever were they'd been deleted. Then I went downstairs, back on to the high street, and got a flagon of cheap brandy. The drink for heroes, as Samuel Johnson described it. Not this stuff. Then I went back up to my room, sat on the bed, and took a couple of swigs before I got started on the personal mobiles, two expensive touch-screens on contract.

Naturally, they were full of stuff. The phone books were an endless list of names and numbers, there were hundreds of texts and dozens of voice messages. I went through them all. Friends, loved ones, relatives; drinks on the town, a birthday to be remembered, a wife's dental appointment, a son's football match, a daughter's sleepover. A girlfriend to take out to the cinema and a sister who had fallen out with her husband. A mate who needed a lift on Thursday night. A mother who was cooking Sunday dinner. It was all there, that stuff, a horrible, mundane, personal intimate glimpse into the lives of the two dead hustlers who were rotting under plastic sheeting at High Farm. The messages were the worst. Some of them got quite tearful towards the end. They must have suspected something; the wife and the girlfriend and the mother and father, in the face of this sudden absence. They had still been trying to make contact this morning.

None of it told me anything about the case, or matched the numbers on the business phones, and it didn't do my theory any good at all. I hadn't really expected any different. I turned off the phones, finished the rest of the brandy as quickly as I could, swallowed a couple of painkillers, drew the curtains on Merthyr, and laid myself down on the bed, eagerly waiting for oblivion to descend. Thinking about the sight of a naked foot, dangling from a bload-soaked sheet, as it was dragged through the long wet grass.

Ryan Davies and John Billingham, their names were.

THREE

SYNDICATION

I

I had given Derek Hughes a full forty-eight hours. It was as much as he was going to get. He sat behind his desk and fretted at the impropriety of life.

'I'd like more time,' he said.

'We all would.'

Outside in the hall five hundred bent heads dabbed their pens, and the caller ran the numbers. I had been awake to see the sunrise, although not the sun, just a fainter shade of grey on the other side of the steep hill. And I had eaten my cereal and read the paper and caught the news, with nothing in either about High Farm, and played the fruits and walked the streets in the fine rain, and drank ever so slowly with the old crowd at the Wyndham, who were still at it, had been for decades, and now it was gone seven in the evening, and dark again.

Hughes shifted in his chair again, looking anxious and concerned, but just a little bit too much of both for me to think it was completely genuine.

'Look, it's entirely your choice. But you have to make it now. My client is in pressing financial need and I am sure there are plenty of people who run cash businesses like yours that would be happy to accept.'

'Local man, is he, your client?'

'No, far from it. He just got handed a stack of fake cash that he cannot bank in one bad transaction. And as you'd expect, my employment is also supposed to protect his anonymity. If you think you can go round the middleman with this one, you've got your work cut out.'

'How much did they hand him?'

'What's on offer is fifty grand in notes that are almost completely passable. The rest of the money he can afford to keep and spend himself over time.'

'What is it? Drug money?'

'Money is money. The only difference is between the money you can spend and the money you can't. But no, it's not drug money. If it was drug money, I wouldn't be here. Drug people could take care of a problem like this. Distribution is something they know how to do. Now, I'm not going to tell you where it did come from, because it would give you a lead to my client. But it was a legitimate high-value cash transaction. If you like, you could think maybe it's foreign racehorses. Or maybe it's a yacht, or a substantial personal debt. And if you were thinking along those lines, you'd be kind of on the right track. That's really where this guy is coming from. And he'd rather use a little professional discretion and anonymity than reputation and brute force. It's an unorthodox offer, but it's coming from a gentleman who's been put on the spot. Not a gang.'

Hughes picked up a biro and jabbed it at me. I took it as a good sign. It meant he felt like he was starting to take some control of the situation.

'And how'd you get involved?' he said.

'You ever met a private detective before? Moneyed families get themselves into fixes like this now and again.

It's possible to scratch a living sorting them out, although it can lead to some interesting conversations. I doubt very much you'd want to do it. But believe it or not, some people think I'm just about trustworthy enough to ask for help.'

Then I leant back in my chair and put my hands in my pockets, like a guy who would be perfectly happy if the next thing he did was to walk out the door and never bother you again. I ran back quickly over everything I'd said, but there wasn't much more I could have put in the mix. A bit of old money, a whiff of class, a little bit of down-at-heel private detective glamour, even a nod towards self-righteousness.

'And what you want for it, then, this fifty grand?' said Derek Hughes, at last.

A couple of months, the doc said. So play on the safe side and call it five, although chance would probably be a fine thing. Two grand a month would see me through, and stick another five on top for jollies and jams.

It worked out to a nice round number.

'Thirty per cent,' I said.

'What, fifteen? And all at once, I daresay.'

'Yup. Simple enough, isn't it? One handover and that's it.'

He didn't baulk, which I was grateful for. A business like his must have traded off a cash float well above that. Use a little personal money to balance it off, for safety's sake, and it was there for the taking. Thirty-five grand, tax-free, in his pocket.

Hughes stroked his chin and then rummaged in a drawer, came out with a notepad and a deep sigh, and started totting up a few numbers. Maybe he was just stalling, or maybe he really was thinking about it. It didn't matter now. We were on the home straight.

'Any movement on the percentage?' he said, trying to sound like the most bored man in the world.

I shook my head.

'Set by client.'

'Come on,' he said. 'Play the game.'

It was my turn then, to sigh and shrug, as if we were talking about council-tax bands or mobile phone tariffs.

'Well,' I said, 'I can knock a grand off it, just to show willing. And that'll come off my end. That's as far as it goes. That do you?'

Hughes looked at me like he expected me to say something more. I just ran my tongue along my teeth and looked at the ceiling. The silence grew and I realised I would have to get up and walk out. I was busy thinking of something smart I could say on the way to the door which wouldn't look too desperate or obvious, but nothing sprung to mind. Then Hughes tore the sheet off his notebook, crumpled it up tight, and flicked it into a small plastic bin.

'All right,' he said. 'Come back in three days.'

I sat there and tried not to look too cheeky and failed.

'What?'

'Three hundred quid for the samples,' I said. 'Play the game.'

I saw myself out after.

In the off-licence next to the fried chicken place I got another one of those half flagons of cheap brandy to steady the driving hands. There was nothing else for it now. No putting it off. I cast a jealous look, on the way back to the car, at all the people behind those bright little pub windows, who could look out on the wet grey world with a little warmth. The Cavalier was still waiting undisturbed in the Tesco car park. It wasn't a car you'd be tempted to break into or take for a spin. Next to it a mother of two small children was emptying a trolley full of groceries into the boot of a Mondeo estate while the kids climbed happily over the back seat, and I unscrewed my bottle and pulled hard. When they were gone I tried the engine, and managed to get the car out of there without hitting anything or anybody.

On a lay-by on the outskirts of town I stopped to use a public phone box, dialling in the number that was supposed to be my own mobile, half hoping to hear Gerald's blustering tones on the other end. Instead a woman's recorded voice explained to me that the person I was trying to call was not available. I hung up without leaving a message, wondering if there would ever be an answer on that number again. Then I got back in the car and pointed it down the curving road that led up over the dark looming contours of the Beacons and into the farms and paddocks of Carmarthenshire, an open bottle resting between my thighs.

I made it back to Llandovery in one piece. The roads were almost empty, except for a few lonely headlights snaking their beams across the bracken. Past Sennybridge there was nothing at all, save for the one meat train rolling east with five hundred sheep. I pulled onto the verge to let it past. Before I could get back on the road some boy racer sped past in a hatchback at about seventy, if not more, hurtling round the bends like a pulse down a wire. Come nightfall the lanes turned into racetracks round here. I waited to see if there was a mate trying to catch up, but there was only the moon, sailing alone through the cloud.

The little town was empty, as usual, and the next thing I was taking the turning up through the woodland and keeping an eye out for the mud track to High Farm. When

I saw it I pulled over, killed the engine and turned off the lights, wondering if there was anybody there now. If Gerald had reappeared, great, but odds on all other visitors would want to hurt me or put me in prison, or both.

I sat on the bonnet by the side of the road, the steep wooded sides of the little valley rising up above me, waiting for my eyes to adjust to the dark. There wasn't a sign of life anywhere, not even the hoot of an owl. The A-road, half a mile downhill, was silent. I peered through the trees in the direction of High Farm and not a light shone. Still, better to be safe than sorry, and shit-scared if nothing else. I set off up the mud track almost on tiptoes, with half the brandy still left.

It wouldn't have taken two minutes in the daytime, if you weren't worried about someone killing you. God knows how long it took me. The mind plays tricks on you. By the time I got to the gate I thought there was an extra car in the courtyard, and I must have stared at it for ten minutes before I remembered it was a skip. For a while the stream, babbling quietly behind the barn, was two people talking at low volume. A lone sheep baaed from two or three fields up, and I took cover by the mossy stone wall like it had been the crack of a rifle.

I edged up past the side of the garage and tripped over some baling wire. I went round the farmhouse once and fell again over a loose drainpipe. And I made it a hat-trick on some wet mud while circling the barn. I was that keyed up I didn't realise how cold I was until I sneezed, triggering a long coughing fit that made my chest ache with that old, familiar growing pain I carried inside of me. Sometimes I swear it was as if I could feel my lungs bleed. After that I couldn't have done any more to announce my presence if I'd used a megaphone, and no one had come out to murder or arrest me, so I heaved open the barn and flicked the light on.

From behind a workbench a startled fox made a break for safety, running out behind my legs, and was gone so quickly I wondered if I'd imagined it. But everything else was exactly the same. The printing press still sat under its plastic cover along the rear wall. I went into the Portakabin and turned on another set of lights. No detectable change there either. The uncut notes were still next to the guillotine. I picked up the top sheet and held it in my hands, cold, damp and full of dew, but it still felt like money. I wondered how long you'd have to leave it here before it rotted. One winter would probably be more than enough.

It was a good job, I thought to myself, that someone was going to stop that from happening. Just as well that somone was going to put it to good use. In the fear-filled early morning, it was a sensation that could almost have passed for virtue. Ennobled by such sentiments I casually laid it out across the guillotine.

Doubtless, it was a job that required a steady hand. I unscrewed the brandy again and took a swig. The pile of uncut notes was at least as thick as a bible. There was no hope of counting it tonight. How many pages was that? Three hundred? At least. Fifty thousand quid was probably an underestimate. And god knows how much more had been printed. You might as well go outside and try to count the stars.

I gingerly ran a finger along the blade, and nearly drew blood. No problems with the kit. A steady hand and a bit of patience was all that was called for. I squared up to it, moved the sheet up against the block with the palm of my hand, and inched the top of the first row of notes up to the cutting line. It sheared in one effortless glide. I trimmed the sides next, and the bottom, and tidied up the top again, because it was a little hard to detect where exactly the white margin was in that light. And you had to get it dead on, of course, dead straight.

A little while later I had the whole sheet neatly carved, thirty-two very passable twenties, six hundred and forty quid near-cash that would pass muster under any human eye, as long as you didn't mind trapezoid currency. And not even Merthyr would accept faintly triangular notes.

'Fuck,' I announced to the empty barn. It would probably be better in the morning.

I walked back down the mud track to the car, marginally less scared now, but still pretty on edge by the time I'd got there. I took the Cavalier off the road and left it in the courtyard, and then went into the farmhouse with my gear and plonked myself on a rocking chair, with a bottle of brandy and a sawn-off shotgun in my lap. What I planned to do with the sawn-off if anything happened I don't know, but I felt it was probably good luck to have it there with me. First thing tomorrow morning I'd take the paper and the guillotine and get the hell out.

And as I sat there in that reeking house, full of cat piss, with nothing more than brandy for company, I got round to some rough mental arithmetic about the fakes in the barn. There was a lot more than fifty grand's worth. Thirty-two on a sheet, over three hundred sheets, came in at a chunk under two hundred grand. The first ten times I did it I'd thought I made a mistake, but no. One hundred and ninety-two thousand pounds, or almost-pounds.

I sat there rocking in the chair trying to get to sleep, but thinking of nothing else. What came after the hundred and ninety-two grand I couldn't tell you, but I could at least add up to it. It was kind of like the opposite of counting sheep. Even so, morning got the drop on me somehow, found me blinking into the feeble dawn that was filtering in through the dimpled window, with the silhouettes of two men stood in front of me.

Well, you gave it a go, I thought fleetingly, and then the heart started to flutter and I didn't think anything at all.

'Just the man I wanted to see,' said one, in a tone that suggested something quite the contrary. 'Got more than a few bones to pick with you.'

It was a familiar voice. For a moment I thought I was going to pass out, and then the two of them came into focus. It was the used-car dealer who had sold me the Cavalier. Next to him was Gary from the White Hart. My overwhelming sense of palpable doom decended a couple of notches.

For a while no one said anything. We were all just looking at the sawn-off in my lap. When I remembered what it was and how it got there I shot up like someone had just spilt a mug of boiling coffee over me, and it fell to the hard flagstones but did not go off, although the empty bottle smashed. It lay there like a thick black slug, all that lethal muzzle velocity and pounds of pressure coiled in the depths of its stubby twin barrels, and still no one said anything. At last I picked it up and put it on the dresser.

What did you say in situations like these? What was the etiquette?

'That wasn't for the likes of you,' I said, in the end.

'I should think not,' said the car dealer, sounding offended. I wondered if it cost him much to sound that nonchalant; if it was courage or just a lifetime in sales.

Maybe it was the context that was missing. I doubt I could have seemed that threatening. I looked at the bottoms of their trousers. If they'd seen the bodies, they would have been wet up to the knees, but there was just a little mud around the uppers of their shoes. Maybe they hadn't even been in the barn yet.

'I heard you and Gerald were up to something,' he carried on, like the gun had been nothing more than a faux pas. 'Where is he?'

'I have no idea,' I said. 'He got himself into a spot of bother and took off.'

'That's illegal,' said Gary, sounding worried, either because he was younger or smarter. 'A sawn-off shotgun. It's illegal.'

'Yeah,' I said. 'It's not mine.'

Like a teenager disavowing a lit cigarette.

'Who else is here?' asked the car guy, steering the conversation away from the elephant.

'Just me.'

'Then whose is the H-Reg Merc?'

'That's Gerald's,' I said, stupidly confident.

'No it's not. Gerald drives a Peugeot. I sold it to him.'

Of course it wasn't. It must have belonged to the lads from Port Talbot. All you had to do was stop and think about it for a second. It was another little reminder that I was not all I used to be. God knows what else I'd missed. But you don't always have the time, not even a spare second. Gary was idly shifting around to my right, as if he was just looking for something to lean on. It didn't bring him much nearer the dresser but it was in that direction.

'Hold on there,' I said suddenly, and lunged for the little shotgun, and I had it in my hands, and my back turned to them, by the time Gary went for me. He got me in a bear hug and I went down like a sack of potatoes under the weight of him, busting my kneecaps on the stone floor, but by the time he'd got the gun off me I'd broken the chamber and I had the cartridges. I stuck a thumb in the perforated plastic cap of each one and poured the powder out on to the flagstones, with him scrabbling over me the whole time. If he'd had any brains he would have clubbed me with the gun, but like I say, you're not always thinking like you should be.

It felt like my kneecaps had split.

'Let's not have any of that nonsense,' I managed to get out. 'Pointing guns at each other.'

And then the white vibrating curtain that had appeared at the corner of my vision folded across the room, until all I could see was this shocking trembling wall of agonising light, even with my eyes closed, and then Gary stopped punching me like a kid brother and everything went black.

I came to within seconds, in almost as much pain as before, but it was going away from me slowly, as I sucked in huge gasps of air, sucking in the dust and dirt from the floor and feeling like a landed fish waiting for the bludgeon. My chest made a sound like a car on a gravel driveway.

Gary wasn't still hitting me. Seeing he wasn't, I gathered up the nerve to climb back onto the rocking chair, but it kept sliding away from it me. Once I'd made it, my knuckles curled around the ends of the armrests; I thought if you can do that, you might as well try opening your eyes again. As soon as I did a series of small explosions started firing in the back of my head. Gary and the car dealer were standing stock-still in front of me with big scared faces as wide as satellite dishes.

Although it hadn't been touched, my left arm started to ache like it had been broken. It could have been, I thought, could have been the impact, and then the exact same pain spread to my neck and my jaw, and I realised it must be something else entirely, just as an invisible belt started to tighten around my chest.

They started talking then, those two, but I couldn't hear them. I wouldn't put it past them if they were thinking about calling an ambulance.

'I'm all right,' I said, with a winded voice. I don't know what they said back. I said it a couple of times. Then I don't know what I said or did. Ten minutes later I was sitting there across the dining table from them, breathing shallowly and chewing down a couple of painkillers. My chest felt like I'd just gone ten rounds sparring at about forty classes above my weight.

'You all right now?' said the car dealer.

'I've forgotten your name,' I said, eventually. Despite my condition, I did notice that I was neither in police custody nor the care of the emergency services, and it was important to conduct negotiations like these from first principles.

'Dai,' he said.

'Oh, yes,' I said.

'Now what's yours? Not what you put on the fucking forms, your real name. And what in Christ's name are you up to?'

He was still a little scared. They both were. But they hadn't phoned anyone.

'Robin,' I said. 'It's Robin. Ask Gary there. Now what was it you wanted to see me about?'

'Don't play funny buggers with me,' he said, and thumped

a fist down onto the table. It was a little hammy, but then people can seem inauthentic when they are genuinely wound up. I blame television myself.

'False name, false address; fair enough. You get that now and again. And then you go and pay me in fake notes. And if I didn't know the cashier, I'd be in a whole lot of trouble, I can tell you. So what am I supposed to do, you tell me?'

I let that one hang for a second too long.

'It's the police,' he said. 'That's it, as far as I'm concerned.'

Funny, I knew exactly what to say then.

'Let's go in the barn a minute,' I told them. 'Just have a look in there first.'

So we went, the three of us, across the courtyard, young Gary's grip like an iron band around my upper arm, the two of them eyeing me like I might suddenly decide to pull off a flying kick and then sprint for the treeline.

They made me open the door, as if there might be somebody in there waiting for them, and I was just about able to heave it to before my legs went. They let me sit down on a plastic drum and I waved them on, too breathless to speak.

It didn't take them long. A muted conversation in the Portakabin, and then ten minutes later I could see they had the covers off the printing press. I leant back against the cold metal of the barn wall and tried a few deep gentle breaths. You couldn't hurry them. It was pretty obvious what it was, but what it meant would take a little longer to sink in.

What did it mean anyway, money? Money always meant something else, a week's worth of food or a sixty-grand car or what have you. Even if you didn't know what to do with it, like I guess I didn't, it was a little claim cheque against the future and the past all rolled into one. As long as there was hope there would be money, although the two were very different things. The stuff was born out of the glint in a huckster's eye, it shimmied forth from the cosmic cardsharp's sleight of hand, an epic genetic grift that the human race seems to have subsconsciously invented for itself. A three-card monte to keep us guessing in a world we would never understand.

Without tomorrow, there would be no money.

'Haybaler my arse,' said Dai, returning, hitching his belt up over a portly midriff. 'I thought that was bullshit. What does Gerald Williams want a haybaler for?'

'Yeah?'

'Yeah. He had an artic deliver that about six weeks ago. Had a new concrete floor laid down for it too, by the looks of things. Must have been some lads out of town. He wasn't running all this on his own, was he?'

'Could have been, if someone set it up for him. He could have bought the whole set-up wholesale from a gang somewhere. It all could have been used before, somewhere else. Was he mechanically minded, do you think?'

'Gerald? Was he in the Royal Engineers, I wonder? Gary! Was Gerald in the Royal Engineeers?'

'How'd I know,' Gary said, still back in the Portakabin.

'I don't know. He left town as soon as he was old enough, and he didn't come back till his old man was almost in the ground. Then he inherited the farm.'

'Not bad going.'

'No, funny thing though, he was pissed off as hell about it for a long time. Because they had a lot of money too, family money, been accumulating for a long time. You know what some of these old farming families are like, they don't spend a penny of it. And the old man gave all the money to the hospice in town.'

'I heard they put Gerald on the board,' I said, thinking that otherwise I might very likely still be handcuffed to a bed somewhere.

'Yeah, big ceremony and that, and him sitting through the whole thing looking miserable as sin, or so I heard. I think he has as little to do with the place as possible, although they all have to doff their cap to him down there. So how'd you get involved with him, then?'

I had no real answer to that, I realised. I had some experience of breaking the law for profit, I was fond of a drop, we were about the same age. Beyond that I was at a loss.

'Guess he liked the look of me,' I said.

'Liked the look of you?' Dai laughed, hard. 'No offence. Gerald didn't like the look of anybody.'

I had no reason to but I bridled anyway.

'I've got a little reputation, you know,' I said, like I thought I was Tony Montana.

'Got some form, have you?'

I shrugged.

Gary was still in the Portakabin. I could hear the faint metal swoosh of the guillotine as he tried out a few experimental cuts. It was only human nature to give it a try. Did it ever amount to anything more than that? Like form was just a question of being in the wrong place at the wrong time.

I shrugged and felt the dull tight knot in my left breast.

'Did he mention anything about other parties, then?' Dai asked. 'Like who else was involved?'

I sat there in the Carmarthenshire countryside, at the

precipice of a bottomless well of money, looking into the black infinite, and I could feel the strands of the web trembling as they reached out across the county and into the connections you couldn't see or had never met or just couldn't remember. Connections that would be moving in already, slowly and bumbling at the very edges of things or pounced an instant away. They could arrive cluelessly in months, dumb and afraid like Gary and Dai, or they could be turning off the A40 at this very moment, with bin bags and gaffer tape for the bodies. But they would get here. It was one of the forces of nature.

'Not that I recall,' was all I said.

'What you doing with a shotgun, then?'

'Well, you can't be too careful.'

'You're starting to sound like Gerald.'

'It was Gerald who gave it to me.'

And I felt a smile, of all things, creeping onto my face, in that rotting hole of a farm, as the trouble closed in and the days shortened. Maybe I wasn't really after the money after all. Maybe I just wanted to see what would happen, and find out what had started it all. Maybe I just wanted to learn something about myself. I'd already found out I wasn't the type to point a gun around, and I didn't mind that at all.

'I'm surprised about Gerald,' I said. 'He looked like he was born, bred and bound to the place. I didn't think he'd really spent much time anywhere else.'

'Oh,' said Dai, lost in thought, 'well, look at the state of the gaff. A twelvemonth here'd turn anyone into Wurzel Gummidge.'

From the Portakabin you could hear the blade of the guillotine travelling swiftly up and down its runners.

'What are you doing in there, young Gary?' yelled Dai, although we both knew full well, and Gary came hopping out looking a little pinker in the face.

'They're not bad, are they?' he said, offering a note. Dai took it and the number of furrows in his forehead doubled.

'They're almost perfect,' I chipped in. 'Except the hologram doesn't shift as much as it should, and they glow just a little bit under UV. Spend it in small quantities and someone might turn it down, but they probably wouldn't be confident enough to call the cops.'

'That's what the lady in the bank said,' said Gary absently, a man trying to think about ten things at once. 'The UV.'

Gary stood there with his hands in his pockets, smiling now like a man who had just got out of trouble instead of right into it. Dai simply turned the note over and over in his hands, as if he was hoping it had instructions printed on it somewhere. I prodded my ribs gently where the ache in my chest lay and wondered where that fox from last night was now.

'So,' I said.

No one said anything. Faintly, through the trees, the rumble of a meat train or timber lorry reverberated up from the A40. Dai went and stood over by the barn door, wide open, looking out into the courtyard and probably not seeing anything out there at all. It wasn't a bad day, as it happened. No morning mist, no dew, no wind. It wasn't even cold, or if it was I couldn't feel it.

Dai came back in and stared at the wall like he couldn't see that either. It was one of those rare moments that come in everyone's life when everything changes all at once. Even if he pushed it all out of his mind and took me straight down the station, even if he was up to playing the good citizen bit, he would never be the same again. The memory of this, and the thought of what could have been, would come back to haunt him at night. And in the mornings and afternoons too. Some part of him already knew it, and I knew it too, and I watched him stumble about like a deep-sea diver, the weight of an ocean above him, looking for a lifeline to the surface. But he would never be going back there again.

I tried a few gentle deep breaths again, raking the sullen air over the hot coals in my lungs, but the fire was dying. I was almost back to normal. In fact, I was pretty relaxed. Cosy must have been something I had never gotten much of.

'There must be hundreds of thousands here,' said Gary, still grinning. He was a young man, after all.

The car dealer massaged the top of his bald head with four fingertips and groaned. He had no wedding ring, I noticed. It was a good sign.

'A little under two hundred grand,' I corrected. 'Unless I've missed some.'

Dai started rubbing the top of his head angrily with the flat of his palm. For a moment I wondered if that was how he'd gone bald in the first place.

'And what do you expect us to do with it, hey?' he said, crossly.

I shrugged. It couldn't be helped. None of this could be helped. It was the world we lived in.

'A three-way split, I suppose.'

Dai left his scalp alone.

'Aye,' he sighed, like a hollow man, as if he had just said farewell to an old friend. 'I suppose we'll have to.'

'Well,' I grunted, shifting off of my drum, 'you better do

the cutting, young Gary, and then we'll divvy up and get out of here. Shouldn't take long.'

He disappeared back into the Portakabin before I'd finished the sentence. Dai didn't move.

It was a funny thing, crime, and the criminal life, or at least it was if you looked at the people outside it. Nature versus nurture, social policy, the breakdown of the family unit, personal moral weakness, genetic disposition, it's all been trotted out, and it's all far wide of any useful mark. The point is, crime finds you. Not everyone, but some. You slip into it, or you just find yourself compromised; it's a dealt hand. After that you just sort of stay in it, or near it, and some make millions and most get sent down penniless, but you stay in it. You stay in it because once you're there, you have no choice but to try and make sense of the world and yourself, because you know that the life you had before was a lie. All that moral self-assurance you comfortably nested in was built on the sheer arbitrary coincidence that you never ever had the chance to pull a fast one that was worth anything. You'll fiddle your tax maybe, and your expenses, and you'll put a claim in for overtime you haven't done and you'll pull sick days and watch bootlegged movies and all that banal, shamefully trivial stuff, maybe even drink-drive or do some drugs; and while you check the overdraft and the mortgage every month you'll console yourself with the thought that you are a decent citizen, whatever that is. One of the fundamentally honest, toiling mob, silently working together to keep us all on the rails.

The truth is you never had the chance to do anything worth a fuck. Something might have occurred to you, something suicidally stupid or just possibly halfway to worthwhile, but nothing came up on a plate, and nothing at a time when the only option worth considering was to take it. And that means you can live with the lie.

When you've fallen through that glass ceiling, the difference between right and wrong is something that becomes a lot harder not to spend much more time thinking about. It wasn't exactly an edifying experience, but, I thought, as I put an arm around my new colleague, it was home. I knew it by something other than memory.

'Come on,' I said, as we walked into the Portakabin. 'We'll need to go over a few things.'

Inside Gary was already hard at work, fast but fastidious, the spare white rag paper piling up at his feet. Even so, it was clear the job would take him a couple of hours. It was enough time to go over a few pointers.

I offered Dai a beat-up old wooden chair and he sank onto it like a deflating balloon.

'Bloody hell,' he said.

'You'll be all right.'

We sat there and watched Gary hit his stride, the odd bead of sweat forming on his forehead. After a while, his hands started shaking, and he leant up against the wall, his arms folded, with pupils the size of casino chips. It seemed like a good time to get started.

'Listen,' I said. 'You take your time over that, but when you finish, we three are leaving here and never coming back. That's the first thing.'

Dai just nodded like he was listening to a doctor, but Gary found it a little harder to swallow.

'You reckon? What about all this paper and ink and stuff? What about that thing back there?' he said, jerking his head in the direction of the printing press. 'That's bloody Stargate that is. That's a portal into another world.'

'You can forget about it,' I said. 'And I'll tell you why. Firstly, assuming you could get it working, there's no way you could handle the quantity of notes it produces. Secondly, if you tried to do anything with all those notes, you would get your fingers burned, and badly. That's if no one managed to crack onto this place in the time it took to get it up and running. Thirdly, it's one thing to find a pile of money and ferret it away, but it's another thing to start up and run an operation like this. You'd wind up having to deal with a type of person you haven't met yet. They would scare you, and if they couldn't scare you, they would hurt you pretty bad and maybe worse. Fourthly, you'd get caught, sooner or later. Unless you can draw a line under things, you get caught, and we're all drawing the line today.'

Gary wiped his brow with the sleeve of his hoodie.

'You could handle the notes,' he said. 'I expect. Couldn't you?'

'I'm not interested. This whole set-up is a time bomb. I wouldn't be happy. And this is the other important thing: this is only going to work – even just taking the money that we've found – this is only going to work if we're all happy.'

'What do you mean?'

'Well, I'm not a problem. By this afternoon I'll be gone from this place for good, and never coming back. In a couple of months I won't be anywhere at all. What with the cancer. If the worst came to the worst, and I got caught, there's no deal they could offer me for grassing you two. They couldn't cut the sentence short enough. With you two, who are both local, it's a bit more complicated. A whiff of trouble, and you'd be racing each other to a full confession.'

'Fuck off,' said Gary. Behind me, I could hear Dai letting out another long painful moan.

Divide and conquer, was what Napoleon called it. I couldn't have the two of them fumbling around something like this. It would collapse before it had started, and I didn't need the attention. And in any case, it was good advice. There were two bodies at the back of the neighbouring field to attest to that.

'That's how it is,' I said. 'Right, Dai?'

'Too fucking right,' he said.

'Right, Gary?'

The barman looked at us both with contempt burning bright in his eyes, but there was resignation there too. He hawked up a glob of defiant phlegm onto the floor and went back to the guillotine without speaking, his hands steadier now that they were dealing with dreams we had made finite.

Sometime later Dai went into the farmhouse – to see if he could find a little tea or coffee, he said, but came back predictably empty-handed. Apart from that the three of us spent the entire morning in the barn, watching the notes pile up. By the afternoon it was done. Dai took out a cheap cigar and the two of us quietly watched him count it up into ten grand bricks while the crows cawed outside. When it was all finished I reached around my share with an outstretched arm, like a big winner in a high-stake card game, and swept the lot into my Cymru sports bag.

To look at us you'd think we'd never known anything else.

'Spend it as slowly as you can, and spend it somewhere they don't know you,' I said, from the barn door. 'Mix it up with real notes. Gary's the one you'll have to watch out for.'

'Fuck off,' said Gary.

'He can come and work for me at the garage,' said Dai. 'We'll get through it soon enough through trade.'

'Yeah,' I said. Like hell they would. He'd be gone before the winter, but he probably wasn't dumb enough to get caught while I was still alive. 'Leave all the off-cuts here, or if you finish cutting somewhere else, burn them. They're evidence. But get the hell away from the place, and don't come back.'

In the field, by the low wall, I could see a couple of crows hopping in and out of the long grass. There would be others there soon, fighting over the entrails. A black cloud of angry birds, and then probably some curious or professionally incurious person. The way of things. Forces of nature.

I put a hand on the roof of the Cavalier and took it all in, the state of the place, from its mossy tiles to the festering pools of old rainwater in the still-wet mud, a smallholding some four hundred years old by the looks of things, hunkered halfway up a toy valley under a sea of grey, pressing cloud, and all of it rotten to hell.

The barman and the car dealer were still in the barn, waiting for the sound of my engine maybe, before they got to arguing. Maybe they'd be able to keep it under wraps for a while, or maybe they'd chicken out and get straight down the station. Maybe the serious people would pass me coming south on the way up, and it would all kick off straight away. Maybe it would go to shit and maybe it wouldn't. Gerald had the right idea, even if his hand had been forced. Get out while you still have some chips on the table.

I climbed into the old saloon and got her running, turned her around in a squealing, squelching six-point turn, and got her back on the tarmac. I didn't look back. I got through the little market town of Llandovery without accident, discovery or any desire to ever return. I made it through the tight, winding road until I broke out onto the top of the Beacons, straight into a thick bank of mist that stayed with me until I came down the other side for my final visit to Merthyr. It looked just the same, right down to the fine rain.

The time was just short of four in the afternoon. I left the car in the supermarket car park again, walked past the same old end-of-line railway station and into the high street. I called Hughes at the bingo from a payphone in the bus station and he told me to come in around eleven that evening and I hung up.

That gave me about seven hours to kill, a working day for some people. The depositors were still queuing outside that busted bank, although there were fewer of them now, and the ones who were still at it had a glint of grim enjoyment in their eyes, exchanging dark mutterings about the state of the nation and drinking from thermos flasks. I wondered how much they had inside. A couple of hundred quid, I guess, would be enough for some people to put on a show, if they had the time on their hands, and there was a lot of spare time round Merthyr. The ones who had any real money to worry about would be talking to solicitors by now.

I found a bank that didn't have a run on it yet and went in to lodge my three hundred unfaked notes, straight into the account of Clifton Detectives. No queues in there at all, not even any customers; it had an eerie bubble of calm like you get in a building that is just about to be demolished, or a dodgy side street you knew you shouldn't be walking down. I went straight up to the counter and filled in a paying-in slip for a jowly matron in pince-nez, a pale blue cardigan over her garish uniform blouse, wondering if she felt it too.

'You're not having any trouble in here, then?' I asked, as she stamped my receipt.

A young man with thick dark hair clippered almost to his scalp strode out from the side office at the end of the counter in a cheap suit and told me in the tone of voice you'd normally associate with a nightclub bouncer that everything was fine.

'I'm only asking,' I said.

'Well, there's a lot of silly people spreading unhelpful rumours at the moment. If you bank with us you've got nothing to worry about.'

He gave me the sort of look headmasters probably used to about forty years ago, and then shared it with the cashier for good measure before going back to his small room and whatever pressing matters required his silent, unseen toil.

Ever so slowly, the cashier leant towards me. At first I thought she was falling off her stool.

'Well, anything could be happening couldn't it?' she whispered. 'We'd be the last to know here, I can promise you.'

'Used to be different when you started, I imagine,' I chipped in, nodding in the direction of her boss. 'That was a good job once, being a bank manager.'

'Oh, long time ago,' she said. 'I'm retiring next week.'

'Well, enjoy it,' I said, and she smiled once, and then settled back into lifeless normality, conserving her energy like some hibernating animal.

I took the stamped slip and headed back to the phone box to ring the Bristol agency and tell them they could get cracking, one background check on a Llywelyn, Robin; a former private detective last based in the Totterdown area. The guy tutted a bit over the lack of paperwork but seeing as he'd already been paid the full whack he didn't kick up too much of a stink. I said he could give me the goods verbally when I rang back in a couple of days, and hung up, wondering what I thought I was doing. I had no memory of Bristol whatsoever. My life felt like the itch an amputee gets on a lost limb. At least there was somebody asking after me now who wasn't trying to do me over. What good it would do me who could tell?

Like a tumbleweed in a Western, a single empty shopping trolley glided past me and came to rest against a vandalised bench, covered in black marker pen and Tipp-Ex. Somewhere a way off, a street or two up towards the Gurnos, somebody was calling someone a fucking cunt. The sky, not yet night, was a shade of red and grey, and the streetlights had come on, their orange glow fatter and heavier in the wet air. The evening had just arrived, all of it in one piece, the mystery of my untidy life was still unravelling, and there was nothing to do but wait.

It was what pubs were made for.

It was not yet six and in the Wyndham the old crowd were in their usual corner, their gravelly voices like a fast, shallow river, coursing down the same worn route it had for years. I perched myself on a lonely stool and listened to it, like the rumblings of an old machine that pulled nothing but time. I just listened. I mean Christ, you wouldn't want them to catch you looking. I drank slow, nursing the glasses, which seemed the only way I could drink now without falling off the world, and waited for the cold wet town outside the small windows to shrink away. After two or three it started to move in that direction, although not far enough. I doubt if I had more than five pints the whole night.

I sat there, face forward and eyes down as the pub grew busy around me. No one talked to me all night, which is unusual for Wales, and doubly so for a town like Merthyr.

But there is something about a man that will make you leave him be, sometimes. Truth was I sat there thinking about what was next. After the money. No one ever really knows what happens after the money.

I sat there in a lively pub, hardly drinking at all, speaking to no one, under the growing and instinctive certainty that nights like this were probably all that every night had ever been to me, once. Cusping on the top of that fourth pint, my happy veins tingling in my parked body, safe and inert in a crowd of lively strangers; it was like coming back to a long-forgotten country. I wondered if I would take up residency there. I wondered if that was all I was trying to do, or if there was something else I had in mind.

I wondered about the two lads from Port Talbot, about Gerald Williams, about the solicitor in Swansea and the car dealer and the barman up in Llandovery and whatever other messes I had made of other people's lives and of my own. Perhaps I was just getting morbid, but I sat there asking myself whether I was fixing to leave it all behind or sort it all out, and I couldn't have told you either way.

It didn't matter, in the end.

When the woman called time I flipped up the collar of my blazer and headed out, past the fights and kebab queues and hysterical women, down past the garage and the roundabout to Caer Bingo. The car park lights and the blue neon lettering were both off, but the foyer was still lit. The pit, vast and empty now, was in darkness, the fruits were all silent and the bar towels were draped over the pumps in the corner bar. In the far corner the door to Hughes's office was still open, and spilling light, and I walked towards it with my sports bag casually clutched in a single hand, trying out a few likely lines in my head.

I went in and Hughes was there in his usual seat, but next to him were standing two bruisers well over six foot, and a fourth, better groomed, perched insouciantly on the edge of the desk, in a suit and overcoat, black hair gelled back tight over his head.

'Christ,' said the man on the desk. 'They said you were in bad shape, but Christ.'

And the door closed behind me.

It was a kind of luck, I guess.

II

It's strange how much silence an empty bingo hall can make. Any place like that, like a railway station or a sports stadium or a factory, that you would normally associate with thousands of busy human lives, and instead there is just nothing.

The smartly dressed man took out a cigar from his inside jacket pocket and tore off the cellophane wrapper. The noise of it filled my ears like I was standing at the bottom of Niagara Falls. I couldn't think.

'So we get a call, from Derek here,' the man said over the din, searching for a lighter now, 'that some chancer claiming to be a private detective has strolled into the office one night and tried to offload fifty grand's worth of fake twenties.'

The man produced a golden lighter, one of the electric ones that make a quiet roaring sound like a housefire behind a faraway door, and worked on puffing his cigar into life over the little blue flame.

'Welsh, was he? we asked,' he said, exhaling a cloud of not inexpensive-smelling smoke. 'Did he look like a sack of shit? Yes? Aye, aye, we said. We know who that is.'

I went round the faces in the room. Derek Hughes,

straightening his tie, almost looked a little bit embarassed. Heavy number one, tall, fat and pig-ugly in a denim jacket and an All Blacks top, was just about angry enough to pop a neck vein; number two (if he was a heavy at all) was as tall, solid and animated as a Welsh dresser, and the guy with the cigar had the sort of expression you get when you walk into your local after a night you can't remember, that tells you you did something very bad, and something very bad is about to happen back.

'All right mate,' I tried.

'Oh, I'm fine, thank you, Robin. Just fine. Let's have a look at them, then, these notes.'

I put the bag on the table and unzipped it, and he took out a single note from the pile that was there and held it up to the light, and I stood there as if I was a punter on the *Antiques Roadshow.*

'You've got a machine for counting this?' he asked over his shoulder, and Derek took a little thing that looked like an electric weighing scale out of a desk drawer and upturned the bag.

'You could have banded them,' Derek said, without looking at me.

'Not someone like him,' said the one with the cigar. 'They're all right, aren't they?'

'I told you they were. Now this might take a while, mind.'

'Fine. Tomos'll stay here in case you need a hand, won't you, Tomos? Gavin and I will take Magnum here off for a chat in private. Got one or two old matters to settle, and people always feel more like opening up when they're in private, don't they?'

Tomos was the hairy lunatic in the denim, it turned out,

which meant I got the bored-looking one. I tried to figure out if that made him more or less dangerous, until I realised I was completely helpless either way. It didn't take too long to get there.

'Come on, then,' said cigar man, turning me around by the shoulders in a way that was not too friendly at all. 'Out to the car.'

The playing pit felt somehow bigger and darker now, although we seemed to cross it in a single accelerating heartbeat, and then we were outside, in the cold biting air, the sounds of the drunken town echoing down to us, and Gavin slid the side door open on an upmarket people-carrier and waited for me and my enemy to get in before closing it shut. It smelt of car leather and chemical pine. When he turned the ignition the soft light of a digital dashboard glowed into life, and the radio started playing a song by Sinead O'Connor at a volume so low you thought you could only hear it in your head.

I was not afraid. Or I was afraid, but not out of my wits. If it had to end like this, it was an ending, at least. It would make some kind of sense. We would see.

Gavin took the people-carrier up to the A470, and the lights of the town, dulled through the tinted glass, disappeared, and the Beacons came on, and I sat there in the middle of the back seat watching the white line ahead flicker on and off in the middle of the black tarmac. To my left, in that misty glass, I saw or thought I could see the dark shapes of the hills undulating against the unlit sky like massive living things, slow and ponderous and portentous, covered in miles of solid coniferous forest where no man ever went.

No one spoke. It must have been a prearranged spot

they were taking me to, and I wondered if there had been others there before me, or if they did it somewhere new each time. They probably did. It was a nice car. It was not an inexpensive cigar. They were probably sensible people.

'It's funny,' I said, cracking at last. 'You'll need to tell me what it was I did wrong. The head's fucked, you see.'

I couldn't see his face, although it wasn't two feet away, and facing me, on the rear pull-down seat behind the drivers, his head nodding gently as the road bumped and turned. I don't suppose I had to have done anything, if I had something they wanted. That was history enough.

'Your head was always fucked,' he said. 'I'm sure it'll come back to you though, when push comes to shove.'

I couldn't see any point in arguing. They would find out their own way. It was the only way people found out anything, if they ever learnt anything at all. And if they didn't, I guess they would go back thinking I went tough, and that was not a bad note to bow out on.

We stopped a little later and turned off into a picnic lay-by, and there was a gate at the end leading into some Forestry Commission property, the sort of gate that was normally padlocked but was not tonight. Gavin got out to open it, came back to take us through, and then went to close it after us before driving another hundred yards or so into the trees. Then we came to a halt and he did the doorman bit again, and I could see from the hint of a moon up amongst the clouds that we were on the edge of one of the old Victorian reservoirs, the still water stretching up the centre of the valley like a field of flat shining ebony.

I got out first, before anyone could shove me, and perhaps it was the adrenalin but in seconds my eyes had adjusted enough to see each stone on the embankment, to see the fake clinker-work on the fibre-glass rowing boat, beached on the grass. There were two beaten-up old plastic chairs on the bank, and an old steel drum; the sort of spot where the rangers would eat their sandwiches whenever they checked the fire breaks – which would be about every seven years or so. It was a lonely spot. The top cat flicked his cigar butt into the waters, and it sounded as loud as a bucket of water thrown on hot coals, up there in the forest. Then he sat himself down on one of the plastic chairs and clapped his hands on his thighs.

'Off you go then,' he said. 'Do your best.'

I reached into my jacket pocket for the pill jar, unscrewed the child-proof lid and knocked back more than a couple of painkillers. No sense in making things hard for yourself.

'Oh no,' I said. 'You go first.'

'Very kind of you, Magnum, but you start. Then we'll do our bit. Be interesting to see how much the story changes.'

Behind me I heard a catch unlock and then the slow hiss of the hydraulic arms as Gavin opened the boot, and then the sound of something like a toolbag dropping onto the gravel.

'I don't think you'll go for it particularly,' I said.

'Probably not.'

Away up in the treetops not too far away some unsquawking bird took silent flight. You could hear the flap of his wings, powerful and steady, like a strong heart. I waited till he was gone.

'I was laid up in a hospice not too far away from here. I'd got one of the doctors to stick me on an intravenous morphine drip, the sort of stuff they put you on when you're in your final hours, you know, so you can just drift off in a painless haze. Really strong stuff. The idea was to shake off the Crown Prosecution Service so they'd drop some VAT fraud and smuggling charges. It worked. Only I was on this stuff for more than a week. When I came to, I had no fucking idea who I was. It was like I'd come down from another planet. I still can't remember a fucking thing about anything that happened before I came off it.'

The man on the chair gave a tired sigh, and slapped his hands gently against his cheeks before rubbing his palms downwards against his face.

'Yeah,' he said. 'That it? And you woke up with a bag full of fake money in your room. The end. That's it?'

'No, not quite. It's a bit better than that. I came to, and there was a guy in the neighbourhood who knew me, who may even have been able to help me out with the deal in the hospice. Someone I had been working for. He had a farm near there and he had a load of counterfeit money and I'd been helping him get rid of it. He's fucked off now. I have no idea where he is. He wrote me a note about it. The money in the bag is just what I'd grabbed from the farm when I got round to going back there.'

'He wrote you a note. How sweet. What was his name, this nice guy?'

I wondered if I had taken enough pills for this, and how long they would need to take effect. Too long, probably. But you had to keep something back. I wasn't just being proud, it was practical.

'No,' I said, 'it's your turn now. But you'll need to be careful.'

Then something metal hit the back of my knees, and the gravel drove itself hard into my face, and then some solid pointy thing started tearing chunks off my ankle, and I stopped making any kind of human noise at all. Someone was talking, but it wasn't me, and I couldn't hear the words, only the wind tunnel of my own pain hurricaning through and around my ears. And my heart, when I noticed, was no longer a heart but another set of jaws, biting furiously at my ribs, and my chest was setting concrete and a sea of dazzling stars appeared behind my tight-shut eyes and I passed out.

Then I was sitting cross-legged on the track, my back against the van door, draped in a blanket from somewhere, with a bleeding left ankle that was already the size of a pineapple. It was a while before I could say anything, and when I finally unclamped my welded jawbone my teeth rattled like dice in a cup.

They were patient enough about it. I could have done with a snap of something from the hip flask, but I guess they had a tone to keep. I told them Gerald's name, the location of High Farm, told them about about the printing press and all the gear. I didn't tell them about the bodies. Gerald could have moved them there himself, and I wouldn't have known. I had a feeling if I told them about the bodies things would accelerate far too quickly for me to keep up with. And the other thing I kept out was Gary and Dai, which was only fair. I'd only got them into it so I could get out, and neither of them needed a midnight visit from these people. What's more they probably thought they were still decent citizens. If they came up against the sort of pressure these boys put on they could cave in and call the police without worrying too much about the consequences.

Gavin and his employer were sitting side by side on the lawn furniture, their overcoats wrapped tight around them. We were all shivering. Much more of this and pneumonia would get me first.

'Shall I give him another go?' Gavin said.

The other one looked over his shoulder and over the water at the vague hint of day which was showing at the edges of the big sky. He got off his chair and leant into my face, grabbing my chin so he could look at me up close and in the eye. I don't know what he saw there. Not much of anything, I expect.

'What's my name?' he hissed. His aftershave smelt of cedarwood and lemons and there was tobacco and stale coffee on his breath.

'I have no idea.'

He took his hand away, but I held his gaze, even though I could barely lift my chin. Right now it was all up to them, everything. If they went at me again I knew I would tell them all about the bodies and the barman and the car dealer and anything else I could, and if that wasn't enough then I guess I'd be out in the boat and over the side, or taken deep into the woods and left there.

'We'll go and see this farm first,' he said to Gavin. 'He was always full of shit. That's the problem.'

'Now?'

'Yes, now. You all right with that?'

Gavin blew out his cheeks.

'Yeah, I guess so.'

'You better be.'

Then we were back in the people-carrier again, none of us speaking, back down the other side of the Beacons again and through the silent lanes. Llandovery and High Farm. I couldn't get away from the place.

I had to give them directions when we were on the other side of town, and when we came to the turning for the mud track the boss man got Gavin to stop on the verge, in the same place I had stopped the night before.

'You better go and check the place is empty,' he said, at the tail end of another cigar. There had been some coffee in a thermos and a something in a hip flask too, but none of it for me. It struck me that I should have been exhausted, but I wasn't yet, although there was tiredness in both their voices. None of them had enough on the line, I expect.

Gavin did that thing with his cheeks again. It was probably the closest to insubordination he ever got.

'All right,' he said.

Then he sloped off and left the two of us sat there looking at each other, him twirling a dead cigar butt around in his gob the whole time. My ankle throbbed so badly I could feel it in my temples, a pulsing pain so intense it seemed strange it wasn't making a sound. I would probably have to cut the shoe and the sock off it somehow, tomorrow at the latest, and I had nothing to replace them with. But first of all you needed a tomorrow to have problems in.

Gavin reappeared panting at the side door after a couple of minutes, with mud all the way up his left trouser leg and the left side of his jacket.

'No sign of life that I could see. No lights, nothing. A couple of cars in the yard but they look like old bangers.'

'Exterior light come on or anything like that?'

'Nothing,' Gavin said again.

No one mentioned the mud.

'All right. Drive us up.'

The gate was still open wide, propped up against the mossy stone wall, and as we pulled into the courtyard there was a Volvo estate there that I didn't recognise. There were getting to be a lot of cars parked in that courtyard. I wondered about it quietly in my head.

Gavin got out again and pulled the door to for us, but

gently this time, and we got out slowly and took a couple of deep breaths as if we might all of a sudden need to be very quiet. I stifled a cough on my sleeve. Over the top of the steep valley there was a ribbon of blue-red sky, and in the faintest light of the first traces of morning the square farmhouse, with its crumbling white plaster and dark windows and big black door, seemed set in a giant grimace against ourselves and the world.

'That the barn?' said the man, in a voice that sounded as if someone had hands around his throat.

'That's the barn,' I said.

The three of us stood there in the biting cold, and I was already shivering again, so I went to open it up myself but he put a hand on my chest and set off to do the job himself, with me trailing a good way behind and Gavin no nearer, despite the fact he had two good feet.

The man opened up both the doors and nothing happened, by which I meant no one leapt out or started shooting, and I caught up with him and turned the lights on for him. When the strip light flickered into buzzing life the place seemed pretty much untouched, from what I could remember.

'That's the Portakabin and that there is the press up against the back wall?' he asked again, still standing at the threshold.

'Yeah. Like I said. This is it.'

And he rolled his head on his neck and lifted his chin high and stepped inside the magic circle, where money might come to mean nothing, nothing but the flick of a switch, and you had to use some other gauge to know what was precious and what was not. I looked out past him at the dawn, and the world outside looked different already.

'Go on in,' I said.

And he kept his hands loose by his side, and Gavin cracked his knuckles and followed suit, both of them light on their feet. They were a couple of steps ahead of me when the pair of them froze stock-still and turned white, and then coloured with a sudden and intense anger. Gavin came back and grabbed me by the lapels and dragged me up past the corner of the Portakabin and there, huddled bashfully in the far corner of the barn, right up against the wall, were Dai and two other old boys from the town, by the looks of things, doing their best not to tremble. Up by the printer, which had its cover off and a ream of paper cack-handedly wedged in the far end.

'They're just some locals,' I managed to get out. 'Curiosity got the better of them.'

'You were always full of shit,' said the cigar man. 'I said it, didn't I? Who the fuck are you?'

Dai stepped up to the crease for the home team.

'We heard the car stop in the road,' he said. 'So we turned the lights off. Didn't know who you'd be, like. We just came up to look around.'

'Fucking hell.'

The three men, each of them the other side of sixty, stood there as passive as children, awaiting the solution to the problem they knew they presented, and hoping it was something that meant they'd be able to go home soon. When the shock wore off, in a couple of minutes, and they got round to trying to talk themselves out of it, things would only get worse.

I did warn them. I warned them both.

Gavin put me back down on the floor and I found myself taking a couple of backwards steps until I had a wall to lean against myself, and stayed propped up there against the corrugated steel like a stack of timber, until I got my breath and my brains back. Dai gave me a pleading look but I waved at him to keep his mouth shut for now.

'So who the fuck are you?' asked the main man, again.

One of them, the better dressed of the trio, who had recently seen the inside of a barbershop and had someone to iron his shirts for him, started off on that long journey from fear to indignation and shuffled forward half a step.

'And who might you be?' he asked. He had a nice, educated tone of voice, although it was quivering a little on the vowels.

Gavin walked up to him with his fist clenched, save for one pointed finger, and stuck it hard into his shoulder and left it there.

'Answer the gentleman's questions,' he said, listlessly.

'We're just from the town,' said Dai. 'We came up looking for Gerald and, you know, we hadn't seen him so we started looking around.'

'What time is it? Is it even seven o'clock yet? You normally go paying housecalls at half six in the morning? And you're all a bit long in the tooth to go round playing hide and seek.'

'You're not the police,' tried the well-spoken one, better on the vowels this time but stuttering ever so slightly on the consonants.

'You think? See what it says in their wallets.'

And Gav flicked out a little black cylinder, no bigger than the palm of his hand, extending it in one twist of the wrist into a baton about three feet long. He took a step towards them and everything started happening very quickly.

'Ask him,' said Dai, breaking at last, jabbing a Sovereignringed finger in my direction, 'he's the one who's in on it all.'

At the same time there was a noise from the Portakabin, maybe like something falling off a table and onto the floor.

'Fuck off,' someone yelled, a loud high-pitched voice that you might hear around a set of school gates, and there was Gary, squaring up, his hands gripped bone-white around the stubby sawn-off shotgun.

'Fuck off!'

Then, just for a moment, maybe not even for a second, everybody was quiet and still. I looked at the gun and wondered if, even with two hands wrapped firmly around it, the barrels were shaking a little bit. God knows how many young and not-so-young men up and down the country would have reacted the same way. A complex, frightening situation that is still unfolding, and the solution, apparently, is to point a gun at it, or wave a knife, and sound off your war scream. Too many movies, I guess.

'You want to put that down,' I said. 'That's not going to help anybody.'

There was barely a shred of hesitation in his voice, except maybe the pitch was a trifle high, and stance-wise he had his gunslinger's pose down perfectly. But that's the easiest thing to pick up there is. In my day the young men would have taken something from the Westerns, I guess, holding it off your hip with your legs apart. Gary stood side-on with his left hand over the top of the barrel, which is what you do when you're firing a sawn-off, because they go everywhere, and I wondered which gangster film he'd seen that in. It must have been British because you don't see sawn-offs in the American ones.

So fair play to the lad it all came over as very credible and authentic until you looked at his face, which I suppose most of us got round to eventually, and then you felt as solid as a brick wall staring at the driver of a spinning sports car just before impact. If you'd taken a head-and-shoulders photo right then you'd have assumed he was simply howling in fear; his mouth locked open, nerves carving deep lines into his young face, the corners of his eyes beginning to tear.

Point a gun around and you think people will just start doing what they're told, but they don't, and you run out of ideas fast. The six of us stood there looking at Gary while the truth rushed up at him. This was probably what had happened to Gerald. You make a play at being the big man and you end up a hostage to fate. The only choices you have are to pull the trigger and derail your life for good, for ever, in an instant, or to back down and put it in the hands of some people who you just threatened to kill. Odds on, you'll disappear just like Gerald did either way.

'Just put it fucking down and relax,' I said. 'It's an honest mistake.'

Gary still hadn't shot anyone. Gavin started walking towards him, slowly but deliberately, until he was right in front of him, shoulder to shoulder. Gary watched him without moving a muscle. Only his eyes moved, to watch the baton as it rose up past Gavin's shoulder, and then descended to crack him, fast as a whip, across the top of his skull.

The boy crumpled at the legs first, kneecaps bouncing off the concrete before him, torso twisting, upper body slumping off to his right, until his face hit the floor – although his shoulder took some of the brunt.

'It's not even loaded,' I said. 'I bet. Break it open. Take a look.'

It was just a frightener from a lad. Nothing more. Let it be.

Gavin tugged the gun from out of the boy's hands, wrenching it hard from the awkward knots of his insensate fingers, but careful to keep its two black holes pointing away from us all as he did so, and out towards the cold dawn of the day.

Still holding the baton in one hand he flipped the catch on the top of the stock and broke the barrels.

'Empty,' he said, looking back at us, running a thumbnail across his brow, and then back down at the body, at the red that was now matting the tousled brown hair.

And before it got any further out of hand I heaved off the wall and stepped through the charged air, and bent over as casually I could muster, like a fielder out in deep cover at the village cricket match, picking up a stopped grounder. I put two fingers to the barman's neck and did my best to keep my arm still.

'He'll live,' I said, although I was shaking too hard to feel a thing. 'He'll be all right.'

He would have to be. Or we'd all be fucked.

Gavin took a peek inside the Portakabin to check for any other vigilantes, and then put an arm out against the door frame for support, still holding the baton and the gun in the same hand.

'That's enough of that,' he said, quietly.

The three old fellas in the corner were keeping a lid on it, which was a good thing. There was already a beermat-sized patch of blood by the side of the lad's head, thick and viscous and growing. Gavin and his boss exchanged an empty glance. I could sense more bad ideas rumbling towards us like thunderclouds, rolling in fast and unstoppable.

'We'd better have a word, boss,' I said. Another ten or twenty seconds and I probably wouldn't have been able to say anything worth a damn.

'Oh, yeah?'

'Yeah, just a quick word. Away from this lot.'

He stuck his chin out once in agreement and jammed his hands into his pockets.

'Something coming back to you, is it? Get their wallets,' he told Gavin again on the way out, who did not move an inch.

We walked across the muddy courtyard and I held the black farmhouse door open for him, and we went in under the rafters and sat down around the round wooden table on rickety chairs, looking at each other across the dust and dirty plates, in the poor light from the small and filthy window, two poker players without any cards.

'What?' he said.

'You know I don't remember who you are,' I said. 'I don't have a clue. I came to handcuffed to a bed one week ago and I've been picking up the pieces since then.'

'Whatever.'

'All right,' I said. 'You're in charge. Fair enough. But I reckon you're stretched pretty thin right now.'

The man gave a tired smile.

'Doesn't look like that to me,' he said. 'Or anyone else here with one eye and half a brain.'

There was a little poison in it now, a little venom around the edges, but it was still a smile. A thin smile with all the latent violence of a coiled whip.

'In case you haven't worked out what you're looking at yet, I'll spell it out. The printing press, a pile of fancy foreign paper high as your chest, enough inks to make the QE2 look like a colouring book, you know what all that adds up to, surely? Only between you and that you've got three good old boys in there too, locals all their lives I imagine, and probably not one criminal conviction between them. Plus the lad, you never know what these young ones get up to. Anyway, the point is, you can't really put the frighteners on them, because they'll just tell the police.'

The smile wavered slightly, and the man crooked his fingers to examine his nails, like he had nothing else to think about.

'Can't I?'

'No, you can't, and you know it. They have nothing to do with this. They just stumbled over it same as you. And you can't seriously expect me to believe you're going to bump the lot of us off, either. This is Carmarthenshire, not fucking Paraguay. So the only way this is going to work is if everybody's happy. And you know what? Everybody can be happy. No one's going to argue about their share. Not even you. Because you can make more money in there than Swansea council would know what to do with. It probably wouldn't take more than a couple of days either.'

The man finished with his fingernails and sat there looking at me like he might say something that was halfway sensible.

'What the fuck are you doing here?' he said. 'Really? What are you doing involved in all this? Why you?'

'I've been around, you know,' I said, trotting out the old lines. 'I've got some reputation.'

'A reputation? Well, yeah, but not that kind. You couldn't organise a piss-up in brewery. In fact, you'd fuck up a round of drinks. What did Gerald Williams want with you?'

I took it on the chin, there being no other way to take

it. He had a point, of course, although not a particularly pressing one, at least not from where I was sitting.

'I don't know,' I said.

'You're not even curious?'

'Got other things to worry about right now.'

He stared over at the milky white light of day, glowing from behind the film of grease on the kitchen window, and waved a dismissive hand.

'All right. Smooth the waters with the old school in there and I'll let you all have a bit of the gravy to take home.'

'And that's the end of it? Of you and me too?'

'If it all goes to plan, and you haven't forgotten to tell me anything, we can part on amicable terms, yes.'

'Sorry, I didn't catch your name?'

Like I was doing the rounds at a garden party. The man sighed, like he was hearing an old, old joke.

'James,' he said. 'James Blethyn. We went to school together, long, long time ago.'

Then we went back over to the barn, twenty-seven steps across the wet mud, and while no one was watching I took the time to steal a glance at the low stone wall, at the end of the top field, at the half a dozen crows hopping around the sheeting where the bodies were. Wondering if they'd got at them yet, and who else they would be hopping over soon, and how soon that might be.

Because that was all we had done. Shoved the trouble a couple of days forward, out of sight for now behind a mountain of invisible money, an uncountable, incalculable K2 of cash, its lofty, cloud-hidden peak up there somewhere scraping the infinite. It would work if everyone was happy, and there was enough to go around for that, but it's not just a question of quantity, not always. I mean no one seems to stay happy forever. But I might have bought enough time for myself: after all, I had a shorter timetable, so maybe.

I went into the barn and they were all still there. The three old boys had peeled off the wall and were standing in a loose and vaguely attentive semi-circle around the lad, who was sitting on the steps of the Portakabin holding someone's woolly jumper to his head, and above him was Gavin, leaning against the doorframe, his baton retracted and pocketed but the shotgun still out, although he was holding it by the barrels, between thumb and forefinger, like it was a dead fish.

I strolled up and opened my mouth and started to lay it all on, as is my wont. It rolled out without effort, the same old tune with a few minor variations, the type of noises you made when you were leveraging a little illicit potential over some inbred decency. The sort of spiel you gave whenever you were getting ordinary people to do the wrong thing.

I told them that James and Gavin had a prior proprietory concern in the enterprise, that their unexpected presence was bound to ruffle a few feathers, that there was more than enough to go around and at least they wouldn't have to worry about any more unpleasant intrusions now that some proper professional security was attached. I said we had sorted out a deal the other end to turn it around, and they could come in with us or do their own thing, and the most important thing was to run off all the materials that we had and get out. I think I even used the phrase 'closing the window of risk'.

It all poured out like I was a top tenor in a male choir. It was, after all, all I ever seemed to do.

No one ever said no.

III

Well, it was as fine a body of men as you could have hoped for, as long as you kept your hopes packed up tight and small and you were ready to throw them off at a moment's notice.

Francis Pritchard was the sort of half-ragged, nondescript septuagenarian you saw waddling about the streets of any small market town, nothing to do but always busy. In Francis Pritchard's case he owned the Easy Shopper franchise in town, a little place with faded linoleum on the floor that sold washing powder and frozen pizzas and fags and was probably the only shop half the town ever saw. He had got his niece and a Polish guy in to do all the actual work, which left him to focus his idle attentions as the whim took him. And it had taken him to High Farm.

He was a slightly bow-legged widower whose tight, curly hair was as dark as it was when he was twenty, although there were flecks of grey in his stubble. And he had that small-town knack of keeping silent when he had nothing to speak about, which will come across pretty sensibly in most situations. In fact he hadn't said a single word the whole time we were in the barn. I could see why Dai had got him onboard, although how he hoped to put ten million odd quid through the till in Easy Shopper remained to be seen.

Simon Hargreaves was the smart one, or rather he was educated, same age as the others but middle-class and proud of it, the one who tried to put a bit of manners on when Gavin shook them all down. He wore a button-down collar and a navy blazer, with thin sandy hair swept over a bald crown, and was a certified chartered accountant, whatever that was exactly, but neither a particularly successful nor an honest one, and he spent his semi-retirement in an office above the high street, trying to sell Spanish time-shares to whatever clients still came in the door. Again, you could kind of see what he was doing there.

Dai's surname turned out to be Lloyd-Bastable, but other than that he was sort of a known quantity already, the Henry the Eighth of the clapped-out hatchback, portly belly in a cable-knit cardigan and chunky gold bracelets, a small brown pork-pie hat on his bald head, sausage-like fingers folded in a stately manner across his chest. No wedding ring on them either, an intestate jack-the-lad whose lonely legacy would be an acre of tarmac and twenty third-hand cars, and undoubetdly the prime mover behind last night's local counterfeiting initative. I didn't expect much trouble from Dai.

Young Gary, on the other hand, was up and about and suitably demure for the time being, until he decided to do something stupid again, as young people do. It wouldn't surprise me if he got knocked about a bit more before I got clear, but as long as he didn't have enough equally young and stupid friends in the neighbourhood to try something himself, he could be kept in line for now. Judging from the amount of time he spent playing with his little electronic games gizmo, we were probably in the clear on that one.

On the other side of the equation were Gavin and James

Blethyn, about whom I had no idea at all, only that they were organised in a roundabout sort of a way, and had been for a while, judging from James's easy and unchallenged authority. Then there was the brother Tomos, who I had seen back at the bingo hall, an obvious lunatic that a professional firm wouldn't have tolerated for a moment. James probably ran a smallish family crew, bad enough in a squeeze but nowhere near big enough to deal with all of this, not straight off-the-cuff anyway. They hadn't settled in yet, but even so I would have been shocked to hear they were seriously considering splitting anything with us lot, except maybe our heads. For now they tried to stay in the background, where they looked about as natural as two Dobermans in a rabbit hutch. What I had done to get in their bad books I had no idea, but from the looks of them it didn't have to be anything more than having something they wanted.

We had a good chat that morning all right, all sat round the kitchen gaunt and careful like mourners after a funeral. I told the boys about myself and the memory, and I'd be surprised if they bought it any more than James and Gavin had, but they were content enough to go along with it. I don't think they wanted to know, they weren't in the least bit curious about their other two new friends, which was pretty sage.

Dai did most of the talking. They had come up last night for a look around, got excited, tried and failed and failed again to get the press rolling, and suddenly it was dawn and they were facing down a couple of full-time naughty boys. The whole night spent poking around feeding reams of imported rag paper into the bowels of an eight-foot-long press and getting nothing but jams, shreds and arguments and then a nasty shock when we turned up.

'Must have wasted about forty sheets, and the bloody thing's still gummed up now,' he said. 'Hell of a complicated bit of kit. We were just curious, you know.'

'It's only natural,' said James, fooling no one. 'We'll take a look at it now. Apart from whatever you've touched the thing must still be set up from the last run.'

Mr Simon Hargreaves, BSc FCCA, looked at his watch.

'It's almost nine,' he said. 'Some of us have places to be.'

'Bollocks,' said Dai. 'None of us have anything to worry about there. It's your wife you're fretting about.'

More than a few of us shifted a little in our chairs.

'You married, Francis?' I asked.

'Passed away.'

'You got a woman, Dai?'

'No mun, I always played the field, you know,' he said, dodging that one with hollow but well-practised bonhomie.

'What you want to do,' he continued, 'is just swill a little whisky around your mouth before you talk to her, tell her you ended up in the pub and got slaughtered and I had to put you up at the bungalow. Tell her I'd just found out I had a disease. Or that you've been stressed at work, you know. That'll go down fine with women.'

'Thank you for sharing your rich experience of married life with us, Dai,' said Hargreaves. 'I think I'll just tell her I slept on the settee, thank you very much.'

'Well clear some time,' I said. 'Get a fishing trip organised or what have you. You'll want to be available over the next couple of days. She can't know anything about this.'

The accountant stood up and pushed his chair in neatly. Out of the corner of my eye I could see James Blethyn visibly stiffen.

'Where you going, then?' he said.

'I am going to my office, if that's all right with you, of course. If that's perfectly all right with you.'

'We're only asking, all right?' I intervened. 'It's a perfectly ordinary question.'

'Well, I don't need to seek permission, do I? I have a life of my own to attend to. And I wouldn't be bothering with all this ridiculous nonsense at all if it wasn't for the fact that our entire banking system appears to be on the verge of complete collapse. Unlike some around this table I have a considerable holding in hard-earned, honest investments that I am now unable to access, thanks to the greed of multi-millionaire chief executives who couldn't do the job of a simple ledger clerk. So if you think for one moment I am at all the sort of person who can be talked down to, you are very much mistaken.'

I put one apologetic palm up towards him and laid the other firmly on the shoulder of James Blethyn, just to stop him from getting up and hitting him, and worked the cheek muscles into a smile. It felt like bench-pressing a car.

'We just need to know where you are,' James said, like he was chewing on stone.

'Well, I suppose you better give me a run into town,' said Francis. 'I'll bring back some breakfast from the shop.'

'If you do you better bring some things to cook it in and eat it off. This house should be cordoned off as a biohazard.'

Neither of them said goodbye. They just got up and walked out, like they hadn't a care in the world. For a moment I thought that someone had seen to the cars, had nicked the distributor cap or loosened the spark plugs, but I heard an engine start up without trouble, and as the sound receded, I realised that James was intent on keeping things civil for as long as he had to. Not that I fancied I would be allowed out myself.

'Don't worry about Si,' said Dai, without looking at anybody. 'He's as bent as a nine-bob note. Si's all right, Francis too, known them both for donkey's years. See them in Rotary every other week.'

'Llandovery Rotary Association,' said James. 'Well, Jesus Christ. We're in the premiership now.'

And we all would have laughed at that, I suppose, if it hadn't been for the tiredness, and the edginess, that was steadily building up around us like a rising river at a levee. It was there and there would be no stopping it. But we did smile a little. We still had our chins above water after all. James Blethyn pulled an empty box of Villigers out of his pocket and peered into it sadly before throwing it onto the heap of crap in the middle of the table.

'Well, we better go and see just what we've got in there,' he said, brushing the dust and the dirt off his overcoat, which was starting to look a long way from cashmere already. 'Stay by the car and keep an ear out, Gavin.'

Dai showed us round, or at least he tried to, putting on the same sort of patter he'd used on me in his forecourt.

'Those are the inks over there, all the colours you'll need, they're all mixed up ready to go… you can tell which trays to put them in because the numbers on the bottles are chalked on to the trays… well, some of the trays, but it's easy enough without the numbers because you can match the colours around the nozzle… the fluorescent stuff is for the hologram, obviously… there's the paper, over there, goes in this end somehow… and in here you put the finishing touches on it… there's a hand press for the watermarks, I guess you have to do that a sheet at a time, and the ink for that is right by it, some metallic grey stuff you water out by the looks of things... and there's the metal crimper and a little light aluminium for the security tag, must be, and the guillotine. Even got some bands here for packing them into bricks.'

James and I followed him, nodding absently, like a married couple contemplating a new hatchback. We weren't listening to a word he said, either, which made it all the more realistic.

'Where the fuck did it all come from?' James said, finally.

'Bought it all off some gang somewhere, I expect.'

'Oh, you expect do you? Don't suppose they sold him an instruction manual too, did they?'

Before we could descend into full-out bickering, Gary strode purposefully into our field of view, his hands mercifully free of weaponry.

'The press is a Heidelberg 1100,' he said. 'It's Swiss. They stopped making them in 1989, although they exported quite a few of them to the UK. But the paper is from a trader in Germany, and the inks come from a printers supply store in Manchester, apart from the stuff they use to fake the hologram, which is actually custom car paint from Halfords. And all of those suppliers are still going. And how do I know this?'

The three of us waited for the punchline.

'Because I googled it. You ever heard of Google?'

It was some compensation for him, I suppose, given his earlier embarrassment.

'Right son,' said Dai, after a suitable period of time, and then we all went into the Portakabin where the fancy work was done, all the cutting and crimping, and poked about in there like we knew what we were doing. It occurred to me that the old man in the home, the tiny hunchback with the bottle-end specs, could probably run all this standing on his head. Ironic, really, all that help locked up in such a spiteful little body. He wasn't the type to take you to an abandoned stretch of roadside in the middle of the night, I grant you, but there was more malice in him than either James or Gavin.

'You never found out where he'd been, old Gerald, all this time he wasn't in Llandovery?' I asked, inspecting a Stanley knife like it was some kind of clue.

'Prison.'

'Ah,' we all said. Apart from Gary, who had gone silent again.

'And Si says he remortgaged the farm not four months ago.'

'Ah.'

'Well, you might be right there after all, Magnum,' said James, bent over the guillotine like a snooker player staring down the baize. 'About the gang. Why would you sell a set-up like this, though?'

I knew perfectly well. James did too, or he did when his mind was working properly. He would have known yesterday. Anyone with any sense would. It was a machine that broke the rules of nature, and if you hung on to it, sooner or later you would wind up dead or in jail.

'You can have too much of a good thing,' was all I had time to say, and then from the courtyard Gavin shouted 'car!' and we all stood around paralysed trying not to repeat the idiocy we'd witnessed earlier that morning.

'Only Francis!' he informed us, when I was almost halfway under the desk.

And we all emerged as if nothing had happened to see Francis step out of his shop minivan carrying four bulging carrier bags and a twelve-pack of toilet roll, and followed him into the farmhouse.

'Got some bacon and eggs and bread and tea and coffee and milk and whatnot,' he said, dumping them onto the flagstones. 'Enough provisions for a couple of days. And a saucepan and frying pan and your basic domestic stuff, and two bottles of Bell's.'

'That's the first sensible contribution anybody's made to this effort since we got started,' I said.

'Well, we'll do better after a bit of breakfast.'

'A bit of breakfast and another go at it,' said Dai. 'With some fresh faces.'

Ever since we had gone back in the barn I had started to see white dots, and whenever I closed my eyes it was like watching a firework display in a black-and-white film. I worked my my around to the Welsh dresser and leant hard against it, taking the weight off my busted ankle, and drew a few deep, rasping breaths that seemed to do nothing. I felt like I was about thirty-two thousand feet above sea level, or possibly fifty fathoms below it. Whichever it was, I needed more than a fried breakfast.

'Well, good luck,' I said to the assembled, with my eyes still closed, opening and necking another small handful of painkillers without looking. 'I'm going to take forty winks. I'll catch you later. Let me know if you're going anywhere, James.'

'I'll be right here,' he said, 'going through this place with a fine-tooth comb. Find out everything I can about your man Gerald.'

'You'll find he was a messy fucker,' I said, and then

James said something I failed to hear, and so possibly did a few other people, and next I was lurching through the doorway into the hall and staggering upstairs like a man who'd just been shot. I found the old family four-poster, its mattress a collection of curious stains, and fell into it. From downstairs you could hear the faint sounds of men talking, casually, at an even timbre, without raised voices or sullen silences, and of coal scuttles and running water and cupboard doors and other innocent things. There would be arguments soon, and heated ones, and then violence, or the intrusion of violent strangers, but not yet. Surely not yet. I felt a wave of warm security descend on me, like a parrot in a shrouded cage, and fell asleep.

It was dark when I awoke, and for a moment I thought I was back in the home, waiting for the squeak of the breakfast trolley, until the stench hit me. I had been too tired to notice it, which must have been very tired indeed, because I was almost gagging on it now. This four-poster bed, dark oak from the looks of things, which could have been in the family since the Civil War, with its mattress probably dating back to the abdication of Edward VIII, had likely become as much a part of the Williams lineage as bookshelf shoulders and Roman noses, and now it was just a massive cat toilet. That corrosive, battery-acid tang billowed over me like mustard gas, and I rolled off the bed and onto my bad ankle and nearly swore aloud, but that would have meant opening my mouth.

Outside the curtainless window the gibbous moon shone just enough, through a break in the rolling cloud, for me to see my way to the landing, and even on the landing you could still taste the stink in your sinuses, even through a closed door. But only when I coughed did I realise how quiet the place was. It was just me and the house now, for the moment at least, and I descended the dog-leg staircase under its stern and watchful silence.

In the square hall a single naked light bulb glowed feebly from a piece of frayed flex, casting shadows into every corner of the room, and outside the cracked fanlight the night had fallen dark again, so that the old glass could almost have been painted the same black as the big front door. I looked fruitlessly for a clock, and scratched absently at the space on my wrist where a watch would have been. It could have been six in the evening or four in the morning.

Off to my left the kitchen light was still on, in the only room in the whole building that we had dared to colonise. In a fake crystal chandelier up between the thick beams one candle-effect bulb still glowed feebly amidst half a dozen empty sockets. Francis Pritchard had brought three bulging bags of groceries into the place this morning, and almost half a dozen men had eaten both breakfast and lunch here today, but all that fresh supply and succour had already blended into the general mess, and you needed a keen eye to see any sign of life. Outside I thought I could hear the sound of them now, working and struggling in the barn across the yard.

Save for thickening the cloud of footprints in the flagstones' grime, and heightening the stack of crockery in the Belfast sink by a few inches, we might never have been there at all. It was that kind of house, and had been for a long time. You could almost feel it, as if the building itself was waiting for that time when it would fall unbuilt and stand proud and unseen in the brambles like all the other forgotten steads and crofts and sheds that tombstoned the spartan crests and troughs of inland Wales. And men were still here trying, seven of us and counting so far, to eke out a fortune from their tenuous tenancy, but the house was taking over. It was winning. It knew just how thinly rooted were the schemes and dreams of all its fleeting visitors. From the barn I heard a discussion peak into a brief, heated argument and then quickly fade.

'They should have put you in the reservoir,' said a deep, even voice that was itself as flat and dead as still water.

My eyes adjusted and he was sat, oddly stiff and proper and contained in the corner on a chair that was much too small for him. All chairs were.

'Tomos Blethyn,' I said, without conscious thought or effort. James Blethyn's younger brother, or half-brother, was it, from the bingo hall in Merthyr, but I knew him from before, too. I had a sense of him towering over me, in some alleyway, or on some council estate; my gaze fell to his hands, clasped in his lap, folded for now, but I had seen and felt them clenched.

It was another piece of me, another fragment from the implosion rolling back downhill towards me. Like the lady doctor had said, Dr Catherine, the one with the round gold-rimmed glasses and carbonara sauce on her jumper: the memory might come back, over time, if there was enough time left. At the current rate, I kind of doubted it, but that would not stop it feeding back at its own pace.

I looked at him with the certainty I had wronged him somehow, like the way you woke up some mornings and couldn't remember the night before but knew there was trouble waiting for you when you went back in the pub. You did not always need memory to remember, or not the sort you'd think, just heart or soul or whatever unconscious emotional well you wanted to call it. Shame and fear and guilt sang their own songs and told their own stories inside you without the recollection of anything specific.

And love too, I guess, might work like that.

'They told me you said you'd gone mad but even if you have that doesn't change what you did,' said Tomos, in his denim jacket and wrestling T-shirt, with bulbous bloodshoot eyes protruding angrily from the tops of his puffy cheeks, his round face ruddy and reddening under a thick wilderness of black curly hair.

I remember I was about to offer up some of the usual glib evasions I emitted whenever I was faced by blanket anger for unremembered sins.

'You fucked us all over,' he said. 'Even your own son.'

And the truth barrelled in like a storm cloud breaching a mountain ridge, and unloaded in a heavy downpour. Maybe it would have been different if I had been able to remember him, just a little bit. Maybe I would have worried about him, about how he was. Instead the first thing I thought was how this would be it, now. This was all it would be. I was alone, and there was a reason why I was alone, and that reason was me.

The worst of it was, I was not that surprised. As hard as it was to take, it sort of fitted.

'Got to keep an eye on you,' he said, and there was an anger in his monotone now, something badly unnatural in its deadness. He had tensed, and was trembling ever so slightly; I wondered (or perhaps I was remembering something) if he was not on some strong medication.

My son.

I didn't know what I felt, save sorrow and shame and rage and regret and wonder, and fear for who I was. Without any conscious impulse behind them my feet took a few tentative backwards steps towards the hallway and the front door. Tomos matched me, step for step, keeping the same distance, with the same simple autistic doggedness. I found myself terrified about what else he would say, what else he would wrench obliviously out of my past and brandish before me. I'd rather he set about my face with a string of straight jabs than this, to have all my crimes and trespasses hurled at me all at once by an idiot.

He could say anything. He was a simpleton. He could say anything and it would be true.

'I'm just going to the barn,' I found myself saying, the cold brass of the doorknob under my hand, the door already ajar. 'See if anyone needs help.'

'You never helped anyone,' he said.

There was a smear of brown sauce on his chin.

Then I was tumbling down the two stone steps into the courtyard, the soles of my shoes slipping on the wet mud, the chill of the night on my cheeks and my rushed, panicked breath clouding before me, presaging a heavy frost on its way. Tomos filled the farmhouse doorway briefly and was gone, back into the depths of the house. He was a shadow receding into a den of shades, a dumb familiar of the entropy pervading the place, that spoke of the ruin locked inside us that awaited us all.

I stood and looked up at the stars, hard and bright in the cool air, and wondered how distant from me these things were: my son, and the woman who bore him, and whatever feelings there had been between us all. I could not picture them nor remember them, but I could sense their absence now, or perhaps just the absence of their memory, and it made my amensia feel like something wicked, like a moral infirmity. I was a moral cripple.

The stars above me, impossibly distant, shone on without blinking. Behind me you could hear them all in the barn, their voices louder now but still muffled, occupied and busy like men on a production line. I turned my back on the house and walked across the yard, wondering how much of the life I couldn't remember had been spent trying to forget, and how you stop such things.

In the barn the lights were blazing, and people were stood in small groups busily talking to each other. Along the back wall I could see the long printing press, still completely inactive but with a few canopy hatches hinged open and portions of its incomprehensible innards on display for all to see. A mess of balled-up paper clogged the far end, tailing off to a thin wedge as it neared the other. A single sheet had made it half-over the finish line, a series of blurred off-colour rectangles flopping out the other end. Dai and his mates were stood around it mournfully sharing a thermos. I stood in the darkness near the door and listened to James Blethyn, his man Gavin and young Gary talking about paper supplies not ten feet from me.

I watched them all, hard at work, labouring over machinery of purpose and design, all pulled along together by the lure of the lucre like they were as inert and integral to the process as the rollers, pins and plates. Some things in life cannot be stopped, I guess. Nature takes its course. I felt to see if my eyes were wet but they were as dry as stone.

Gavin was the first to clock me, when I stepped inside.

'If you know anything about how this works, now would be a fine time to share it.'

'I'm not really up to speed on that side of the operation,' I said.

'I downloaded a manual for a similar model off the

internet,' said Gary, 'and we've been trying to work off that, but it's in German.'

James and Gavin let that slide.

'We're going to need to get some professional talent in to get that started,' said James. 'No doubt about it.'

'Are you sure?' I asked.

'We've got time,' said James, stressing that first word, making it ring with a little exclusivity. 'We have got time. Gary here has been checking up on the supplies you need to run this machine. They're all legally available. Could be quite a project. Would probably work a little better if you kept it going, milked it out at sensible levels, got it ticking over nice and smooth. We've been trying to build Rome in a day here. Strikes me the only one who's in a hurry is you.'

'And we know why that is,' added Gavin. 'Only got to look at the state of you.'

I stood there with the three of them looking at me, even Gary, looking down at me now like I was just a bit-part player. A day in bed and the balance of power had shifted a long way. Or maybe that was just how it had always been.

Behind them I could see the three Rotarians gaze up and over at me, without a glimmer of recognition between them, before they went back to their musings at the broken business-end of the money machine. Behind me there was nothing but the night and the little valley, hundreds of acres of fucked-up farmland and rotting timber, all the way down to the A-road, which was silent. Everything out there was silent. It must have been the early morning, and not for the first time I wondered if I was ever going to get out of Llandovery alive, and if I did, what with and what for.

'I need a word, James,' I said, like I was a middle manager calling in an errant clerk. 'In private.'

A man should have some pride, after all. It will do him when there is nothing else to speak for. James shot a wry glance at the others, so they could see he was acting indulgent, but I knew he would come. Underneath that bossman's front he was still scrabbling cluelessly the way all people do when they think they can see the keys to the big house on the hill dangling in front of them.

'What?' he asked, out in the cold air, once we were a good few steps from the nearest ear. I shut the front of the barn and then turned to check the farmhouse entrance but there was nothing there but a big black door.

'What is it? I didn't think it would be possible, but you look even worse than you did this morning. You're not doing to die tonight, are you?'

I wondered if he knew my son, and if he knew him at all well. But there was too much to ask about, and the trust between us was like our condensing breath in the near-winter air: it appeared, insubstantial as a vapour, when we spoke of it, and then vanished into nothing before we closed our mouths.

'Did you find out anything about Gerald? When you searched the house.'

'No,' he said, but for a moment his face went as blank as white paper. 'That what you wanted to talk about?'

Off down by the corner of the rickety garage, I saw that fox again, perfectly still, its tail down and its nose an inch off the ground, looking up at us with its yellow eyes, before sloping silently off into the night. They could make me disappear just as quietly, I thought. There would be no questions, not from anyone that was interested, a shrug or two at the very most and no one would ever talk about me ever again. For a moment I wondered stupidly where Gavin had put the shotgun, but the panic passed.

'It's gone to your head,' I told him. I didn't expect him to listen. 'You've hardly been here any time at all and you're full of big plans already. That's the effect it has on people. I never meant to come back here, but I did. I came back a couple of times.'

'Don't you worry about my head,' he said. 'You're the one who's not thinking straight. Do you know what you've stumbled on here? Listen to what the lad was saying. The machinery is all here and the materials have been traced back to the original suppliers. I'm not saying we stay here, maybe we relocate to an industrial unit somewhere, but this is a gift from fucking god. And you want to cut and run like a teenage ramraider. Hey, I'm sorry you've got the cancer, but that's not my fault.'

He couldn't see it.

'Have you got a torch?' I asked.

Without speaking, James went over to the people-carrier and took a black Maglite out of the glove compartment.

'Well?' he said.

The barn was still shut and the farmhouse door was closed.

'Give me that,' I said. 'It won't take two seconds. Follow me.'

Although it had not rained that I could tell, the long grass was still wet. The ground was still as slippy, but I was ready for it. James nearly tumbled, and called me a daft old prick, but he came on. After all, he had nothing to fear from me. I could feel my trousers clinging damply to my legs below the knee, could feel the resistance of each foot as I lifted it from the mud. We were there in no time at all.

We stood before that small heap of ex-humanity, the black plastic gleaming in the torchlight, and to my surprise, as my hand reached out to a corner of the plastic, I felt nothing at all, perhaps because I was almost dead myself, and just as trapped. James must have already guessed, although he said nothing, I felt a tightness in his silence. I tore back the plastic and shone the torch directly on. The light did not shake or tremble. I felt my stomach shrink and harden but it passed. There was an odour, but it was almost winter, and it was nothing more repellent than any of the other odd smells you might come across on a run-down farm.

I heard a sharp intake of breath, and then a gag, and James was bent double vomiting, his hands on his knees. He came up once, coughed, then turned around and went down again just for the bile, and stayed there, his eyes firmly closed.

'It's not a gift,' I said. 'Not if god has anything to do with it.'

When he straightened up he set off straight away, striding with difficulty through the field towards the light of the courtyard like a man wading up a fast-flowing river. Halfway back he pulled himself together and stopped in his tracks, and when I caught up with him he slapped me across the face, just once, but hard and fast enough for me to go down onto my arse.

'What else have you been holding back, you cunt?'

Even with my arse in the mud, I could feel the fear in him behind the anger, and in the safety of the darkness I felt the corners of my mouth lifting into a grin. I got up and faced him without speaking a word, and even when he grabbed the lapels of my jacket I was still buoyed by the sensation of some small victory.

'Who are they?' he said.

'Calm down,' I said. 'You wouldn't want the boys in there to find out about it. You couldn't carry the local citizenry along on this if there were bodies involved.'

The hands came off the jacket, slowly, and with a little hesitation.

'They're just some guys who were after the same thing you want. They found out about it, somehow, just like you did, and wanted a piece of it. And from the looks of them, they must have got into an argument, some shitty falling out about a percentage, and lost. You wouldn't think it, would you? But then maybe you would. You're not an idiot. You know the story. Plenty for everyone, if everyone shares, and nothing if everyone doesn't, and it always gets to be nothing, doesn't it, somehow?'

From the barn came the muffled sound of the press grinding into life again, and then cutting out, just as quickly, like a mower that had rolled onto rock.

'Who are they?' he asked again, his voice calmer now.

'No idea. They're from Port Talbot, is my guess, and they were taking a chunk of the counterfeits. They haven't been here more than a week yet, and I reckon people will be starting to make serious enquiries after them about now. It was enough for Gerald Williams to take off, and it was his show. He didn't grow it all out of fertilizer either. Christ knows how many other people are onto this place.'

'Fuck it. We'll take the whole lot off. Move the entire operation. I'll get an artic down here.'

'Don't be a cretin. That'll add on another four or five people straight off, and the locals won't stand for it either.'

'Watch your fucking mouth,' he said, but it was just a reflex. His hands stayed by his sides. 'Well, we'll see what they'll stand for.'

'You're still not thinking. Get the machine runing, use up the materials that are here, and get out before you get into some sort of fucking bush war. Or before the law gets here. We could all be out of here in days, which isn't much more than it would take to relocate anyway. And let's be honest, there's enough in there. There must be enough there for thirty or forty million, at face value.'

I swallowed a little empty air myself on that note. It was the first time, I think, anyone had ever tried to put some numbers on it, and they were not the numbers that normal people were ever supposed to use: thirty or forty million. They felt obscene on the tongue. But they were in there, waiting, in a normal farmyard barn.

'You're going to have enough of a headache turning that into usable money as it is,' I ploughed on, 'and another one when it comes to spending it, not to mention keeping everyone on board. Keep it in perspective. As it is, we don't even know if that thing will work properly at all again.'

I would have kept at it, I think, only my breath ran short, and I felt that old familiar pain inside my chest, pressing down and bursting out at the same time. I took a few breaths and sounded like a fat man snoring.

'Well what do you suggest?' said James. 'Apart from leaving at the soonest possible opportunity.'

Fuck it, I thought. You had him in mind all along, and with any luck it will give the old fucker a heart attack, or somebody'll hit him.

'I know a guy who might be good for the printing,' I said. 'If we can take the plates off the press ourselves. Presumably there are printing plates on there for the offsets of the notes, and they must screw off or something. If we can make it look halfway legitimate we can tap him out tomorrow. He's not far and I doubt he would ask too many questions if we can get him in.'

'I can meet him first?'

'You better had.'

He dragged the back of his hand across his face, and in the quiet country night you could hear the stubble against the skin. Then he turned and tramped off, back to the muddy yard, and I followed a little way behind him.

He went into the kitchen, with me after him, and from one of the plastic bags in the pile on the floor he produced a whisky bottle which he uncapped and swigged from. A full bottle of Scotch: I had missed it amongst all the general detritus. Tomos was back on his chair, sitting as primly as a newsreader, if broadcasters ever hired sloppy over-sized psychopaths to read the news.

'All right,' said James. 'I'll wind things up for the night. It's gone three in the morning. Now piss off a minute.'

I headed off to the barn to see the others, but seeing as there weren't any curtains on the kitchen window I hung around in the courtyard for a minute. Long enough to see James bark at his brother, who stood up meekly and took a fist in the face without flinching. I couldn't hear what he said.

When I heaved the big door open there were five pairs of eyes watching me, and I sauntered in with as much insouciance and brio as I could muster. They were still in two distinct groups, the older men at the back and Gavin and Gary at the front, the barman slouching back against the Portakabin as if the last twenty-four hours had made him a fully fledged member of the criminal underworld.

'I've put him straight,' I couldn't resist saying, loud enough for everyone to hear. 'Too much bullshit from you was the problem, I expect.'

Everybody was too wise to say anything.

'Listen Gary, did you get in touch with the hospice after, like I asked you to?'

'Worried, are you?'

'Well, did you?'

'Yeah,' he said, giving up the pose and reverting to teenage taciturnity.

'They give you any bother?'

'No.'

'Good lad.'

And then James staggered in, still in the same suit and overcoat, but not looking quite so smart any more. In the barn's harsh industrial light his black stubble stood out like iron filings, grey in patches, and as he moved towards us the shadows danced across the tired features of his face.

'That's enough for today,' he said. 'We'll take this up tomorrow. Gavin, Robin, Tomos and me are staying here the night. Anyone else wants to stay, help yourself. Otherwise I want to see you or hear from you tomorrow morning.'

Without dissent or query our informal night shift disassembled, muttering without rancour about sleep and showers, jammed rollers and blocked feeds. No one said anything about money. It was too much to think about, or it was the wrong time and place to discuss it. I stood in the courtyard and watched them go, their red tail-lights disappearing through the trees. I was listening to the sound of their engines travelling away down the A-road when the rain started, nothing torrential, but heavy enough to splash up a little mud, thinking how nice it must be to have a normal life to go back to.

'You're not serious,' Gavin was saying. 'You don't want me out in this?'

'Better safe than sorry,' said James. 'I'll send someone out to relieve you in a hour or two.'

'What am I supposed to do if anyone comes, then?'

The argument ran on for another minute or two, although I was too busy trying to get the back seats down in the people-carrier to listen in. When I'd found the right handles there was more than enough room for me to stretch out, and I was settling in for the night, wondering if I'd sleep at all, when the driver's door opened.

'Don't want to leave you with the car keys,' sneered James, his hand reaching around the steering column. 'Although it's not like you're in any state to do a runner, is it?'

And he laughed again, that tired mechanical laugh, and went into the house. It echoed around my head after he had gone, and I thought of the old machines you'd stick a penny in, and watch the dusty curtain part so a shaking dummy behind a glass screen could tell you your future. I thought of seaside piers and sunshine, of ice cream and innocent elation, and how we all turn out in the end, when all is said and done and childhood packed away for good. I wondered if it was a memory, or just something I'd seen in a movie; if I'd ever seen one of those laughing dummies myself, or taken someone else to see them. And I had no way of knowing. I thought about it, with eyes open and shut, with focus and intent; there was nothing but a sharp and soft pull upon the heart, and you would get that, I suppose, either way.

I popped some pills and tossed and turned upon the

seats, smelling the cigar smoke and the fake pine, and listening to the faint sounds of Gavin shuffling around the courtyard; the occasional click of a lighter, or a footfall in stagnant water. I got up on my elbows once to look, and saw nothing but a dark shape and a lit cigarette end, hovering like a firefly, somewhere by the broken-down gate that led to the rutted lane and the big wide world. Despite what James had said, I could have made a break for it, I think. If I'd picked my moment I would have said the odds were in my favour, if not by much.

If I could make it to the treeline I could stay in cover, maybe even hobble a couple of miles towards some distant houselight, or hole up in some roadside bushes until I could flag a car. And then what? Briefly, I tried to picture where the locals might be right now; their homes, their families, their weekends. It was like trying to see me on that seaside pier. It was like trying to see my son. I lay there on a folded seat in the back of a Mitsubishi Grandis in the darkness of High Farm, and couldn't think where else I ought to be.

We stick with what we know, sooner or later, because we know that sooner or later even that will go. And so we ride it out, all of us, hoping for a little resolution before it does, some denouement. Perhaps even the blind and immobile at Howell Harris, shrunken in their beds, perhaps even they lie there with a little summoned hope that the clouds will part before the light finally dims.

IV

There was a rapping of knuckles against the window.

'Wakey, wakey, rise and shine,' said James, a little more rested but still unshaven.

I was awake -- had been awake to see the sun come up, somewhere behind the clouds, high above the steep hill, as the sky changed from black to light grey and stayed there, a dull glow behind the billowing cumulonimbus, like a bedside lamp behind a faded curtain. It was the sort of morning where you lay there looking at it and knew it was all the light you were going to get all day.

Outside a fierce wind was shaking the trees, sending the leaves spiralling down across the yard. I got out and stood there shivering with my blazer buttoned and my collar up while the men slowly emptied out of the house and into the barn, carrying mugs of coffee and finishing off slices of toast.

'We'll see about getting those plates off,' said James, shouting a little over the wind.

I ducked into the farmhouse to see if there was anything left of breakfast, and found an old whistling kettle still on the hob, half full. It was warm in there; they had got the wood-fired stove going the night before, and I pressed up against it so hard it looked like I was climbing inside. After my front had warmed up I put my back to it, and when I turned I noticed Tomos, still grounded by the looks of things but trying to look busy, absently tidying up some of breakfast, and succeeding only in moving small piles of rubbish from one part of the room to the other. The only way you could achieve any discernible difference in there would be to burn it down. He had a black eye where his brother hit him that was almost closed up all the way.

We didn't speak.

Tomos shifted a pile of dirty plates from the table onto the sideboard, and then, when they looked a bit precarious on the cluttered countertop, back to the table again. I turned my back on him then; the warmth from the oven was still coursing through me, but not enough of it. The heat had started to ebb, and I could still feel the night cold in my joints, the start perhaps of that residual chill that slowly builds in the old and infirm and other people near the final exit door, and never entirely leaves. I unhatched the stove door with a broken chair leg from the nearby wood basket and crouched down to bask by the flames before I fed it in.

Old women used to say you could see your future in the flames of the hearth. I didn't see anything, except the remains of a yellow Prontaprint packet, and the shrivelling corners of thirty-six colour exposures, mostly ash now. From what was left of them it was easy to see what they were. I watched the hem of the bride's dress turn to black and disappear. Why burn a set of wedding photos? I felt inside my jacket pocket for the shot I had already taken from the pile, the one of Gerald with the happy couple, and it was still there, though I didn't take it out.

I shoved the stove closed and got up. Tomos was still occupying himself out of sight behind the table, so I slipped outside. It didn't seem a good idea to say anything.

In the barn Gavin and Gary were busy unscrewing bits of the press while James looked on in his normal supervisory fashion. One of the plates was already standing on end against the wall, a solid chunk of steel about as big as the rear shelf in the back of a car. I watched them take off the other three, just by loosening a couple of screws and some butterfly nuts, and carry them over to the boot of the people-carrier.

'Got to keep a hold of my investment, haven't I?' James explained. Exactly what James had invested, and how that made it his, he didn't say. 'Tell us about this printer then.'

'Oh, he's only down the road. Retired, you know, but he seems pretty knowledgeable. Offer him some cash to prep it all and show us how it's done and I doubt he'd be the sort to get curious. Too long in the tooth.'

'Yeah?'

'Yeah,' I said, hoping to god that the old man would cotton on and get the pounds signs in his eyes like everyone else. Just the thought of his smirking virtue taking a tumble made me smile. 'Tell him it's for restaurant menus or something.'

'Sure. Just give us the address and we'll see what he's about.'

'Yeah, but I think I better go with you. You'll need an introduction.'

James turned at last to look at me, a long square look of contempt, tempered with a little pity.

'From you?' he said. 'You look like you've been sleeping on a bench for a week.'

'You don't look too fresh yourself. I'll need to get some bandages for the foot too.'

'I look better than you, and I've got a weekend bag in the car. You better see if there's anything in the farmhouse. I've still got to make sure the rollers are wiped down and put all the paper and paint drums out of sight. And hey,' he said, grabbing me by the shoulder, 'how do you know him, if you don't mind me asking? Only you're supposed to be a fucking amnesiac.'

'He's sort of a handyman at the hospice I was staying at,' I said, trying not to squirm as his fingers dug into the soft flesh under my collarbone. 'Looks after the boilers. Like I said, he's retired.'

'I'm sure he's real cutting edge,' he snorted, but he didn't say no.

I went back into the farmhouse and climbed the stairs to the spare room, where I moved a couple of bicycles out of the way so I could get to an old oak wardrobe. Inside there was nothing but old dresses and the faint, camphor smell of very tired mothballs. On top of the wardrobe was a tartan suitcase though, which turned out to have some Sunday-best items in the men's line. I put on a white dress-shirt so old you could have poked a finger through it, which hung on me like I was wearing a sail. Then I fastened my tie around its oversized collar and took the dirt off my suit and shoes with the clean corner of a wet dishcloth and waited in the barn obediently for my chance to get at James's electric razor. I would have washed, but the water wasn't heated and came out brackish and deadly cold, no doubt from somewhere deep under the black hills.

All the incriminating evidence was locked up, carried

away or wiped off in less than forty-five minutes. The set-up still looked suspiciously out of place, like an operating table in a butchers, but it wasn't as obviously illegal as to require out-and-out collusion. Gary was giving it a once-over while James and Gavin were in the house. I went over to him.

'I meant what I said, you know.'

'About what?'

'Don't think you can get involved in all this for any length of time and not get hurt, or locked up, or worse.'

And he looked at me like I'd told him to tidy his room.

'Listen to what I'm saying. I've been around a bit.'

'Yeah, the only problem is you can't remember where you've been. If you're that worried about it why don't you fuck off?'

It's not the young people who think they know everything. Not always. Obviously, it doesn't make them any less annoying.

'What I'm trying to say,' I said at last, as the nerves closed in, 'is that it's kind of a vocation. Are you coming to Howell Harris House with us? You're supposed to be my nephew or something.'

How easy it would be for Gavin and James to get rid of me, once I was off-site. They could just tell everyone I'd jacked and left, if they had the stomach for it.

'Someone's got to stay here and keep an eye on this stuff. Anyway, didn't you say you'd pay me two hundred a week for keeping you out of there?'

I gave a shit-eating grin and a high-pitched laugh that was the closest thing to an apology I could muster, and went out to wait my turn for the electric razor, feeling like a man who was waiting his turn for the electric chair. In the end it was just the three of us who went. I knew it would be.

I got them to stop in town for some bandages and a new pair of socks, which I put on in the castle car park under the faceless statue of Llywelyn Ap Gruffydd Fychan. It wasn't a pleasant experience. There was no sign of gangrene, was about the best that could be said. Squeezing my foot back into the shoe was the worst part; it had ballooned to the point where it looked like a leg of lamb but I was adamant it was going back in. Which it did, but I couldn't see properly for about five minutes afterwards, and I expect I made a fair bit of noise. Naturally, James and Gavin were a bit concerned.

'What the fuck is up with you?' said James.

'Just give me a minute, please.'

'Jesus Christ. It can't hurt as much as it smells, I can tell you that.'

Gavin pressed the buttons for the front windows and turned the radio on, which was playing a song by some old nineties boy band that finished and turned into a dial-in talk show on the war in Afghanistan. James went to kick his heels down by the statue, where he lit another one of his cigars. It was a Welsh radio station, and by and large no one had anything good to say about the soliders we had over there, apart from a woman from Llandeilo who said we'd probably be doing a lot better if everyone stopped moaning and the government kept the casualty figures secret. I sat there getting annoyed, which is all radio talk shows do to any normal person, and realised that if I was that bothered by it I was clearly over the worst of the pain, so I gave Gavin the nudge.

'Who the fuck is that?' said James, climbing back into the car. 'Llywelyn Ap Gruffydd Fychan?'

'Oh, some guy who got involved with the wrong crowd

back in the days of Glendower and thought the better of it. He ended up giving the English the wrong steer so the rebels could escape up north.'

There was the genteel sound of creaking leather as the two of them turned in their seats towards me.

'How the fuck do you know that?' said James.

'Dunno. Don't they teach you all that at school?'

'Oh, I remember something about it. Turned out to be a good guy after all, did he?'

'I guess. When they found out they ripped his heart out and cooked it front of him, I think.'

'Christ, can't you remember something useful instead?'

'That's education for you.'

In less than five minutes we were churning up the gravel outside Howell Harris House. I was almost grateful to be back. We sailed through reception no trouble, because there was nobody in it, and I led them down the corridor to the day room. If we'd gone in and carted the residents out a dozen at a time the front desk would probably just have thanked us for it, assuming they even noticed.

It was just the same, the empty green chairs under plastic sheets, the daytime television, the three old women parked around the place like little figures in a landscape painting, except they wheezed. The old man was not there.

'Fucking hell,' I heard James say, under his breath. 'You sure this bloke's still alive?'

'Yeah, it's fine, he sort of works here.'

Behind the rolled-down screen over the canteen counter on the far wall you could hear the sounds of the kitchen staff washing up after breakfast. I went over and gave it a polite tap, and it rolled up about ten inches.

'Sorry love, breakfast's over,' said the thin woman who

had once searched the whole house to find me change for the phone, her face horizontal in the gap.

'That's all right,' I said, crouching down some so I could talk to her. 'Have you seen the old fella? The seven-year resident?'

'Oh,' she said, 'he'll be down in the boiler room I expect. He likes it down there. In the basement, door at the end of the hall. You're not supposed to go in there, but you're a visitor now, aren't you? I'm sure it'll be fine.'

'See?' I said, as I took them both down another long hallway. 'I told you. He works here. Looks after the boilers.'

At the end, underneath a flight of stairs, was a blue door with a plastic 'Staff Only' sign nailed to it. It was already ajar, and I pushed it all the way open to see a set of concrete steps leading down to a corridor with a linoleum floor and scuffed white walls, lit by a string of naked bulbs. We went down and the still stale air had the smell of a crypt. The only door that didn't have boxes piled up against it was wide open. I walked in, and there he was, the seven-year resident, the old-timer, sitting on a rickety chair in a square underground room with the light off, absently wiping his hands with an old rag, over and over, his absorbed mind opaque behind his heavy lenses. The only light came from the corridor and a small mildewy window up by the ceiling. There was a stack of newspapers on the floor by his side, although the uppermost edition looked far from recent, and big black lines around the walls where the boilers must have been, before they were ripped out, a long time ago.

I stood there and watched him, awestruck at his self-containment. I'd always thought he was just a bitter old fool full of lies, but to look at him then it was clear there was more than a touch of the ascetic about him. Maybe the two traits aren't mutually exclusive. In India, I understand they go and sit up poles for thirty years. Maybe in this country they just find a basement, or a shed. Because no one else would want to fucking talk to them.

I was about to cough when he trained his hugely magnified eyes on me, two massive inscrutable irises, and I found myself a little lost for words.

'I thought you'd found some family daft enough to take care of you,' he said, carefully folding up his rag and tucking it into his dungarees.

'I have,' I said. Lying was a knee-jerk reaction. 'But I was talking to my nephew the other day, and this gentleman here is an acquaintance of the family, a businessman, and it came up that he needs a printer, just for a small job, and as he was passing he was kind enough to give me a lift in, actually, because I have to see the doctor here, and I thought he might like to have chat with you, seeing as you were in that line of work.'

I watched those two black moons blink on and off while I caught my breath, the face underneath locked in its perpetual grimace.

'Oh, aye,' he said. 'Gentleman's a businessman, is he? What's he doing with you, then?'

And I pressed up against the door while James and Gavin strolled brazenly in, neither of whom seemed to be particularly impressed either. Here we go, I thought. I couldn't bear to watch.

'I'll leave you all to it,' I said. 'You won't need me for this. I'll just go and see the doc for my prescription.'

Anything to get away.

'Well, make sure you come straight back,' said James. 'I'll be waiting out front.'

I took another look at the day room, then went through the conservatory, and then took the stairs up to the second floor. For old times' sake, I guess. It wasn't like anybody could stop me now I had left. But then they probably never could: it was an odd realisation. Although the place had felt like a prison it was nothing like it. It was a nexus of care, half-arsed sometimes, occasionally misplaced, and wrapped up in bureaucracy, but it was here for the right reasons. It wasn't the walls that kept people in. It was weakness and age and the lack of anything elsewhere, the emptiness outside. It was a sad, bittersweet kind of revelation. A prison you could kick up against, the way I had and countless other grumpy wards probably did, out of blunt wrong-headedness or plain delusion. But the desert your life had become, that wasn't something you could bang your head against.

I was musing on such joyous truths when I found myself outside Hilary's room, the door wedged open and the bed stripped. There was no sign of any of her belongings. I went and stood by the bed and tried hard to imagine her son had taken her in, and failed. And now there was nothing, just the dust motes floating in the light. The last time I saw her she had been sobbing as she walked up the main staircase away from me. And instantly I was back in that self-conscious dichotomy, of knowing that the entire business of this building was to look after people, and at the same time hoping it burned to the ground.

I didn't linger long. It felt like standing on a grave. I walked off without any direction in mind, and ended up back in my old room, I don't know why. It was the last place I had felt safe, I suppose, but it was already occupied. I pushed the door open with a single finger only to discover some heavily tanned old man with peppery hair in the bed, staring at the ceiling with his arms by his sides.

'Hello,' he said, struggling to raise his head.

I stood there with my mouth open like a fish, grappling with the realisation that there was no going back now. I could, I daresay, have made a show of pleading my case, coming back with my tail between my legs and begging for mercy, but Gerald wouldn't be on the board to throw his clout now. The die was cast. I was out.

'I'm sorry,' I said. 'I'm not supposed to be here.'

And I closed the door, as gently as I possibly could. On my way downstairs I bumped into my old nurse, the peroxide blonde from Eastern Europe.

'Visiting old friends?' she said, her hands on her hips.

'Just checking in,' I said, with a wink. 'Making sure everybody's behaving themselves.'

She tossed her head and gave a boisterous laugh, like it was all a lot of fun.

'I tell you what,' I said, playing along, 'how'd you like to be my private carer? Good money, not so much work. You could tuck me in and cheer me up.'

That was about the funniest thing she'd heard all week.

'Oh, you,' she said, delighted, and I grinned at her, and winked again and made that suggestive clicking sound with my mouth, and walked on by. At the top of the stairs she called out to me.

'Two hundred and fifty a week, if it is live-in,' she said, without a trace of humour on her face. Never joke about business with someone from an ex-Soviet state.

Back on the ground floor there was no sign of James or Gavin, either in reception or out by the car. God knows what spiel they had decided to use, down in the basement, talking to my last frail hope of getting this thing to run vaguely my way. I paced about like a father-to-be outside a maternity ward.

They had gotten round to replacing the phone I'd torn up, although the canopy was still cracked. To be honest, I was impressed I'd had it in me. I stood there jangling my change absently in my pocket and then it occurred to me to take a quid out and feed it in. I still had the number for the Bristol detective in my jacket, and I dialled it, without any great expectations.

'Yeah,' said the bloke, when I got him on the line, 'we did look into him. To be honest, I knew of him myself, although I only met him once or twice. Not really what you'd call a professional investigator. Turned up in Bristol sometime in the early eighties, tried to get into the police force and failed, ended up working as a debt collector. No great shakes at that, just did the door-to-door stuff for maybe nine years, worked for a local firm called Carmel. Got involved with the police again somehow, probably as a low-level informant, then got involved with a bent copper or two, and one of them gets him a job with a very small firm of private investigators in south Bristol, where he's playing second fiddle to a one-man band. Shortly after he gets arrested, handling stolen evidence, we believe, most likely drugs; anyway, he turns grass to get the charges dropped and gives up his bent copper friends, all of which makes him pretty much useless as a private detective. By the time all this ends his boss is dead and he ends up running the practice on his own, muddling along with a bit of divorce work and whatever else he can scrape up. They took his driving licence off him, so Christ knows how he survived. He left town about two years ago, no one knows where. Avon were running another investigation into police corruption at the time, so it's possibly related to that, if I was going to speculate. He's back in Wales now, is he?'

'That's not bad for three hundred quid,' I said.

'Well, like I say, a few of the lads here did know him a little. He never amounted to very much.'

'I expect that's what he wanted everyone to think,' I said, thinking of the file from my solicitors, about the duty evasion and the VAT scam: a warehouse full of booze and tax fraud that ran into seven digits. 'Keep a low profile and all that. From what I hear he had his fingers in quite a few pies.'

There was a burst of incredulous laughter on the other end of the line.

'Robin Llywelyn? No, not him. Complete piss artist, and a pain in the arse, and that's it. If he ever made any gravy it was from bagwork.'

'Well, you never know, do you? Not with the smart ones.'

'You're the customer,' he said.

'Any enemies?'

'I should think so. Avon Constabulary and the Regional Crime Squad would be a good place to start.'

'Any family?'

'Not that we know of. Certainly none in Bristol, at any rate. Do you want me to send you the file? We've got a bit of paperwork here, it's got all the names and dates on.'

'I'll let you know.'

'So,' he said, 'you going to lend him that money then?'

A woman in a beige tabard walked past, wheeling a tea urn on a trolley.

'Everyone deserves a second chance,' I said, and hung up. Then I put the receiver back on the hook, without breaking or smashing anything. I didn't even punch the wall.

I didn't sound like the sort of guy who managed an import business, or ran a warehouse, or took on the taxman, or a captain who went down with his ship. I sounded like a patsy. And none of it really surprised me, but none of it resonated either, just like everything else I'd heard or read about myself. Because what it really sounded like was someone else. After all, people do change. They do. Things can happen to your head.

They had replaced the phone, and they had replaced the canopy, but the backing board was still the same. It still had the same numbers on it, all the guff that people had scribbled down so they could get hold of their nieces or their nephews or the Chinese takeaway. One of them was in my handwriting. I stared at it as if the numbers were words, and then remembered. My Swansea solicitor. The reason I had smashed up the phone in the first place. What had he said, before I hung up?

Facing the music isn't the same as paying the fiddler, Llywelyn. I went and waited meekly in the day room with the rest of the spinsters, and watched a documentary on the Eisteddfod with the sound turned off. I'm pretty sure it was better than with the sound turned on. I don't know how long he'd been standing there next to me before he spoke.

'I don't know how anyone stands a single minute in this place,' said Gavin, his face a picture of absent disbelief, eyeing the mute television like the rest of us.

On the screen that summer's bard was giving an

interview in a book-lined study with the crown still on his head.

'James is still in the basement,' Gavin added, consoling himself. 'He asked the old guy if he knew anything about printing and now he's getting a lecture on the four-colour process.'

'Did you find anything out about Gerald, after? When you went through his stuff?'

His expression instantly changed.

'You'll have to ask James about that,' he said. 'I'm going to wait in the car.'

A little while later I followed him.

On the way out I noticed that one of the receptionists was actually at the desk, wrapping a strand of mousy hair around her finger while she pored over another tabloid glossy, and just for old times' sake I went and stood in front of her with my hands on the counter, leaning all the way over until I was reading it with her: a little piece about how a soap star was letting herself go because she'd gone to the shops without her make-up on.

'Hello,' she said in a way that was not at all friendly. I gave her a blank smile and watched her while she tried to remember who I was.

'Any mail for me?' I asked. That did it.

'You're not staying here any more, are you?'

Overhearing this, her slightly larger colleague came out from the back office, sensing the threatening possibility that one of them might be asked to do something, and keen to nip it in the bud.

'No,' I said. 'I checked out. I wanted somewhere with a pool.'

It's just possible that the corners of her mouth turned up ever so slightly.

'There was someone here looking for you,' said the other, and the hair on the back of my neck went up. 'Can't remember their name now.'

'A solicitor from Swansea,' said the larger one. 'Good-looking man. Nice voice. We didn't know where you'd gone, though.'

I felt my pulse steady again.

'That's all right,' I said. 'The gentleman's friends have since been in touch.'

'No,' said the mousy one. 'Not him. There was somebody else, just yesterday. Not that we could help him either.'

'What did he look like?'

'Shortish man, narrow face. With a scar on it.'

The two of them looked at each other, their eyes narrow in thought. Mine probably were too.

'Yes,' said the other, finally. 'Didn't say who he was though. Where are you staying now, then?'

I was about to embark on some nice flight of fancy when James walked in with the old man marching proudly beside him; he didn't come up much further than James's waist. So I gave the two of them a nod and tapped the counter in goodbye.

'He's not coming, is he?' said the old man, his bristly jaw jutting out in disgust.

'Afraid so,' said James.

The three of us went and joined Gavin in the people-carrier, and I was allowed to sit in the front seat for once, so James and our special passenger could enjoy each other's company in the back. I looked at him in the rear-view, perched there on the back seat fussing with his seatbelt, and

I'm not sure his feet even touched the floor. And behind him was Howell Harris House, disappearing. It still looked grand, in a forlorn sort of way. Must have been the delight of the county set at one time. But I bet none of them ever had to stay there now.

We travelled back to High Farm without speaking, our new recruit gazing out of the window at the passing countryside. I don't think he could have set foot outside the grounds for some years. What it all meant to him was impossible to tell.

We pulled into the courtyard and Francis's shop van was there, and he was standing out front along with Gary and Tomos and looking about as happy as a horse at a knacker's yard.

'Where have you been then?' he asked, all bow-legged defiance. 'What's all this?'

'What's all what?' said James. 'I've been taking care of some business.'

At the same time, with the flick of a pointed finger and a nod of the head, he motioned for Gavin to usher the printer away into the barn before the conversation could get indelicate.

'Where's the plates? And who exactly is that?'

James stepped up to him and pushed the same finger into the middle of the shopkeeper's chest.

'You watch what you say now. That's the printer. He's going to get that machine running for us, and he doesn't need to know what it's for. He's on flat rates. And the plates are in my car, because I didn't want to leave them here for anyone to run off with.'

'Well, that's no way to carry on. We're all in this together. You should have spoken to us about it first.'

James closed in till he was breathing down on Francis, staring hard from inches away.

'I haven't got time to do this by committee, all right? Don't go trying to get on my bad side when I'm doing you a favour.'

Francis crumbled, but the spark of resistance did not burn out entirely.

'Well, Dai and Simon Hargreaves are not happy at all.'

'I'm sure they'll see the light the next time they come in for a little chat,' said James. 'What do you all expect, anyway? You're all just part-timers. Somebody around here has to make things happen. Now watch your tongue.'

And with that he strode off towards the barn, with all of us trailing after him. The old man was already scaling up the side of the press like a cat burglar, flipping open panels and hatches as he went, and we all lined up to watch, just far enough away to make sure he wouldn't land on us if he fell.

'You've made a right pig's ear of this,' he said, singling out Gavin for some arbitrary reason. 'Go and fetch me a stepladder, will you?'

Gavin shrugged at us and then went off to look for something he could stand on.

'Do you think you'll be able to get her up and running?' asked Francis.

'It's a Heidelberg four-colour,' the old man said, without turning round. 'Practically a ship-of-the-line. An industry workhorse, this one. Have her going in no time as long as you haven't broken it already.'

'Well,' James said, a tad too loudly, 'just as long as she's up and running in time for us to print these supermarket coupons by tomorrow we should be in business.'

'We'll see,' said the printer. 'You've got sixteen rollers on this, all with their own speed and direction settings, and god knows who's been at it but you don't have two of them set the same.'

'Oh dear,' said James, herding us all out at the same time. 'Why don't you piss off out of it?' he hissed.

'All right,' said Francis. 'But you'll need to spare an hour later on for the meeting.'

'What meeting?'

'Simon wants to go over the accountancy of it all. He's got some ideas about what do with all the money, you know, so we don't have to keep it all under our mattresses. And we still need to settle how we're splitting it all up.'

'Oh, sure,' said James. 'I'm sure that'll be really helpful. He'll be the man for that all right. Bugger off.'

'Serious,' said Gary. 'We want all that settled soon as.'

James pinched the lad's cheeks like he was a toddler.

'Later,' he said. 'Now fuck off. All of you.'

And muttering out-of-earshot complaints, Gary, Francis and I went to join Tomos around the kitchen table, with the sudden feeling that we were all surplus to requirements. I didn't think anybody would say anything though, not while we had a Blethyn in our midst – there'd just be a lot of uneasy faces. But I guess feelings were running high.

'I'm not happy,' said Francis.

'Do you think it'll be all right?' Gary asked me.

Tomos turned and glared at them with his nostrils indignantly aflare.

'I'm sure James will let you have a little slice when all this is done, providing you don't make a nuisance of yourselves,' I said. 'Right, Tomos?'

Tomos snorted, bull-like, at the effrontery of us all.

'That's not what we agreed,' said Francis, jabbing a dirty butter knife at me. 'That's not what we talked about at all.'

'I wouldn't get worked up about it. And it's not my fault, remember. We're all in the same boat.'

'Yes. And we're all due an even share!'

Tomos snatched the knife from his hands and flung it into a corner of the room, and then got up from the table to grab a handful of Francis's still-black hair.

'Shut your mouth,' he huffed, and then took his hulking frame out into the courtyard, where he couldn't use it to hospitalise anybody, pausing only to punch Gary in the back of the head on the way out. It was an admirable display of restraint.

It was a problem that I suppose would have cropped up sooner or later. When fine upstanding voters like these walk into a criminal enterprise they carry some funny expectations with them. Like everybody is supposed to play by the rules, their rules, the law of the direct debit and annual pay rise and the evening in front of the television. They'll put a little something on the line but they'll never cross it, and the most they'll ever sacrifice is a few nights' sleep. If the shit hit the fan, I'm sure those four would all get off with suspended sentences. None of them ever woke up handcuffed to a hospice bed. None of them ever got taken on a midnight ride to a mountain lay-by and had their foot attacked by screwdriver. None of them counted themselves lucky, and half of them probably wanted the death penalty brought back.

'Keep a little perspective,' I said, once the flush of anger had left Francis's face. 'This could still work out well for you.'

'Well, we all know what side you're on,' he said. 'You brought them here.'

Actually, they made me take them here. They got me in a car and took me up somewhere in the Beacons where the hikers never go and hurt me till I told them what was going on, and right now I'm too busy wondering if I'll get out of this alive to sit here thinking about a new conservatory and arguing about the take. And if I told you any of this you'd take fright and have us all in a cell before you had your dinner.

'That's pretty far off the mark,' was all I said.

Francis found another bit of pointy cutlery to play with, and sat there like he was going to kill someone with a greasy fork. After a minute his phone rang, and he went into the front room to take it. When he came back he was wearing the sort of expression a traffic warden gets when he books a sports car. He managed to keep it to himself for about a minute and then he couldn't resist it.

'Well, we'll have to see what Dai and Simon have to say about that won't we?' he said. 'They'll be here in a minute. And they're bringing Doc.'

Soon after we heard a car coming up the lane, and then everyone bar the old man was out there struggling with the fight-or-flight response. But of course it was only Dai and Simon Hargreaves, as predicted. James and Gavin were already drifting back to the miracle-in-waiting back at the barn when one of the back passenger doors opened and a third man got out. They didn't even have to look at each other, the pair of them were over there breathing down necks by pure synchronised instinct.

'Who the fuck is this?' screamed James.

The passenger was a short but square-shouldered man, about five-eight, with close-cropped black hair, a bald pate and a thick moustache. He had a beard about two days old and he wore a Barbour jacket, jeans, and a pair of black leather boots; his small eyes looked demurely about as the histrionics built up around him. I had seen him before somewhere, and I felt a twinge of excitement at the possibility I could be remembering someone I'd known from before the hospice, and then I recognised him. He was the old squaddie from the White Hall Hotel in town. We had swapped some bullshit the night after I'd moved the bodies, but I hadn't said anything about any of this. What Dai, Hargreaves and Francis hoped he would pull out of the bag for them was by no means obvious.

'We've asked Doc here along to help us out,' the accountant was saying, 'after all, who the hell have you got in there? You just upped and left and brought god knows who into the picture, and took the plates with you, so I don't see what your problem is.'

James was spitting angry and Gavin was the same. It was fairly clear that at least one person was soon about to get badly beaten.

'Donald in there doesn't know a fucking thing about what we're doing here, he's only here to get the printer fixed, and he's not going to find out either,' yelled James. 'And he's on a flat fee!'

'So's Doc. You've got your man and we've got ours. Now fair's fair.'

'Fair? Are you deliberately trying to wind me up?'

Simon Hargreaves, in his navy blazer and chinos, was doing his best to pretend that James wasn't grabbing him by the lapels, and Doc just stood there like a guy who'd much rather just go home now, if that was all right with everyone.

'Well, he's here now,' said Dai. 'So let's all just calm down.'

For a moment, I thought everyone would. Then James dropped Simon Hargreaves and walked over to Dai and slapped him hard across the face. Doc pretended not to see it and Dai was so shocked he probably hadn't realised he'd been hit yet. I looked over at Francis, but all I saw was that same idiotic grin he'd been wearing round the kitchen table, like he was standing in the home end of the Vetch, watching his team coming in over the try line.

'What's he fucking for?' said James, with one hand around Dai's neck and the other around Simon's. 'Is he your fucking muscle, is he?'

Gavin took that as his cue to square up, and he was a good foot taller than the new man with probably an extra six inches on the reach. He backed up behind his front left foot and the same hand came up and jabbed straight out from under his chin. It would have done some damage, if it had connected, but the ex-squaddie took a half-step back and leaned clear, just as Gavin came in for a right hook, which would probably have been just as bad only he ducked that too. Then the two of them stood there looking at each other before Gavin closed in for a couple of short ones to the body, both of which came through, although Doc had turned side-on and moved his arms down to take some of the blow, almost like he was letting let them through. Then he took a couple of quick steps backwards and put Dai's Vauxhall between them, and he stood there not quite looking at anybody, that lost-Labrador expression still fixed on his face.

'They just asked me here to help out with the lifting and that,' he said, in a small hollow voice. 'Being they're not young men, you know. I don't want any trouble.'

'Hit 'im,' yelled Tomos, like a child at a wrestling match.

Gavin still had his fists balled but the steam was out of

him now. He looked over at James for the lead but the head Blethyn had got command of himself. He let go of the two old boys and pretended to dust off their shirts.

'I'm not going to lose it this afternoon,' he said. 'Not with two new faces around. But you gents are out of favour. And you've made a mistake. If you're that worried, you shouldn't piss off every half hour. So let's all stay put for now, and once we've sent our little printer home, we'll all have a good talk. All right?'

Simon Hargreaves said nothing, and Dai only put up a hand to touch his cheek, as the truth finally dawned.

'Get the car keys, Gav.'

Gavin opened up the driver's door but couldn't find them in the ignition, so he came round to Dai and held his hand out, and the salesman dropped them in it without a word.

'Good lad,' said James, to a man at least twenty years his senior. It was only Hargreaves who showed any sign of life, filled as he was with some sense of middle-class mission.

'All right then,' he said, tugging his shirt sleeves straight. 'But I expect to resolve all this today. I'm a fully qualified accountant with a considerable amount of professional experience, and unless I'm very much mistaken, your abilities lie elsewhere. There is a substantial amount of financial organisation needed here, and I have put no small amount of my own time and effort into a plan that will benefit us all. So let's pen in a meeting, right away, as soon as you're free, and after that there will be a lot less confusion all round.'

If it hadn't been so laughable I've no doubt he'd have got his jaw cracked.

'Sure,' said James, patting his cheek. 'Now you get in there out of the way and I'll be in when I've freed up my timetable.'

And like nothing had really happened, James and

Gavin went back into the barn, and we all trotted into the farmhouse, and I would have rushed to forget it all myself except for the way Francis patted Doc's back as he walked through that big black door; like he was the outsider who knocked out the champ. I could just about believe he was handier than he looked. He was awfully fast, after all.

'I think there's probably some whisky left around here somewhere,' I said, rooting around a pile of seven or eight carrier bags, the rubbish and the food all piled up in one big mess. 'Francis?'

Francis didn't say anything. No one did. It would take them a while to build back enough pride to talk again. In a bag that contained two empty boxes of custard tarts and the wrapper from a bag of sausages I found a bottle of High Commissioner, two thirds full. There were no glasses, or nothing you'd want to use, so I unscrewed it and took a swig straight from the neck. Hello, old friend. I fought the urge to drain off another three or four inches and pushed it into the middle of the table, like that would help.

'Have a slug,' I said to nobody in particular.

Eventually, like it was the most arduous task in the world, Dai dragged a coffee mug towards him and poured himself an inch or two. He took a sip and let it spread.

'Where is he?' he said. 'Gerald.'

If he was going to be civilised, I wasn't going to let the side down. I took a cracked teacup off the dresser, blew off some of the dust, and helped myself to another shot. And downed it in one, without meaning to. It didn't make anything any clearer.

'I don't know. Done a runner. That's what he told me. He was smart enough for that, I guess. He must have made enough to get away with.'

'Think we'll ever see him again?'

I shook my head.

'Doubt it.'

I wondered if anyone would. Trouble tends to run with you. Dai pulled the bottle back towards him, and for a moment it felt like we were attending a wake.

'He always said he was going to move to Spain,' he said, 'when his boat came in. I thought that was what he'd remortgaged the farm for, to be honest. Did you know him well? How did you come to know him, anyway?'

'To be honest,' I said, staring forlornly at my empty cup, 'I don't really know.'

My hand found its way into my jacket pocket somehow, and felt the presence of that single photograph. Gerald Williams and the happy young couple. I pulled it out and looked at it. They were all still smiling. I dropped it on the table and slid it over like it was a poker hand.

'Who are they?' I said.

Dai's eyes shot up at me.

'You leave them out of this,' he said.

'Look,' I said, very nearly laughing, 'I'm not with those boys out there. I'm not into the rough and tumble. Well, maybe at the receiving end. It was those two who did my foot in.'

And I pointed down at my ankle, thick with bandages, and already yellowing.

'It wasn't my idea to get that sort down here. They just sort of caught up with me.'

'I see,' said Dai. 'It's like that, is it? Well, now's a fine time to tell us who we're involved with.'

Francis got up to rinse out another mug, giving Doc an admiring glance on his way to the sink.

'Not that we didn't have our doubts,' said the shopkeeper, wrenching open an old and creaking tap. 'They might be top dog down in Swansea or wherever they come from, but they don't mean anything up here. Right, Doc?'

Doc looked at his shoes and said nothing.

'Where did you serve, Doc?' I asked.

Doc just kept looking at his shoes, without seeming to find them especially interesting.

'It's his sister's kid,' Dai piped up, holding the photo between his thumb and forefinger. 'Can't remember her name. It was the only one of his family he had any time for, and in fairness, she was the only one of his family who ever had any time for him. The rest of them never spoke to him since he went off the rails.'

Francis came around our side of the table to take a look at it, helping us wear down the whisky another couple of notches as he did so.

'Yeah, that's Joan's girl. Shame about Joan. Her husband hung himself in the garage the year Thatcher got in, was it? He was always a queer fish, mind.'

'No,' said Dai, 'you're thinking of Gareth Bowen, ran the chip shop. Dave Bowen got hit by a car walking back from the Castle Hotel.'

'Oh, yes. And Joan had gone and got MS. She lasted about another three years. So the girl ended up with a foster family, I think. Not the best of starts for a little kid. She used to come up every summer. Came in the shop a couple of times.'

I sat there listening to their easy talk and hazy recollections and thought how nice it was to know people, real people, who weren't trying to play you in some way or just plain hurt you.

'Yes,' he went on, still squinting, 'that's her. And her fella. Lad from down Swansea way. They had a kid then got married about, oh, seven or eight years ago. Wedding photo by the look of it. He wasn't too lucky either. Mother died of cancer, forget which, and the father fucked off when he was little. Ran off to become a policeman, would you believe.'

'Never,' said Dai, chuckling. 'Doesn't get much lower than that.'

'Well, thing was, he didn't even get in, so I heard. Became a debt collector instead.'

Dai was laughing outright now.

'I take it back, that is worse.'

I wasn't laughing. I was looking at the square of his brow, the colour of his eyes, the gloss and thickness of his hair, the shape of his ears and the set of his jaw, reading the young man in the photo for the first time.

'I think Ger had sort of taken the two of them under his wing a bit,' said Francis, when the laughter had died down, although I kept hearing it for a while afterwards. 'She might know where he is, you know.'

The shape of his cheeks as he smiled, the spacing between his front teeth, the set of his shoulders, the way he might walk.

'Yeah,' I said. 'That was why I got it out. I think.'

The features I had lent that meant nothing, nothing except a message now for me, and me alone, echoing back to me, ringing with the long, empty years. About lives that touched somewhere and moved away. I could not remember him, as I could not remember his mother, or my mother, but we could not have been close.

There is no intimacy without trust and there is no trust down here. There is no trust in the land where I live. There is something wrong with us here. Weakness is strength, strength is weakness. Love is a spasm.

'With respect,' said Simon Hargreaves, in a tone that suggested none at all, 'family histories are not our prime concern at present. Neither is Gerald Williams, wherever he is. The man had a long record of disappearing whenever and wherever he caused trouble, leaving things half-done or not done at all.'

I looked at the young man in the photo and gazed upon the outlines of another life, a life I could have led, and glimpsed too in fuller, terrible relief the life that must have led me here. To end up alone, like this.

'In the unlikely event that he returns, I doubt very much he will come and ask us whatever happened to all that he abandoned. And if he does, well, he has forfeited his rights to that. You cannot run off the moment the whim takes you, or as soon as difficulties arise, and expect otherwise.'

No doubt, I thought. No doubt.

'Something like this requires careful management. Now as you know I have a great deal of expertise in handling complex transactions and investments, and I have looked into our situation in some depth.'

While Simon Hargreaves took a rare pause for breath the whisky went around the table again, and the old boys exchanged glances, and settled in for a good sensible dose of professional authority.

'Right you are, Si,' said Dai, emptying his mug with one finger pointing off behind him to the pile of bulging carrier bags. 'I think there's some more whisky in that lot somewhere.'

Not without difficulty, I put the photo back in my pocket and got up – although I'm not sure I was the nearest – to wade into the mess like a scavenger tackling a rubbish dump. I caught a glimpse of bronze collar and plunged an unflinching arm deep into the crud, diving like a buzzard that had sighted movement, and brought up another untouched bottle of budget Scotch. I took a draught, a deep one straight from the neck, not caring, then filled my mug, and passed the bottle on without looking at anybody.

'Everyone should have the opportunity to take qualified advice,' said our accountant.

And he went on then, and on, about different types of bank accounts and regulatory structures and the Money Laundering Act and Christ knows what else. Foreign company registrations and offshore trusts and something called a law debenture company. Nigeria was mentioned, and a place called Macao, and Jersey and the Isle of Man. We saw there and listened, or did not listen, as the short day descended into darkness.

The upshot was that once the fakes were converted into real money we could have it all in the bank and no one would be able to prove where it came from or take it away from us.

'Well, thank you, Si,' said Dai, after what felt like an appropriate pause.

'That's quite all right. It's a professional service. I mean, it is my intention to charge you all a fee for it. Five hundred pounds a head plus set-up costs, you know, something around there.'

'Not up front, presumably?'

If they had any Scotch in their mouths they would probably have spat it out.

'Of course not.'

'Unbelievable,' said Francis, emitting a low animal howl that only eventually turned into something like human laughter, and then not by much.

'What it goes to show,' Simon continued, 'is that some of us can maintain an objective finanical attitude however daunting this may all seem to you.'

Francis had his face about an inch off the table. When he surfaced there were tears in the corners of his eyes. For the first time that day I was conscious there was a rich and rising ride of hysteria not too far from any of us.

'Priceless,' he said.

Unhearing or uncaring, Simon slammed a triumphant fist down on the table.

'And how do I know all this?' he asked. 'Because it's exactly what my bank did with all those dodgy mortgages.'

'Yeah,' said Dai, 'and your bank is going bust.'

'But that's because they used it to hide liabilities, not assets. They wanted to pretend they had more then they did, so they could lend more than they should. In fact, before the panic they were trading at a leverage of fifty to one. For every pound they had in deposits, they owed another fifty.'

I don't know why, but I snapped out of it a little then. Perhaps it was my conditioning, a legacy of all those years as a debt collector, knocking down doors and carting away fridges and what have you.

'You wouldn't put money on a horse with those odds,' I said.

'No, it's not what you expect from a bank, is it? There's no reason for it, other than greed.'

One of the things you always assumed about usury was that the people who were exploiting you actually had the money to lend you. It sort of softened the blow, to think that they did. There may not have been much justice to it, but it suggested a certain order to the universe.

'Hundreds of billions of pounds, and it was never there,' said Simon. 'People's pensions and savings and investments, mine included. Not that it matters to us now.'

'Hold on,' said Francis, leaning forward on his elbows, and already visibly warmed by the whisky, 'are you charging that lot in the barn five hundred pounds a head as well?'

'If I can show you some of the paperwork,' the accountant deflected. He pulled up a battered briefcase and did just that. For what felt like an hour. We sat there and said nothing, our minds elsewhere, one of us nodding if he ever paused for a moment, watching the whisky in the bottle slowly diminish. None of us stopped him. The endless drone of his voice, his descriptions of filing deadlines and subsidiary tax law, were probably the only thing we had to remind us we were still in the real, mundane, boring, normal world. Twenty yards away was a machine that could, theoretically, soon make us all millionaires, not to mention three violent men who had taken the car keys. As I said, you could feel the hysteria around your ears, like the low air pressure before a storm.

Doc seemed to be the only person who was exempt from it. He stood there looking like he was waiting for a train, not moving, not speaking. Then we came unexpectedly to a lull in the conversation, a sudden well of silence, and the tension was unmanageable.

'What?' I said.

'The only weak point,' Simon said, 'is the first signatory. Whoever holds the first account, the one in the UK, might possibly be tracked down for questioning at some point. If he's still in the country.'

Francis Pritchard lurched forward, a good belt of Scotch in him by now.

'No,' he said. 'The real weak point is those buggers out there. There'll be trouble from them before we get round to any of this.'

'Is it still going to be an even split?' said young Gary, who had been cradling the same mug of whisky for sixty minutes. 'That's what we discussed.'

Again, nobody spoke, because I guess everybody knew what it came down to.

'I'm sure they'll see the business sense—' Simon began.

'I'm not sure they'll see any sense at all,' said Francis. 'Whatever they are they're not businessmen, I can tell you that.'

He looked at us all, with his red eyes full of fervour, and stood bolt upright, his chair falling over behind him, his hands clenched into fists.

'I'm not sitting here any longer. Come on!'

No one moved an inch.

'Come on!' he said. And then he was gone.

Bedgrudgingly, we got up and followed him, at a safe distance, like adults minding a straying toddler, ready to pull him out of harm's way when he tumbled. Ready to drag him back into the farmhouse and apply the bandages, once the way of things had hit him a few times in the face. Only it didn't happen. He made it four steps into the barn and then froze. I thought at first he'd bottled it, but there was a noise I hadn't heard before in there, the quiet even hum of expensive machinery running smoothly and efficently. And there it was, the Heidelberg four-colour, running at maximum output, whipping out blank sheets every twenty seconds. It took the the top copy off the stack at one end, whirled it clockwise and counter-clockwise through a set of rollers at varying heights, went through four different presses and shot out into a slatted wire tray at the other, like a playing card from a conjurer's sleeve.

Donald stood watching it, his hands black with grease, and it was the only time I'd seen him smiling.

'Well, I'll be,' said Dai.

James and Gavin didn't seem to mind the intrusion. In fact right then I think I could have pissed on their trousers and they would have just giggled.

'Told you I'd get it running,' said James.

'You'll want to do a couple of test runs when you get the plates,' Donald said. 'The central screws on the two sides of the housings are for vertical and horizontal adjustments. A few millimetres either way and you should have it in line.'

'Thank you, Donald,' said James. 'Gavin here will give you a lift back and pay you your fee. Take the Vauxhall, Gavin, we'll be needing to get some gear out of the Mitsubishi.'

On tiptoes almost, as if a cough would send the whole thing haywire again, and with the silent reverence due to a holy totem, the locals crowded round the press, eager to bask in the aura of an approaching miracle. Gavin quickly ushered the old man out into the courtyard before anyone could say anything stupid.

'What did you pay him?' I asked.

'Union rates, he wanted,' laughed James. 'Eighty quid.'

'Think he suspects?'

'He's been a printer for bloody fifty years, so I should think he suspects something. I told him we were part of a brochure business, you know, for the caravan sites and what have you and he was happy enough to go along with that.

To be honest I think it was the chance to spend another day working, more than anything.'

I thought of him in the boilerless basement, standing guard over a pile of old newspapers, running a cloth over his clean, dry hands.

'I expect so.'

'He won't be any trouble.'

I went outside and watched Gavin strap him into the front passenger seat. His head barely came over the dash, but it was high enough to see his face, locked again into that habitual visage of grim acceptance, his thick black spectacles turning his myopia into something that looked quite the opposite now, like you were looking up at him from the slide of a microscope. It was not a happy face, or one that was at all pleasant to see, but it was I suppose what people generally looked like when they had set themselves the difficult task of waiting for death instead of just rushing towards it, or trying to buy it off. In less than a minute he was gone, his brief visit to High Farm over, the only person to get involved in any of this who you could be sure would never get locked up or killed. Union rates for a day's work and nothing else. Behind me, Doc and Gary started carrying the plates out of the Mitsubishi before the car had even disappeared down the lane.

For those next few hours, High Farm was no longer a derelict and abandoned set of buildings. It was home to something that felt vital and tremendous and daring; something which, looked at through half-closed eyes, from far enough away, seemed like a noble endeavour. The men there no longer seemed like criminals, there was no greed or violence or argument, just sweat and teamwork, as if they had known and trusted each other for years. It was if there had been no slaps, no punches, no shotgun, no bodies, no threats, no greed; as if any possible downside, like the risk of sudden discovery or attack, was more than justified by the ambitions of our attempt. It might sound grandiose but I doubt any one of them in those short, fervent hours thought for a moment about gain or advantage or anything at all to do with something as sordid as the future.

The plates were unloaded and dusted off and fastened, the paper pallettes unwrapped and sorted and stacked, the drums of paint rolled out, the trays filled with ink, the rollers brushed clean of dirt, and no one talked of offshore banks or sports cars or how he brooked no shit from lesser men. They were, just for that brief time, engaged in something that was far from mercenary, something that defied and confounded the everyday rules of normal, meaningless life. They were like men scaling Everest, or preparing to scour the bottom of the Mariana Trench. It would be wrong to describe it any other way. They were normal people, about to print money, and there was a terrific intensity to it all.

Unless I really lose my mind, they will never be far from it, those few hours, straddled between the end of the afternoon and the early evening, at the onset of the Welsh winter, when I stood and braced myself for my initiation into money. I can recollect them almost in their entirety without the slightest effort, hours that at the time seemed to be over and ended as suddenly as a stopped thought. And as we gathered around the business end of the machine with our repressed expectations, I wondered if I was really ready for this. There we were, about to barge in on the chief executives and the premiership footballers and all the other people in that magic world where money wasn't a problem unless you really felt like making it one, huddled round that empty paper tray like rookie paratroopers around a plane door.

James gave the nod to Gary, over by the controls at the opposite end, and he flicked a switch and a single test sheet flew though, up and over and under the rollers, and we flinched when it came out. I wasn't able to look at it straight away. When I did, the colours were all over the place. Elizabeth looked like she was wearing a badly fitting wig.

'Plates are a bit out,' said someone, in a voice as tight as wound wire.

Gavin came over, looked at them without speaking, and then opened a canopy and took a spanner to the bolts around the first plate housing. He closed it and gave a thumbs up to James, who gave one in turn to Gary, who flicked the switch again, and once more we held our breath and waited for the miracle. And kept waiting.

The Queen now looked like Phil Spector.

'It's worse,' somebody said.

Gavin came back round, glanced at it once, and went back to the same canopy, turning the bolt the opposite way, and the signal went down the line until the press whirred into life again. The hair was more or less back on her head but the lettering was still out. And so it went.

We must have wasted enough security paper on the run-throughs to print enough for a small family house. Everything had to be adjusted, and everything went the wrong way first. It could easily have gone on till morning, and I have no doubt we would still have stood there the whole time, frozen in focus, none of us speaking except for the tersest observations on the obvious, and moving only to make small, nervous adjustments to the hair-trigger settings in the bowels of the machine.

It must have been **near** midnight when we did it. Nobody really spoke then either.

'Perfect,' someone whispered, and they were, all thirty-two of them. We gazed upon them with the reverence due to scripture. They were holy and flawless. One last time, James's thumb went up, and Gary flicked the switch to full. The machine hummed into life, and the white paper shot through like a flight of doves, the stack of printed twenties building up under each ejected sheet, flying faster than you could see. Even that looked distinctly unnatural, like you were watching it in time-lapse photography or stop-motion film. And we reacted then. We could not hold our poker faces up to fate any longer.

I saw Dai bent double, his hands on his knees, breathing deeply. I took a few steps backwards until I could put a supporting hand out against the wall. Francis Pritchard could look nowhere but the ceiling, and Simon Hargreaves closed his eyes and looked nowhere at all. Gavin stared at the spanner in his hands and Gary seemed like an old man who had forgotten where he was. And slowly, laughter crept upon us. Our little tickets to freedom, in their tens of thousands, were flowing, rushing towards us like a flood tide across shallow sands, and we could see our lives for what they truly were, now that they had started to back away from us. Lives where choice was mostly illusory, where values were just a crudely crafted booby prize, where you sat and made decisions about things you would never do. The lives of most people, other people. The subjugated majority. We were leaving them now, and we laughed. Our tired sallow faces creased.

It didn't stop. We laughed so much our jaws hurt, with wide and frightened eyes. There was no humour in it except for absurdity. There was little triumph, save perhaps from Tomos, yelping as he punched the air and stamped the floor. Euphoria was a long way from the rest of us. We had built something that in some small way would break the working of the world, and our taut nerves had collapsed. They had been under strain for days. And the tensions and contradictions and fears we could not stand poured out.

We, the barn, High Farm; none of it had any semblance of normality about it again that night. At some point Francis Pritchard produced a slab of lager from the back of his van, and another bottle of whisky, and on the Welsh dresser in the farmhouse kitchen James and Gavin gave young Gary his first go on cocaine. It could have been a celebration, but I think we just drank to keep up with the seeming sudden drunkenness of our existence, to become as eccentric and nonsensical as the reality we were witnessing. We congregated around the kitchen table and talked constantly about nothing, with one or two of us leaving only occasionally to keep the printer fed and empty the tray, hanging the wet sheets on the mesh of wires that hung where the walls met the roofspace. It was all that needed doing.

There were the hints of the trouble that would certainly come, jokes that riffed off veiled arguments, dark threats that bubbled under innocuous observations, differences that were plastered over with hollow bonhomie. There would be a reckoning, and it would come soon, but not tonight, while everyone was still in shock.

I went out to do my bit and saw it all on my own, all that intricate engineering working away in an empty barn, without anyone really needed to oversee it, the pristine uncut notes churning out endlessly in serenely ordered rows. It was only once I was alone I could admit it. Each sheet needed drying, then cutting, then hot-foiling. There would be a falling-out before the ink was dry, and it would not be an amicable difference of opinion. And that was assuming we would be left alone, that there would be no more intrusitons, accidental or otherwise, not to mention the rest of it, the conversion and the laundering. But the future was unthinkable to them now, and maybe it would have been to me too, if not for the cancer. They were barely in the present, and to talk of breakfast would have made you a seer. It was the hidden truth that had lain under the hysteria all this time, the emotional warp that had shopkeepers half-convinced they were criminal masterminds.

I caught the slightest hint of movement at the periphery of my vision, and turned to see Doc shifting his weight, standing guard at the far end of the press. He was the only one of us who had been visibly unaffected by the evening. He almost looked bored. I wondered if perhaps he'd never been fooled by it at all, the tantalising, fantastic prospect of all this imminent wealth, or if he simply didn't care. I nodded at him and he looked back at me, as passive as a plank.

Then it was just me, outside in the courtyard in the cold dark. I watched the first hint of a gentle rain in the light spilling out from the barn door, and felt a rising wind in the chill on my cheeks. Behind me you could see them in the kitchen, jabbering at each other inaudibly, the lit window like a television screen with the sound turned down: and I thought of the TV set in the day room, and its oblivious audience, infirm and lifeless enough to seem stoic. And maybe one or two of them were.

Ironic, the panic I had felt at my loneliness, and the

strangeness of this place, this farmyard and this town, when it must have been in some tenuous way the pull of family which brought me here. Of neglected blood. There might be the agency now to change things, and if there wasn't, if it all fell through, at least I had seen it. All those notes spouting out in countless abundance. Christ, it would have taken more than a day just to figure out how much was there. I had stood at the start of the yellow brick road and gazed up at the castle. If it wasn't enough to die happy, it was something. That was what I was thinking when I heard the approaching engine, and saw the main beams glaring through the trees, and watched the branches shiver in its light.

Two men got out gun first, pointed pistols in their hands, and I had seen one of them before. David Knight, of Avon CID, a shortish man with a narrow face. Had a scar on it.

David Knight.

'Give my regards to your cancer.'

When they saw me their hands dropped to their sides, and they advanced smartly and quickly towards me. When I was about to say something, god knows what, a hand shot up and down and out, and I glimpsed the metallic flash of a pistol butt as it bore down on me like a bolt of lightning, and then came the flash, and all the stars went out at once.

V

You wake up in a room you don't recognise, wearing a cheap suit that is too large, slumped on a rickety wooden chair that would barely hold the weight of a boy, at a kitchen table covered in dross. The floor is nothing but bare flagstones, covered in muck and mud and the shoeprints of a dozen men, and on the wall hang some framed samplers. Blessed are the meek, and Guide me, O thy great redeemer. There is a stark square window with no curtains, and outside is only the blackness of night, a blackness that seems to seep in through the glass.

You wake up and a middle-aged man walks in, overweight but alert, with pale blond curls and fierce round eyes, and an automatic pistol in one of his hands. He says nothing. You decide to get up and stand on your feet, but instead you end up coughing blood, and you reach into your pockets for a tissue but your suit is soaked in mud. And you want to say something to this poised and dangerous man, but your voice is thick with phlegm and fear.

And the man walks up to you, and lifts your jaw up until your eyes meet, and says:

'You haven't pegged it yet, then.'

And you want to scream but you have no mouth, you

want to run but you cannot move. The man stares at you quite openly and then walks out, dangling his gun absently by his side, and your shock begins to subside, in that empty fetid kitchen, so, slower this time, you get up to follow him. But before you are upright you are stopped short by a searing pain in your foot, and as you topple sideways you look down to see a mess of soiled bandages around your ankle, covered in brown stains made by something other than mud, and then there is a dizziness that is almost blinding.

'He's conscious,' calls the man from somewhere just outside the doorway, and then there is the sound of splashing footsteps before a small man with a narrow, scarred face appears, wearing civilian clothes but a police baseball cap, and there are flecks of blood about his clothes and face that are not his. He rubs a spot of it from his clean-shaven chin while he looks you over.

'What is this?' you croak. 'What's happening?'

But he leaves too. You wake up alone, in a room you do not recognise, and you know only that something very important is happening, right now, in this moment. And you steel yourself and hobble out after him, and you find yourself slouched against the doorframe of an old run-down farmhouse, staring out across a muddy courtyard, at five men of varying ages leaning prone against the wall of a barn, their hands spread and feet apart, two armed men standing over them, and down on the ground two badly-beaten bodies, on their side and on their front. And you raise a hand to your own poor cracked skull, under a throbbing bump that makes your teeth jangle as soon as your fingers touch your sticky, matted hair, and it comes back.

It all comes back.

It pours forth from the nowhere inside of you, from the space where it had always been, days and months and years and decades telescoping in. Summer mornings and spring afternoons, late nights and lie-ins, you can remember not remembering and everything before that you know is there within you, recollectable, on demand, under an ocean of time, and a sea of booze. Under a thick welt of regret. A wasted life. Robin Llywelyn, Private Investigator.

'I'm feeling better,' you blurt, as if it matters to anyone.

DS Gilboursen and DI Knight of Avon CID exchange glances, and Knight tucks his pistol into his trousers and puts his arm around your shoulder and steers you back into the kitchen.

'Well, well,' he says. 'Who'd have thought it. Let's have a little chinwag, shall we?'

The next thing you know you are sitting opposite each other at that big wooden table, and Knight has put his gun down on the cardboard backing of an empty slab of lager and is looking at you over folded arms. There is still blood on his brow and collar, on his shirt and the lapels of his jacket, on his knuckles, and on the butt of his gun. The only part of him you can see that isn't dotted red are his jagged yellow teeth when he opens his mouth.

'Well, we've got the wideboys knocked out and the locals are shitting themselves. Strange crowd to be involved in something like this. Of course, they've got a couple of things in common. The first is that they're all adamant that none of them really have anything to do with it, and the second is it's all your fault.'

You can remember Detective Inspector Knight. He is violent and he is corrupt, and there was a time a few years ago when you were careful to do everything he said, otherwise he would lock you up or bury you. Some people get a choice between the carrot or the stick. Lonely private investigators just get stick and more stick. The last time you saw him, back over the bridge, he was facing an internal investigation. He must have passed that. You didn't help him to.

DI Knight's weasel teeth dance as he laughs.

'What on earth made you think you stood a chance at any of this? This isn't your level. You're a fucking bum. You couldn't sell a stolen radio without getting your legs broken. What did you think you were doing? Did you think you were the kingpin all of a sudden? You're a useless fucking bum. You know you are.'

It hurts to smile, and it will probably hurt a lot more soon, because it's far from sensible to do so, but you smile anyway.

'I guess I just forgot,' you say.

'I guess you did,' he says. And he reaches into his pocket and pulls out a very dog-eared business card, and hands it to you. You don't need to read it. You know it's yours. It was the last one you had.

'Where did you get this?' you ask.

'Funny old world, isn't it? Turn it over.'

You turn it over, and there it is, Knight's mobile phone number scrawled across the back. The number he wrote down in the hospice, on the card that Gerald took.

'He rang me up. Thought I was you. Left some dipshit, drunken message on my phone, a lot of garbled shit about presses and plates and lying low. Couldn't figure out for the life of me what was going on, although I knew it had to have something to do with my little visit to your old digs, to see you stuck on the drip and drooling. So, the wonders of modern technology being what they are, I sent him a little text. Wondered if he fancied meeting up to talk about it person. I won't tell him about the mistaken identity, I thought, he'll understand that soon enough. So we all meet up in the Severn Services, on the English side, naturally. And we get to talking.'

Gerald Williams is dead.

'He wanted to go to Spain,' you say.

'Yes, he must have done. Only he tried to swim there. You know that big cliff they've got behind the services up there? That was where he took the plunge. He just didn't want to talk to us at all. So we ran a trace on him, and you know what it's like. You put the order in and you wait and you wait while some little clerk goes through the motions. We only got the address today. And here we are.'

And here they were. Just the two of them in the middle of the night, in a civilian car, to go up against an organised crime outfit. They couldn't have reasonably thought it was anything less, even if it had Robin Llywelyn attached to it. And it dawns on you that they haven't come here to make arrests.

'So what was he protecting, hey? Not you. I don't even know why he hired you in the first place.'

And you know now, why he picked you. You know because you remember: because of the wrongs that needed to be put right. But you just shrug and put on a show of false modesty.

'When I'm sober I can bullshit pretty well,' you say.

'So the old farmer disappears and you bring in a new crew and take over. What about the old crew?'

'It was just him and me. I never saw anybody else.

I'm pretty sure he must have bought the entire set-up in wholesale.'

'Well, that mob out there haven't seen a whiff of anybody else in all of this but you, and you don't have the clout to frighten anybody off, so it's not unbelievable. And the force up in Birmingham collared a counterfeiting firm late summer, but they couldn't lay their hands on the kit, so, you never know. These things get sold on from time to time.'

Knight picks up his gun, and etches a few abstract lines in a puddle of congealed gravy with its barrel.

'You know, it occurs to me you're not long for this world. This doesn't have to end unpleasantly if you feel like making yourself useful. If you want to sign a few documents for us, things like that. Help us with the paperwork. You know that banks can be awfully pedantic. We won't be able to let you out and about that much, of course, but you'll be comfortable. We'll look after you.'

You have nothing more to say to this man. You cannot even bring yourself to speak.

'All right? Good lad.'

Then he heads out, like you had no other choice, and you think about Gerald's final leap of faith and wonder if it will be honoured. If you will be able to justify it.

DI Knight and DS Gilboursen confer quietly with heads bent, and then Gilboursen walks up to the prone men and yells,

'Right, Llandovery Rotary Assocation. We've got your names and addresses. If you're local you can fuck off. And don't you talk about this until we tell you to. This is an ongoing investigation, and if you compromise it we'll have you in the dock for counterfeiting and obstruction of justice. It'll be a ten-stretch for all of you. Now piss off out of here.'

They do too, scuttling back to their cars with their eyes to the ground. Within minutes their little convoy has bounced gratefully down the wooded lane to the banality of their everyday, humdrum lives. The shopkeeper, the accountant, the car salesman and the barman, all out of the picture, and thankful for it.

Tomos and Gavin, the only ones likely to cause any trouble, are both out cold. James is still up against the wall, the right side of his suit drenched in blood and dripping with it.

'Right, you,' says Knight, grabbing the bossman roughly by the neck. With his face now visible you can see it looks barely human, it's bloated with bruises in a swollen parody of a man's face. He has one good, unclosed eye but it cannot stay fixed in any direction; the nerves behind it are shattered, and it darts about like a nervous animal's.

'This is the deal. If you can load your buddies into the back of your car, and you can drive it back to sunny old Swansea, we'll let you go. You can run around down there to your heart's content. But a peep out of you to anyone and you're up against the biggest firm in the country. All right?'

Without talking, perhaps unable to, James takes a stab at closing the distance between him and his unconsious brother. He has the pride still to keep his head up, and when he finds himself on his knees, he has the guts to get himself back up. You wonder how much of it must be thoughtless instinct, how much of him is driven by something beneath his own consciousness.

When he gets to Tomos it is all he can do to lift his arms. Even that has him groaning, and even his groans are wounded, muffled by the strange set of his jaw. Tomos must weigh about sixteen stone, and he does not move. Knight and Gilboursen watch without comment and do nothing.

For reasons that are not immediately obvious to you, you help him. The police officers make no objections. The best part of an hour goes by, and there are moments when you think you can still see the stars in the winter sky, although the sky is overcast now and your eyes are closed. The big sliding door of the people-carrier is the only thing that makes the job possible. When Tomos and Gavin are lying in the back like mailsacks, you check their airways are open while James climbs into the driver's seat. He has stopped groaning now, but his breathing has become a loud and erratic rasp. As he did with the old printer earlier that day, you fasten his seat belt for him. And after you've done so, you take the photograph out of your jacket.

'This lad,' you point. 'This young lad here. The groom. He's my son. I know he is. He's my son.'

And James Blethyn, the boss, nods his head at you, although he has to bend his back to do so, because his neck is shot. And you shut the door for him, and watch him, as he grinds the gears, and stalls, and stalls again, as he reverses and then lurches away. There is an awful silence in his wake. You are alone with DI Knight and DS Gilboursen.

'Okay,' says Knight, 'anything you want to tell us now? You must have been laundering it through someone, or planning to. If we get any surprises about any of this, we're going to stop being so friendly, and there must be something. Tell us about the loose ends.'

You stand there, thinking about Gerald, about your son and daughter-in-law, and wonder why *Fuck off* is so hard to say. You begin to think it might be impossible, and then somone speaks.

'I can show you the loose ends,' says a voice as even as a spirit level. And you turn to see Doc, in his ragged moustache, in his wax jacket and his surplus boots, his face as expressionless as a brick wall, his small eyes as neutral as marbles, and in his hands, down by his hips, there is the black metal and green plastic of a British Army assault rifle.

'Don't move your arms at all,' he says.

They don't.

'All right, it's up at the top field, what I've got to show you. Up by that stone wall up there. You go first.'

Nobody moves. For what seems like the whole night, nobody moves.

'I don't want to go,' says Gilboursen, and you cannot see his face, you don't want to see either of their faces, but you think he might be crying, quietly.

'What are you worried about?' says Doc. 'Big lads like you. Come on now.'

And strangely, terribly, almost innocently they go, one after the other, and you are completely on your own, and you do not know if it's the wind, but your eyes are streaming and your nose starts to run, and you want for none of this to have ever happened, even to them.

There are only two brief pops. It sounds just like a cork being pulled from a bottle. And then he is back, and you understand for the first time that immobile face, and those blank eyes, and you look at him and see the Falklands and Belfast and the Gulf, and he is still holding that rifle, down by his hip, with both hands, and he is pointing it at you.

'I don't like witnesses,' he says, in his odd recorded voice, and you close your eyes and if your life hadn't already flashed before you, perhaps it would have done then. You close your eyes and you can hear the wind in the trees, and the life rushing through your own veins, and the steady machine hum of the Heidelberg four-colour, still running.

'So keep your fucking mouth shut.'

It kept running, that press, for the next five days solid. The men from the town crept back before the weekend, once they'd got a sniff that we were still there, and there were no policemen waving guns around. They didn't even ask where they had gone. But James Blethyn and his boys never reappeared. Their records must have been too long to take the risk.

You should never underestimate the criminal who can consider himself a half-honest man. And who knows. Perhaps we were.

Four

Snapshot

I read the newspapers and I do the crossword. I take *The Times* and the *Mail* and the *Telegraph*, whatever's there. I have a book of sudoku. I watch a lot of television now too, I see the news a couple of times a day, and some of the sports. It is rugby season, after all. Wales seems to have remembered how to play it. Boxing, golf, even tennis, I'll watch anything now. I tried reading, but I don't seem to have the patience for it, or the concentration. I don't have the time these days for other people's stories. I think too much about my own. It is what happens to most of us, I expect.

I try to get outside once a day. I can't walk far, but I won't use a chair, not yet. I can make it to the end of the street and back just fine for the time being, and it's a mild winter, or so they tell me. You can go out in a light jacket and you'll be fine. On the days when I can't be bothered, there is the always the balcony, and below it the whole pantomime of Puerto Banus, the Porsches and the yachts, the restaurants and the champagne bars, the models in miniskirts and the inarticulate, unreasonable men in designer suits. The Mediterranean can look as vulgar as cheap jewellery sometimes, and other times, of course, it can be the most tranquil, beautiful, civilising thing you will ever set eyes on. I have stared out at it for hours on evenings like those.

Anastazja will bring me the first drink of the day, but never before six, usually a cold bottle of San Miguel with a big tumbler of bourbon and ice, and sometimes she will watch the sunset with me, and talk about her life and family, about growing up in the Soviet Union, about her brother the systems engineer, about finding a husband, and the salon she would like to own, how the Med is better than the Baltic. She has sniffed the money, but I think she would tell me anyway. Neither of us know anyone here. Sometimes I will spin her a few heavily edited tales about myself in exchange.

I have tried drinking down in the marina, but it was an unpleasant experience. Whatever I have in the bank and in trust I have nothing in common with the people down there. You always heard a lot about the Costa Del Sol, about how the old East End thugs came here to hang their boots up, and on the whole they aren't too bad, that crowd. Old men, mostly, and retired, a bit loud perhaps, a bit stupid, but not too bad. I have sat next to them, with their walking sticks and faded tattoos and exhausted violence, and conversed innocuously about the weather, about which boat was King Abdullah's and which was Lakshmi Mittal's. But they are in a minority now, those men. The majority of criminals here, and there are plenty, are far from retired. You sort of get an eye for it, having spent a life around it.

The whole coast is full of them. There are are gangs of English, Irish, Dutch and Russians, there are Latinos and North Africans, and there are the Spanish as well. Forty miles away, across that gorgeous slab of dark marine, is Morocco, and the Rif mountains, covered in hashish, and past the straits of Gibraltar the sea lanes stretch all the way to South America. In the hotel bars along the seafront there are plenty of hungry captains with idle crews and uncharted yachts, and in any case, there's always space onboard any boat for a couple of hundred kilos of something. Last week an officer of the Guardia Civil came over on the ferry with a quarter tonne of resin in the door wells of his car, and they only caught him because it was the dealers who grassed. There are shootings every other week, and too much flash, and too much mouth. They too are people with problems money can't solve.

My own is almost all locked down now, in trusts and funds and shares. It looks so legitimate you'd think I had my own family crest. Changing it into real money didn't prove too difficult: turns out the sort of people who are happy to take millions of fake notes are pretty much the sort of people who are happy to take real ones, although we had to suffer some swinging discounts. There's just no honest way to spend that much cash, just as there's precious few honest ways to make it. It was largely a matter of approach, the chief lesson being not to send anyone alone into a private venue, which was something I had already learnt. And the laundering, as Hargreaves said, was mere paperwork.

As soon as I could I took my share out of the Jersey pot and ran it through a few trusts of my own. There is an English solicitor in Marbella with an office near the hospital who I used to fix it all up. My son and his wife get two million in three months' time. I wanted to make them wait six, just to stop anybody making a connection to High Farm, but three months is a long time to worry about money when you have a family. The grandkids get a quarter of a million each when they turn twenty-five, although God knows what a twenty-five-year-old will do with a quarter of a million quid. None of them have any idea that it's all there waiting for them. None of them even know where I am, or what happened to Gerald, and the machinery in the farm was all junked before they came to repossess it. I could be putting them in harm's way if I made contact, and worse, they might refuse, and I can't have that. It is all I've got to give.

I have no guilty conscience, at least not about the money. Five men died for it, and four more were beaten halfway there. Over a dozen of us put our liberty on the line for it. It was a bigger commitment than turning up to a boardroom three days a week. It isn't fair, it isn't right, but it's been paid for, in a way. You'll have to make the same choice yourself, sooner or later, when you get a hooky twenty in your wallet: do you pass it on, or hand it in? I don't think many people will be making that trip to the police station myself. And the government and the banks are with me on this one. Quantitative easing, I think they call it. The world makes no more sense when you have money, although you can stand it a little easier.

So I'm not too bothered about High Farm. Although when I lay me down to sleep some nights, I can still hear the messages on those two mobile phones, the tones of loved ones changing from anger to fear and then to grief; women I don't know crying about men I never met, except to carry them through the long grass to the low stone wall. Doc moved them and the two coppers over a couple of nights the following week, I don't know where. We never told anyone else about them.

On nights like those, when I cannot sleep, and the old things still gnaw at me, I will put on my gown and go out to the balcony, and sit there with a cognac in one hand and the photo in the other, the photo from High Farm. The late Gerald Williams, my abandoned son, a daughter-in-law I have never met, and a grandchild I have never seen. And it is enough. Because I have my insurance against the shortening days, the best that I could manage.

One day, when I am gone from here and all the money has chanelled safely through, years after that, my solicitor will send it back to them, with another photo enclosed. A shot of me, before the wheelchair and the oxygen, while I still have a bit of weight about my face, and my young bottle-blonde carer, sitting in one of those horrible bars down in the marina, with ridiculous cocktails and even more absurd smiles, heavily tanned in the playground of rogues and billionaires. Trying to look the part. And when they are secure in their fine houses, with their kitchens stocked with good food and their loved ones all cared for, they will look at it, maybe even turn to it in a family album, and they will say

Yes,

that was him,

bit of a black sheep, that one.